PAGE ONE

A Novel of Love, Lust and Lost Souls in an L.A. Newsroom

By
Kirk Honeycutt

WISE
MEDIA GROUP

PAGE ONE © 2019 Kirk Honeycutt

www.HoneycuttsHollywood.com

Cover concept created by Mira Advani Honeycutt
Cover design by Tatiana Vila
Interior layout by Brian Schwartz
Project managed with AuthorDock.com

ISBN: 978-1629671680
Library of Congress Control Number: 2019919148

Rev 2.25

ADVANCE PRAISE

Page One is an absolute delight. I had so much fun reading it. Kirk Honeycutt is an immensely enjoyable writer.

—Mark Johnson, Academy Award-winning producer

Kirk Honeycutt is one of the finest film critics who ever plied the profession. His experience working at a daily trade paper brings a startling verisimilitude to Page One, a page-turning, multi-character, gripping story. Not only is the writing peerless and in parts mordantly funny, not only has a new novelist been unleashed, but the depiction and description of L.A. and its car-trapped denizens, in the eyes of this long-time Angeleno, is rendered with breathtaking realism, reminiscent of Chandler and Macdonald if they were writing today. There are so few novels about southern California that ring true, but Honeycutt has vividly painted the meretriciousness and speciousness of L.A. that you know it's coming from a true insider.

—Rex Pickett, screenwriter, director and author of the novel *Sideways*

As he did while a top Hollywood movie critic and reporter, Kirk Honeycutt can combine his sharp, often witty observations about people and life, with his journalistic ability and his gift as a storyteller in Page One. His novel perceptively provides insights into a once glorious profession – newspapering – during the tricky transition from analog to the digital age.

—Alex Ben Block, journalist, author, show business historian and former Editor of *The Hollywood Reporter*

This multi-faceted tale of seasoned, colorful and sometimes down-on- their-luck newsroom characters, reminiscent of days gone by, is an enjoyable weekend read.

—Joel Cox, Academy Award-winning editor

A rollicking romp through a big-city newsroom, chock-full of larger-than-life characters — the jaded, the ambitious, the hard-nosed and the touchingly human. Honeycutt has concocted a vivid, hard-to-put-down account of a disappearing time and place: you can practically smell the newsprint.

—Elizabeth Guider, editor, journalist and novelist

Kirk Honeycutt's *Page One* is a gritty fiction vividly realized by an experienced journalist's unromanticized vision of the darker side of sunny 1980s Los Angeles. It's all here — a city haunted by serial murders and a newsroom filled with characters who face life with deadlines, grim routine, and a search for scoops, mixed with barroom banter and professional camaraderie that can lead to on-the-job sex — experiences set against the knowledge that exposing the truth is important, even if it isn't always what it seems.

— Jon Wilkman, documentary filmmaker and author of Picturing Los Angeles, Floodpath and Screening Reality.

SYNOPSIS

Page One is a seriocomic tale about journalists engaged in a newspaper war long before the current 24/7 news cycle but not before a willingness to forego personal integrity was creeping into "the media," and the line between genuine importance and celebrityhood was starting to blur.

The *Los Angeles Morning News*, known to everyone in its newsroom as The Morning Snooze, is locked in a losing battle with the city's leading newspaper. The employees have a motto: "If it's news in L.A., it's news to us."

Then new blood enters the newsroom. It isn't long before the newcomers discover *The Morning News'* dirty little secret: it is not the distinguished paper of record. So it can attack news the way it wants to with splashy celebrity coverage, sticking up for the little guy and perhaps uncovering a serial killer hiding in plain sight.

ABOUT THE AUTHOR

Kirk Honeycutt is a longtime journalist, film critic, teacher and author, who most recently wrote the biography *John Hughes: A Life in Film*. He served as a senior reporter and then chief film critic for *The Hollywood Reporter* for 20 years.

He has written two produced screenplays including *Final Judgment* (1992) starring Brad Dourif, Isaac Hayes and Karen Black. He has written for the New York Times, Los Angeles Times, Newsday, the Christian Science Monitor and American Film and Cosmopolitan magazines as well as other publications.

As an adjunct professor at Chapman University's Dodge College of Film and Media Arts, he taught a variety of film courses. Kirk has appeared as a commentator or guest on many network and local TV shows including CBS This Morning, the O'Reilly Factor, CNN, the BBC, MSNBC, REELZ, NBC in Los Angeles and Access Hollywood along with numerous radio appearances.

CONTENTS

Advance Praise
3

About the Author
6

Chapter One // Nothing Ever Happens in Ecuador
13

Chapter Two // Rum and Coke
25

Chapter Three // The Ax
31

Chapter Four // Dino and Trixie
35

Chapter Five // Big Bob
51

Chapter Six // Coroner's Case 87-03694
59

Chapter Seven // Temple of Doom
67

Chapter Eight // The Mad Bomber
79

Chapter Nine // Sly
91

Chapter Ten // It's Murder
103

Chapter Eleven // Sophie
113

Chapter Twelve // Bodies
123

Chapter Thirteen // Alex
135

Chapter Fourteen // The Good Doctor
143

Chapter Fifteen // Gina and Reggie
157

Chapter Sixteen // Murderers
167

Chapter Seventeen // Repercussions
173

Chapter Eighteen // Human Events
181

Chapter Nineteen // Covering the Circus
191

Chapter Twenty // New Evidence
197

Chapter Twenty-One // The Jumper
215

Chapter Twenty-Two // The Restless
223

Chapter Twenty-Three // Reviving Dr. Death
233

Chapter Twenty-Four // True Confessions
249

Chapter Twenty-Five // Sources
263

Chapter Twenty-Six // Gum-shoe
275

Chapter Twenty-Seven // 30
289

Also by Kirk Honeycutt
295

DEDICATION

For all the journalists I've had the privilege of sharing newsrooms with. Rest assured, you will not find yourself portrayed in this tale. Well, maybe one or two might...

CHAPTER ONE

NOTHING EVER HAPPENS IN ECUADOR

The moment Danny Evans walked into the newsroom of the Los Angeles Morning News, he could feel his blood boil. Bad enough that he worked in such a stink hole. A newsroom, in the chief copy editor's never humble opinion, contained some of the lowest life forms known to mankind. As far as Danny could determine, no one was employed in a newsroom unless he was a bleeding-heart, pot-smoking, granola-and-yogurt eating, Save the Whales, gun-control freak. The only red blood in this rag, as far as Danny Evans was concerned, was the stuff now boiling in his all-American veins.

But what he saw on his desk—or rather what he didn't see— stoked his anger further. What sort of despicable degenerate moral scum would steal his hand grenade?

For the three years of his employment at the News—a fact documented by his desk sign reading "Tour of Duty Began 8/14/86"—Danny's grenade sat unmolested to the left of his video display terminal. For three years no one had so much as touched it. Now, returning from lunch, he discovered the grenade missing.

Missing, for Christ's sake. A hand grenade.

Danny's souvenir from his Vietnam tour of duty was a soothing prop at the Morning News. For one thing, a grenade made a terrific paperweight. It secured all kinds of documents on his busy desk that would otherwise wander off. More crucially, Danny discovered when reporters agonized over their prose long past deadline, verbal abuse alone had less impact than threats delivered with the grenade resting comfortably in his hand.

A short, stocky man in his late-fifties with rapidly thinning hair, horn-rimmed glasses and pitted skin, Danny worked the early shift at the News. He was responsible for all the early forms, meaning Features, Entertainment, Food and Fashion. He manned his desk from 9:00 a.m. until, as he liked to put it, the cows came home. Most days he made damn certain the bovines got into the barn around 6. By 6:05, Danny wanted to be in the American Legion bar across the alley for a quick beer. Then he would head to his home in a trailer park in the San Fernando Valley, which he shared with his pet rabbit, Mortimer.

The sooner he got home, the better. To hear him tell it, working in a newsroom was a somewhat less savory occupation than cleaning toilets in an opium den. Danny professed a fierce disdain for anything smacking of culture. He nurtured intolerance for politicians, criminals, athletes, shrinks, writers, entertainers, animal rights activists and other "indecent" folks — in short, the kind of people newspapers invariably wrote about. He didn't have too many kind words for society types either. Nobody truly decent would have more than a few thousand in the bank, he reasoned.

Danny had a dirty secret, though. When he returned to his trailer-park lair, he spent most evenings painting. It was his one true passion, the one time of the day when he felt at peace. While working on a picture, Danny would lose all track of time. The night would go by in a blur as he struggled to get powder-puff clouds to float in a sky turning from angelica green to soft blue.

Color was his obsession. He mixed and re-mixed his oils to find the right color and would not hesitate to scrape away any disagreeable color with his palette knife. A thing had to be perfect. Painting is not like the newspaper business, where you go to press every night whether you get that late ball score or not. A painting isn't finished until the artist says it's finished.

Danny Evans lived, in effect, a double life—guardian of redneck virtues by day and moral degenerate by night. What's worse, except for hoisting a nightly brew at the American Legion bar, he rarely drank. And a journalist who didn't drink is akin to a Pope who refuses to pray.

To Annie Ledbetter, a fellow resident at the trailer park with whom he occasionally slept and quite possibly the only living soul aware of his double life, he would simply say: "I'm not gettin' older. Just more complicated."

Danny began his hunt for the grenade thief in Metro. Larry Beale was certainly a suspect. And Danny would consider Bill Boyer guilty until proven innocent. Hell, even if Bill could prove his innocence, he was probably guilty. Some people are just that way.

Danny's detective work came in the form of inquiries that sounded more like an accusation and in language littered with expletives. A refugee from Georgia and later the Marine Corps, Danny would exaggerate his Southern accent to the hilt. He carefully crafted his speech pattern so most obscenities were hyphenated and references to barnyard animals frequent.

Maneuvering through the crossfire between rock critic Winnie Yankovich and her bitter enemy, entertainment and features editor Ruth Treadway, Danny confronted Beale. The fuzzyheaded reporter was hurrying through the newsroom on his way to the Criminal Courts Building. Danny nevertheless blocked his path and accused the depraved Jewish son-of-a-bitch of pilfering his grenade.

"Eat shit and die, you Southern scumbag," Larry cheerfully retorted.

'If I ate shit, you'd be a headless wonder," Danny reminded him.

Beale shook his head, giggled slightly and made his way around the inflamed editor. Danny turned to see Bill Boyer heading his way. If he wanted to get any real information out of Bill, Danny realized the confrontational approach would get him nowhere. For Bill's behavior in recent weeks was cause for alarm.

Last Tuesday, when the office goldfish died, Bill demanded a full funeral service that went well beyond the point of being a damned good joke. When he smashed up a rental car while on assignment in San Diego, he insisted he was avoiding illegal aliens dashing across the border. Then a week later, he returned three hours late from lunch with the explanation he lost his car in Disney Studios' parking lot.

No, at this delicate and dicey time in Bill Boyer's life, a gentle approach was called for. Which is exactly the tact he took when he intercepted the journalist on his way back from the coffee machine.

After patiently listening to Danny's query, Bill suggested, "Maybe the grenade exploded." A slight whiff of gin came from the reporter's breath.

Danny's neck immediately justified his reputation. "Would you see my mother-fuckin' desk if the damn grenade exploded?" he fumed. "'Fact, would ya'll see anything but hellfire and destruction if the grenade had exploded, boy?"

"I'd check with Jorge then," said Bill brightly.

"Why would the cleanin' kid take it?"

Bill shrugged. "Maybe he's in a gang. You told me the other day all Mexicans were in gangs."

Bill turned and ambled back to his desk, leaving Danny without a comeback. For Danny had indeed voiced that opinion the previous week. No, locating the thief was not going to be easy, Danny told himself. Maybe he *should* check with Jorge.

Bill's phone rang. It was a call from Nate Shaw, chief deputy to the city councilman for the Ninth District. "Bill, how are you?" inquired Nate with that peculiar false sincerity only a politician can muster.

"Not bad," Bill replied noncommittally.

"Good, good," lied Nate. "Look, Bill, I feel bad about the other day. I rarely lose my temper like that."

"We all do. I understand," said Bill.

"But that's no excuse," Nate insisted. "I wanted to call and apologize."

Oh sure, thought Bill, just like you want to get caught with an underage hooker by Hollywood Vice. Bill enjoyed nothing as much as getting yelled at by one of L.A.'s power brokers. Or, better yet, someone who thought he was a power broker. Bill had several stratagems on such occasions. Usually, the sound over the telephone of his clicking keyboard as he took down threats verbatim swiftly silenced their outrage. Only that tactic had failed in the case of Nate Shaw. So instead Bill tried another avenue: he repeated what the city councilman's chief deputy said to him to virtually everyone he talked to for the next few days. Apparently, word had gotten back to Nate.

"Let's bury the hatchet over lunch. It's on me," said Nate.

"I could squeeze in a lunch tomorrow at the Pacific Dining Car," said Bill.

There was a pause on the other end and then a short laugh. "I see I will be eating rather expensive crow," murmured Nate before hanging up.

Bill felt satisfied. He not only had hustled a free meal, he had fulfilled, for the moment anyway, something he had read in a Hemingway novel about how an important part of ethics in the newspaper business is that you should never seem to be working.

Bill glanced at the clock. He hadn't finished polishing this morning's story on Alan White. Normally Bill was indifferent to deadlines. He knew they were always more flexible than editors pretended they were. But since the Morning News had a new managing editor, it wouldn't do to miss a deadline this early in his regime. Maybe next week.

Fortunately, the story was a pretty good one and Bill had excellent quotes. Alan White was a thirty-three-year-old man in the Crenshaw neighborhood, who collected cans and bottles every morning to recycle for cash. Only the day before, a young man wanted Alan's bottles of beer and when Alan indicated an unwillingness to part with his hard-earned stash, the young man shot and killed Alan.

According to police deputies, White was killed around 7 a.m. Sunday not far from where he lived with his parents. His mother Eustice intended to add Alan's photo to those of two brothers and a sister, also killed by guns, in a memorial collage she had hanging in her apartment hall. Bill had the foresight to have the Morning News photographer get a shot of the memorial with Eustice standing beside it, clutching a photo of her latest dead child. The story was certain to land on Page One of Metro.

A few desks away from Bill, Andy Reynolds, a young and black J-school grad from the University of Southern California, was begging for a new assignment. Somehow he had the "car crash" beat. Not that it was ever called that. But every time a pile-up occurred at the Four Level Interchange he got the assignment. Every time a stressed-out father or teenage hype changed lanes far too quickly on the Hollywood Freeway, guess who went to the scene?

If he was going to make his mark in transit, he wanted to cover the transit beat. The constant political battle over the city's multi-billion-dollar subway through quake-prone earth and NIMBY neighborhoods or the fight to get better bus service with buses that actually ran in East L.A. would furnish him with great clips to attach to his resume when he applied to the Times in another year or two.

But, no, those stories belonged to more seasoned reporters. (Or over-seasoned and under-baked, as he likes to mutter to himself.) He did, of course, understand the pecking order. He was only a few months removed from classes at USC. What galled him though was that his assignments were more like ambulance-chasing than real reporting. In theory, he was a general assignment reporter, ready to dash to the scene of any spot news. However, lately, it seemed that vehicular manslaughter was his métier.

He was getting real tired of mangled metal and blood. He was running out of ways to describe how a forty-ton eighteen-wheeler can rip into a passenger car, he grumbled bitterly to city editor Don Hazel, moments after returning from such an accident in the Antelope Valley.

"Shot, how many times can you write 'jangled metal' or 'crumpled like an aluminum can'?" he asked Don. "I want to do murders or something. I can get behind one dude shooting another because he didn't like the way the guy looked at his girlfriend. But these dumb fucks who drive a station wagon full of kids onto the tracks in front of a train going eighty miles an hour because they're racing home to catch "Leave It to Beaver" reruns on cable TV, who wants to report on these dickheads?"

Hazel was not sympathetic. In his opinion, there were many creative ways to describe how a forty-ton eighteen-wheeler rips into a passenger car that Andy had yet to explore.

***

At his grenade-less deck, Danny Evans had found a new reason for fury. Grabbing his grimy phone, the chief copy editor punched a four-digit interoffice number and proceeded to pore his finest Cracker sarcasm into the receiver.

"Hi, Photo? This is Danny Evans in Editorial. That's upstairs on the third floor in the building right across the alley from ya'll. Know where I'm at? Good. Now I want to know where my Fashion art is?" After a moment's pause, Danny softly purred: "Five minutes now. Not five months."

He slammed down the phone receiver. Glancing at an early layout for the Fashion section, he snapped at his patient assistant, Jenny Rotenberg, "I need a five-inch throwaway. Got a hole to fill on Three."

"Right, chief," she chimed.

Danny hated to be called "chief." He was no fucking Indian.

"Hey, Danny, a croak notice is coming," called out another assistant copy editor, Elijah Jordan. "We gotta make room somewhere in Features.

"Why can't it go in Metro?" demanded Danny, who wanted desperately to get Features closed before its 2 p.m. deadline.

"Guy was an old-time movie director," explained Elijah.

"Shit, why do people always die at deadline?" he asked no one in particular. "And here I am up to my ass in alligators with all this Friday stuff."

Suddenly very tired, Danny looked around the third-floor newsroom as though he were searching for God. Had he located the Almighty, Danny would certainly have given Him an earful. The bedraggled newsroom had scarcely changed in decades. Other than the fairly new video display terminals or VDTs, of course. That and the disgusting youth of most of the reporting staff. Danny swore reporters used to be older and wiser than this current crop of underachievers.

The Los Angeles Morning News, known to everyone in the newsroom as the Morning Snooze, was locked in a losing battle with the Times, the city's main paper. Indeed, employees had a motto: "If it's news in L.A., it's news to us."

Not that this battle didn't feature the occasional victorious skirmish with the Old Lady of Spring Street. For the Morning News had a secret weapon: it was *not* the distinguished paper of record. While the pompous Times went about its solemn duty of explaining the social and political elite's view of the city to its readers, the News flew under the radar. It depicted people's daily struggle for existence. It investigated corruption at City Hall, provided hotlines for readers to bitch about the system and dished out plenty of splashy celebrity coverage.

The paper saw itself reporting on what people talk about in elevators, bars or coffee klatches. One way it did this is by turning the lives of people such as jailed Hollywood madam Tina Bonaventure, Dodgers manager Alfredo Hernandez, Mayor William Warren and police chief Ned Sinclair into pop caricatures called Naughty Tina, Alfredo the Great, Hizzoner and Nutty Ned—caricatures Angelenos could easily detest or admire.

The News could take on the cops, nail politicians, rip the Dodgers, go after real estate interests and pan Hollywood's bloated entertainments without fear of offending subscribers. Few readers—and, more crucially, advertisers—would protest. Why this was true became painfully clear to Duke Whitcomb, the new publisher recently installed by Thornhill Corporation, when he pleaded with the head media buyer for Robinsons-May department stores to advertise in the Morning News. The woman politely explained to Whitcomb the facts of life: his readers were her shoplifters.

The News occupied an ancient structure downtown, six floors behind an Italian Renaissance façade of gray granite. Except for the third floor, the building was a mass of tiny offices dimly lit through dirt-encrusted planes. What stories these grimy, peeling, cracked walls might tell, thought Danny, if their aged stone and mortar could be given voice.

The pumping heart of the building was the third-floor newsroom. It was an enormous space that stretched through the entire floor, lined with rows and rows of gray metal desks atop which perched telephones and VDT terminals. Television monitors, usually silent until the 5 p.m. local newscasts, sat on elevated stands above the newsroom. Near one was posted a sign that read: "The Only Sacred Cow Here Is Hamburger." Such sentiments have never been true in any newspaper at any time in history. But the sign did serve to boost office morale.

News of earthquakes, riots, floods, fires, air crashes, freeway accidents, gang warfare, police shootings and political corruption moved through the newsroom with little visible effect on the people within other than the increased energy and raised voices when a big story broke. Horror was an accepted part of the daily routine. The only noisy reaction from the newsroom came when VDTs lost contact with the server, an event that transpired with increasing regularity as the inadequate, overburdened server threatened to die with each new day.

Journalists' copy would often be swallowed whole, their prose lost to the ages with no chance of retrieval. Columnist Francis Sylvester, known to everyone as Sly, was virtually incapable of referring to the Snooze's woebegone server without mentioning the Anti-Christ in the same breath. A monumental turmoil occurred one day when the "I" key on Sly's keyboard got stuck. A columnist with a malfunctioning "I" key, Sly was heard to remark, dwells in a wordless Hades.

The Morning Snooze had come late to the party that was the computer revolution in newsrooms. Above and beyond the capital expense involved in switching over to electronic publishing, the Snooze's general manager, Ike Maynard, distrusted technology. While Times reporters were learning how to cope with Video Display Terminals in the late 1970s, Snooze reporters continued to labor not even on electric typewriters but on Underwood manual typewriters.

Maynard didn't like electric typewriters. He contended that should there ever be a power failure in the city, the Morning News would have a tremendous advantage over the Times. Maynard dreamed of that glorious day following an all-night citywide blackout where the only paper on the street would be—thanks to his foresight—the Morning News.

It never happened though and, eventually, the Morning Snooze did switch to electronic journalism. Not that the transition was an easy one. The older the journalist, the less willing he or she was to quit the beloved typewriter.

One old guy on the copy desk named Hal Franken labored at a VDT station long ago disconnected from the server. He was being allowed to complete his final tour of duty at the Morning Snooze without ever touching hot stories in Rim. He simply edited wire copy and, unknowingly, sent it off into oblivion.

Even in his youth, Franken never seemed to read what he edited. It was as if English were a foreign language to him. Management was forced to remove him from writing headlines after several gaffes, the best of which lined the corridor to the men's room on the third floor: "Man Sentenced to 30 Years in England," "Include Your Children When Baking Cookies," "Prostitutes Appeal to Pope" and "Couple Slain; Police Suspect Homicide."

***

Danny broke away from his duties a few minutes before the 4 o'clock budget meeting. No one could remember when the practice of Danny Evans sitting in on these daily meetings began or why. He simply did so.

As editors gathered for the meeting in his office, Big Bob Patterson, the new managing editor of the Morning News, jammed a Twinkie into his cavernous mouth. The ME sat at a desk piled with a jumble of story lists, wire-service photographs and page dummies with the "news holes" he must fill. Along with Danny, there was the Metro editor, the assistant managing editor, lead editorial writer, photo editor, political editor and heads of other sections.

Occasionally, a reporter attended budget meetings, although Big Bob frowned on the inclusion of reporters unless absolutely necessary. This was the meeting where section editors decide on the lead stories for the next day's edition and reporters, Big Bob reasoned, only get in the way. They invariably argue the merits of their individual stories over the others and too much time gets wasted. Besides Big Bob didn't like reporters.

The meeting began when photo editor Guy Rutledge placed two staff photos in front of his boss. Every morning, Guy sent his troops into the field with the clarion call of "Bring me the bazooms!" He loved photos of women with bazooms and these photos found their way into the back pages with such regularity that several women lead by Winnie Yankovich were threatening to make an issue of this. Guy also liked pictures of crowds on the theory everyone in the shot would buy the paper.

"We have two pretty good photos from that fire on Arlington, Bob," Guy was saying. "The gutted building after the fire and a shot of the grieving father who lost his son."

"Go with the father," Big Bog said instantly. "It emphasizes the human dimension of the fire, not the property damage."

"About this story on Canadian politics—"

"Spike it," snapped Big Bob interrupting Sidney Wersching, his political editor. "Nobody gives a shit about Canadian politics."

Before Wersching could recover, city editor Don Hazel chimed in: "A sheepdog in Parker Ranch went crazy and led 100 sheep off a cliff."

The meeting suddenly came alive. Everyone recognized the opportunity this presented. "Jesus, we gotta get a great headline for that," said Big Bob.

Ideas came fast and furious: "Bo Peep Nightmare." "Woolly Jumpers Buy the Farm." "Mutton For Sale." The final choice would depend on space and typeface.

Ruth Treadway reminded Big Bob that Darlene Temple's gossip column needed a Front Page pointer since her lead item concerned an alleged lesbian affair between soul singer Louella Jones and actress Tammy Lyons.

"How much space we giving to that earthquake in China?" Hazel then wondered.

"As little as possible," said Big Bob.

"Shit, Bob, 1,272 people died," declared Hazel.

"And our readers didn't know a damn one," said the ME. "Look, here's the sliding scale the Morning News will be using from now on for disasters and unexpected deaths: One American is a story. Two Englishman is a story. Fifty Germans is a story. And nothing ever happens in Ecuador."

CHAPTER TWO
RUM AND COKE

An hour-and-a-half later, Danny strolled across the alley separating the main Morning News building from its photo lab and circulation offices and sauntered into the adjacent American Legion bar. The unremarkable stroll was, in fact, remarkable: here in crime-ridden downtown L.A. was an alley that was so well guarded and heavily trafficked by News trucks and delivery personnel that female reporters felt safe walking in this alley at midnight. Of late, its population had markedly increased following Duke Whitcomb's dictum that the News was a smoke-free building. Nicotine addicts huddled in twos and threes in the alleyway no matter how cold the day.

The American Legion bar supposedly served only Legionnaires but by long-standing tradition was open to all Snooze personnel, mostly reporters. The tavern was a plain, unvarnished affair with a shiny pool table in a corner, a battered jukebox, faded booths, a calendar from 1968 and cafeteria-style tables and chairs. Its ambience was zero, but at least it was dark and stank of stale beer so staffers found it a convivial gathering spot.

Danny nodded hello to Bill and Sly before ordering his beer. Bill and Sly had become great buddies since Bill's wife dumped him. This was, in many ways, a renewal of friendship. When Bill first joined the News five years before, Sly took him under his wing. He taught the young reporter such tricks as how to fill out an expense account in a mature manner so as not to kill a good thing and how to call the floor nurse instead of a hospital PR officer to get a line on a biggie's condition. Most pivotally,

Sly taught Bill Boyer that a journalist's natural tendency is toward melancholy and paranoia and that the world was made to enrich his despair.

"Just the man I was looking for," intoned Sly as Danny sat at their table. Danny would normally have avoided the two journalists for any number of solid reasons. But as they were the only News employees in the bar at the moment to ignore them would be rude.

"You are a veteran of the newspaper business," said Sly. "So tell me: why are newspaper headlines almost always in present tense but all newspaper stories written in past tense?"

Danny took a sip of beer and studied the columnist. Sly knew the question would irritate Danny since the copy editor preferred to leave his work behind when he entered the Legion bar.

"Ya'll didn't take my grenade, now did you?" asked Danny, his eyes focusing steadfastly on the columnist.

Sly laughed. "A diversionary tactic. I knew no one could answer that question. It's right up there with the meaning of life."

"What do I get if I answer that question? A friggin' dining room set?" asked Danny.

"You receive my deepest gratitude and admiration as this question has troubled me for years," said Sly.

Francis Sylvester, a bulky man of about six feet and two inches, weighing approximately one-hundred-and-ninety pounds and around forty years of age—everything was imprecise when it came to Sly's vital statistics—favored red bow ties and florid, old-fashioned mannerisms. He liked to think of himself as a lineal descendent of Ben Hecht and H. L. Mencken. So old-fashioned was his approach to his craft that he was the last writer on the staff to master the computer.

Sly was a consumer. He drank gallons of beer, ingested copious amounts of food and read voluminously. He devoured life. Everything about the human condition interested him. His brain and soul absorbed the minutiae of the City of Angels, its quotidian rhythms, its sounds, smells and sensations. But he drifted through this world without ever being a part of it. He was a journalist, not a player or participant.

Most of all, Sly enjoyed thumbing his nose at authority in general and politicians in particular. In his column, he created the impression that he was out to uncover the rip-off artists, the fakes and phonies of public life. He was on the "people's" side and only the churlish would wish to point out that, in general, Sly despised people.

Sly was a man who worked best amid chaos. The noise of the newsroom was sweet music to his ears. And a noisy bar even sweeter. Thus, Sly was in his element and not likely to budge for a long time unless someone suggested a pub-crawl. Which is exactly what happened next.

After Danny left — and rather swiftly too — Winnie wandered in and Bill suggested they all go out drinking. Since Winnie, for once, had no rock concert to attend, she agreed.

"Let's wait for Jessica," Bill added hastily. The Jessica in question was Jessica Tannenbaum, a reporter newly arrived from the Snooze's Valley office.

"Forget it," said Winnie. "Jessica volunteered to handle a late-breaking story. She'll be tied up for another hour."

"So we must be off. Liquor awaits no man," said Sly.

The trio — each in true L.A. fashion driving his car — rendezvoused at a bar on Third Street, not far from downtown. It was called the Windsor Arms but was known to everyone at the Morning Snooze by Bill's designation — the Women of Color bar.

The Sinatra-era cocktail lounge featured fake rock walls and a sheetrock ceiling sprayed to resemble cottage cheese. The scruffy, indifferently lit interior contained a long bar backed by a mirror and TV set. Most of the bar's neon beer signs and promotional cutouts were decades old and probably worth a fortune to collectors, a fact to which management remained oblivious.

Sometime in the 1970s, the word "Entertainment" had been added to the cocktail sign outside. A wooden runway was installed where a pool table had formerly been between two rows of Naugahyde horseshoe banquettes. On this now well-worn runway "exotic" dancers from Thailand, Vietnam, Jamaica, Central America and Mexico took their turns dancing for customer dollars. A multi-tattooed white woman from North Carolina and a strange, melancholy Russian named Ludmilla occasionally showed up; otherwise, the dancers were all women of color who wore trashy lingerie and cheerfully exposed their breasts for tips.

When not dancing, the women sat with customers to hustle drinks or money slipped into bras or panties. Most of the customers were Latino men, and the thin Asian women complained they could never hustle money from patrons who preferred the fleshier dancers from El Salvador and Guatemala.

One young woman—who hailed from Saigon and went by the English name of June—slipped onto a stool next to Bill who ordered a Bloody Mary for her. Bill was on rum and Coke this evening while Sly and Winnie stuck with beer.

"I need money, honey," whined June to Bill. He ignored her and continued talking with his companions. After a couple of rounds, the trio decided they needed new surroundings. To be polite, Bill asked June to join them.

"I get off nine o'clock," she said.

"You can't take off a little early?" asked Bill.

She shrugged. "Maybe. You have money?"

"I have money."

"Who your friends?" she asked.

"Writers and artists," he replied.

"That's no good," she said.

Nevertheless, when the writers and artists quit the Windsor Arms, June left with Bill. The little party hit Michael's Los Feliz restaurant for food, then found themselves at the Dresden Room on Vermont. Two jazz musicians were running through old standards for the lounge's hipsters, giving the club a camp vibe, which the writers, artists and bar girl ignored.

Everyone found stools at the bar except Sly who preferred to stand. Bill groped June enough to let her think he lusted for her, which he did not, and the three journalists let shop talk give way to ruminations about art and love. Rum and coke nearly always caused Bill to get maudlin about his wife.

"Women leave and that's the end of it," he was insisting.

"What fucking crap," Winnie shot back. "Like men don't leave?"

Sly chuckled and said: "I don't know which is worse—a person desperate to get into a relationship or a person desperate to get out of one."

"Tell me about it," groaned Winnie. "I'm tired of all these really bad relationships I get myself into. By my age, I should be in a really bad marriage."

"I don't remember who said it," mused Sly, "and I wish it had been me, but someone once said, 'I've tried women and I've tried men, and there really should be something better.'"

Bill for once was in no mood for Sly's sly aphorisms. He launched into a heated monologue on love's riches. The monologue lasted for several minutes. Sly listened intently, his left eyelid drifting downward, leaving the right eye bright and alert. Sly sipped his beer slowly and nodded on occasion, not so much in agreement as an acknowledgement of having understood his opponent's arguments. Once Bill finished, Sly opened the slumbering eye and looked directly at Bill with the full force of both eyes.

"You are simultaneously idolizing and trivializing women with all this crap about the glories of love," said Sly. "Love is mostly a hormonal disturbance that passes quickly enough and leaves but an agitated embarrassment that refuses to acknowledge its true reality. Unfortunately, this embarrassment demands institutionalization in the act of marriage. Which is the fossil of love, not its flesh and blood."

"You sound like one of your goddam columns," snapped Bill peevishly. "'Fossil of love'—what a neat phrase. If I hadn't had so much to drink, I'd tear your arguments apart."

June fidgeted. The men were using words she didn't understand and for all the money flowing from their pockets for alcohol, precious little was making its way into her purse. She ran her hand along Bill's thigh and her index fingernail along the bulge in his pants. Bill suddenly realized he hadn't been laid in several months.

Sly ordered another round for everyone. When it arrived, he hoisted his stein and in an exaggerated Irish brogue intoned: "May you be in heaven a half-hour before the Devil knows you're dead."

Everyone drank deeply. Silence descended on the group. Bill extracted himself from June's mercenary embrace to take a leak and Sly joined him. At the urinals, standing side by side with Sly, Bill sobbed. Astonished, Sly glanced at his co-irrigator.

"I still love Renee," murmured Bill. "I miss her. I miss the sound of her voice and the smell of her cologne and the smoothness of her skin. I miss sex in our huge bed and waking up beside her and gazing at her mused hair. I miss breakfast with her. I miss our life together."

Touched by Bill's confession, Sly was moved to grasp his colleague and offer words of encouragement that bore little resemblance to his just-concluded sermon on human frailty. Bill was genuinely touched by Sly's gesture although he would have preferred that Sly had finished his business at the urinal before embracing him.

CHAPTER THREE
THE AX

After the two returned to the bar, Bill said he had to go and offered to drop June. Her face clouded and angry Vietnamese words followed. Bill gave her a fifty-dollar tip, which mollified her so she switched back to broken English.

After dropping her near Koreatown, Bill piloted his white 1986 Honda along Franklin Avenue, riding an invigorating wave of rum and Cokes. He knew all along where he was headed.

Just before Beachwood Canyon sat several aging apartment buildings opposite an enormous mansion owned and operated by Scientologists. In one six-story structure, Bill's estranged wife Renee had taken up residence after moving out of their mutual home in the Hollywood Hills. The building was reputed to have been built by William Randolph Hearst as a hideaway love nest but somehow Bill doubted the rumor. It wasn't nearly grand enough. The other rumor involved Charlie Chaplin. Between those two, they seemed to have owned every building in Hollywood at one time.

Bill parked in the Mayfair Market parking lot, picked up a bottle of red wine at Victor's Liquor and strolled past the French bistro. The apartment building's security system was easily circumvented by the veteran journalist. Bill waited only a few moments down the street before a middle-aged man approached the front door. Then clutching the wine and waving a set of keys, Bill came up behind the man. A cheery fellow in a coat and baseball cap, the man, who spoke with an accent, said his name was István and even held the door. Bill nodded graciously and made a quick joke that produced a roar of laughter.

The lobby featured a high ceiling, an ancient elevator and a vestibule for a doorman who no longer existed. Bill rode the elevator up to the third floor and pounded at Renee's door for a solid minute before she called out, "I'm not home!"

Eventually, she relented. Her concern was less for her estranged husband than irritated neighbors. Bill blew past the opened door, stumbling slightly in his drunkenness, then launched into a bitter argument with her that picked up where the last one left off.

Renee Boyer was a small, dark woman who acted like a Southern belle despite the fact she was from Southern California. She grew up in Valencia and the whiff of provincialism clung to her like bad body odor. This, combined with her Scarlett O'Hara routine, made her seem aloof and demanding when, in fact, she was rather shy. Men kept their distance. As a consequence, when Bill first asked her out, she didn't understand.

He wondered if she wanted to see the new Woody Allen movie and she said she was thinking about it and may go in a week or so when the crowds died down. Only after he persisted about this damn Woody Allen movie did she realize he was asking *her* if she wanted to go see the movie with *him*. She said that would be nice.

In those days, Bill cut quite a dashing figure. He was always going to parties, whether invited or not, and when he entered a room people turned around and noticed. Women especially seemed to enjoy his company so the attention he paid Renee was flattering.

To her amazement, he got her into bed in less than a week. Even more amazing, she enjoyed sex for the first time in her life. She found herself conspiring to get into bed with him as often as possible. When they got married six months later, she couldn't help giggling. This was too good to be true.

Which, of course, it was.

Bill still went to parties only she was often not included. Work absorbed more and more of his time. Also, his charm contained higher proof of alcohol than she had realized. Much more problematic was the state of their finances. Bottomline, journalists earned shit. Renee didn't want to work but with Bill's income, it became a necessity. She worked for a real estate company in the Valley, a job that often kept her out late at night and on weekends.

When she tiptoed past thirty, the view on the other side blackened her spirits: everything in her life seemed so unrewarding. She had nothing to look forward to and precious little to look back at. She took a lover without Bill ever noticing. That lasted no time but the experience transformed her. Another man's desire awakened long-felt needs. She still loved Bill, but what she wanted he no longer could provide. A part of her, untended for too long, was suddenly alive and demanding more. She tried to ignore these demands but gave in with a second lover and this time she moved out.

When Bill found out about the lover, he went berserk. She insisted the man was not the cause of their breakup. That didn't prevent Bill from buying an ax, which he carried in the trunk of his Honda. He wasn't sure what he intended to do with it and it certainly wasn't a weapon of convenience. Still, the vision of the ax descending on Renee's boyfriend's head filled him with quiet satisfaction.

A few days after the purchase of the ax, Bill grew worried so he visited a shrink listed with the Morning News' health plan. After he told her about the ax, though, the therapist became alarmed and refused to see him until he disposed of the ax.

"But that's why I'm coming to see you!" he remonstrated.

Nevertheless, Dr. Helen Linquist adamantly refused to see anyone who roamed the streets with an ax in his car. So he never went back to her.

As the argument with his wife grew more heated, his thoughts kept drifting back to the ax. He faced a dilemma, though: if he excused himself and returned to the car for the ax, he knew she would never let him back inside. So he would have to break down the door with the ax to gain entry by which time the neighbors would be aroused.

Bill was prepared to be arrested and to spend his next few years in prison for tearing up Renee's apartment. Only tomorrow he had to polish and file his three-part series on Tina Bonaventure.

No, his arrest and arraignment would have to wait for a more propitious day. After several more minutes of arguing with Renee, Bill drove home, exhausted, with the ax resting comfortably in his trunk. He did feel better knowing it was there, though.

CHAPTER FOUR
DINO AND TRIXIE

Her lifeless body was covered with scars. The back of her head was punctured. Blood vessels had burst in her eyes, indicating asphyxia. Her right hand was broken. Officially, the cause of the nine-year-old girl's death was an overdose of drugs and alcohol—the tiny body had a blood alcohol level of 0.15. But the girl's mouth was bruised, indicating the possibility of force-feeding.

Laurel's forty-five-year-old aunt, Ruby Danvers, who was her guardian, had been viewed as a godsend by county social workers. She had generously taken in all five of her sister's illegitimate kids. No one from the Department of Children and Family Services had bothered to perform an extensive background check on Rudy before placing the children in her care. None seemed warranted. Plus everyone's caseload was much too large. Had they done so, they would have discovered a family history of drug and child abuse, one suicide and another sibling, Ruby's brother Alvin, in a mental hospital.

Jessica Tannenbaum had fought to cover the preliminary hearing, but David Brassel drew the assignment. She was infuriated.

The case would have landed her on the Front Page of Metro and maybe even the Front Page itself at least twice. There was the whole issue of background checks and, even more exciting, the mystery of who and what killed Laurel Nugent. Could the woman who cared for Laurel as if she were her child have forced alcohol and antidepressant drugs down her throat? Or did Laurel, a troubled youth with a junkie prostitute for a mom, try an experiment that went awry?

Yes, this was a great story. But, no, David Brassel got the assignment. David Brassel, whose major contribution to American journalism consisted of a Thursday Food section story the previous year on the last meals requested by death-row inmates before execution, a story memorable for the bold headline on the Food front which shouted "Just Fry and Serve."

An hour after Don Hazel had rejected her plea, Jessica fumed at her desk. Next time, she promised herself, she would go directly to Big Bob and use whatever feminine wiles she possessed to persuade the ME to give her a solid assignment. For whatever reason, such tactics fell flat with Hazel.

At this very moment, interestingly enough, her feminine wiles were having a powerful effect on a colleague. From his desk three rows down and an aisle to the right from hers, Bill couldn't help stealing glances at her flushed face.

The first time Bill saw Jessica Tannenbaum, he fell in love. Newly transferred from the Valley bureau, she strode into the newsroom as if she had the deed to the place tucked away in her purse. At twenty-four, she was headstrong and ambitious. She wore an Anne Klein skirt, a Jones New York silk blouse and an Ellen Tracy jacket. Her long, dark curly hair made a dramatic contrast to a pale white face. Her eyes were clear and bright with the white heat of intelligence.

He didn't ask himself if she were beautiful. The question was insignificant. The nose was slightly larger than fashion dictated. Her breasts were small and hip almost boyish. Her hair had more shades of brown and red than most women would have wanted. Bill made no judgment as to her beauty: he was obsessed.

He got up from his desk and strolled past Jessica's, ostensibly in quest of a third cup of the battery acid that passed for coffee in the Snooze newsroom.

"We missed you last night," he murmured as he hovered near her desk.

Startled, she looked up. "What?" she asked.

"We missed you last night. Sly and Winnie and I went out for a few drinks," said Bill.

"Oh yeah, I got caught with an extra assignment. It would have been fun." Her eyes refocused on her monitor.

"How's tonight look?" he persisted.

"Not good unless you want to grab a quick drink at the Legion after work," she said, her mind clearly on other things.

"Sounds good," he said. "What are you working on?"

Her eyes rolled. "Celebrity jogging. Can you believe it? I get the shittiest assignments."

"Well, a good reporter should be able to turn chicken shit into chicken salad," said Bill. He was quite pleased with his witty remark.

"Why should I want to make chicken salad when I'm capable of *coq au vin*?" she replied.

Bill reddened, managed a brief laugh and hurried to the coffee machine. Jessica had a way of unnerving him as few women did. As Bill struggled to puzzle this phenomenon out, his route took him through the no-man's-land between Winnie and Ruth Treadway. Most Morning Snooze reporters learned from experience to avoid this area of the newsroom. Sure enough, as Bill passed Winnie's desk, a Threadway volley shot past his ear.

"Winnie, for God's sake, where's your copy?" screamed Ruth.

Winnie was past deadline. But then it was every editor's contention that Winnie was born past deadline. There was a standing bet at the copy desk—actually, a pool to which everyone contributed weekly that amounted to several hundred dollars—as to the time and day *and year* Winnie might make deadline.

Other than this annoying habit, most Snooze employees genuinely enjoyed the company of the bedraggled, twenty-three-year-old rock critic who always looked like she had spent the night with the Beastie Boys. But Ruth simply couldn't tolerate Winnie and the feeling was mutual.

"Ruth has had her vibes tied," Winnie once insisted.

Ruth knew virtually nothing about rock music and cared even less. That Winnie or any rock critic was employed at the Morning Snooze was a necessary evil as far as she was concerned. But what Ruth—a forty-year-old woman who thought of herself as an arts editor—couldn't tolerate was a twenty-something person prone to writing language that contained words such as "chillin'," "def," "rad" and "fly." And there were other words that sounded nothing like the English found in the Associated Press Style book.

Ruth naturally had other suspicions about anyone associated with the music business. She would frequently refer to Winnie as "a woman of substance." Winnie's defense of her lifestyle was simply that it is better to burn out than to rust.

At the moment, Winnie sat transfixed in front of her terminal, neither burning nor rusting. After Ruth's shout, Winnie bit fingernails that were already so chewed it was a wonder her teeth could get a purchase on anything remotely resembling a nail. She looked over at Ruth.

"Sorry, sorry," she said. "It's comin' really slow today. You'll have copy in…ten minutes."

"Ten minutes!" screamed Ruth. "Winnie, it isn't literature. It's birdcage liner!"

"Okay, five minutes," replied Winnie.

"Why do you have so much trouble coping in the newspaper game?" wailed Ruth.

"Fear of success," she replied.

Bill poured a cup of coffee he did not want and skirted the war zone, which regrettably meant missing Jessica's desk. He wondered why she had only time for a drink. What the hell else did she have to do? Was she seeing someone?

Bill shook his head. He must wake up. The fog from last night's drinking still encircled his brain. It was a fine morning though. The newsroom was about to kick into overdrive and he needed to be alert.

***

A newsroom has a life of its own. It gathers energy as the day progresses. Early in the morning, reporters wander in on different time schedules and with different deadlines. Each, in turn, picks up a copy of the Times with trepidation and quickly scans the Old Lady, looking for bylines of reporters on similar beats. It's the quickest way to ascertain what story a journalist missed the previous day. When one's counterpart at the Times has no byline, these are moments of deep satisfaction. It means, if nothing else, another day of employment.

After coffee gets poured and phone calls returned, fax press releases hit followed by phone tips and breaking news. It is hard to detect when newsroom gears finally mesh and forward momentum is achieved. But once it does, the energy level continues to build through the early deadlines for Features and Entertainment, the later deadlines for Metro and on into the late night when the Front Page and Sports are put to bed.

Sound levels are not what they once were in the news biz: the cacophony of typewriters banging away and Linotype machines guzzling lead had long ago been replaced by VDTs with whisper-quiet keyboards and a back shop that take columns of text printed by phototypesetters on high-resolution film, which are then quietly cut and pasted onto photographed final prints.

Gone too were copyboys who passed among reporters to pick up their precious prose, and the brass pneumatic tubes that ran overhead through which, with a hiss-like noise, copy rolled up in cylindrical containers whisked its way to the back shop after being slugged and edited. Now copy whizzed about electronically from reporters to city desk to the back shop. "Spike," which once meant a sharp steel skewer sitting on an editor's desk, on which failed stories got impaled, was now simply a cue in the computer system.

For Bill, there was no more romantic spot on earth than a newsroom. Growing up in San Francisco, he learned to read from newspapers. He climbed the newspaper chain: Street sales. Circulation slugger. Copyboy. Cub reporter. The newspaper was his grade school, high school and college. Journalism got him out of the housing projects where his family lived on welfare.

One of Bill's greatest assets was that he happened not to look like a reporter. He had a shock of brown hair over a handsome, open face. His frame was athletic with broad shoulders and narrow hips. He seemed more like a lawyer or banker than a scribe. He also possessed a certain charm through which he could get answers without having asked too many questions.

He learned too. As a rewrite man one weekend, he handled a story about a murder. He wrote in his lead that a nude and mutilated body of a young woman was found in the woods near Mill Valley. The city editor offered an improvement. He added that she was "beautiful." The lesson sunk in. All young women whose dead nude bodies were discovered were beautiful.

His devotion to the craft of reporting was absolute. It was like fire in his belly. There was also in Bill Boyer something of that unscrupulousness which makes a good newspaperman — slyness and opportunism, a tinge of cynicism and the faintest willingness to abrogate personal integrity.

Unfortunately, San Francisco was a dead town for a newsie. Great for columnists and pundits but zilch in terms of real news. He left the Chronicle after putting in a couple of years on various city beats and soon found himself four hundred miles south in Los Angeles working for the Morning News.

Other reporters in California pretended disdain for the Morning News. It was tantamount to having credentials as a juvenile delinquent. But the truth was a lot of reporters who wrote about the bond market and political redistricting would prefer to spend their time doing Bill's job.

***

Bill's lunch with Nate Shaw served only to make him tired. He had eaten far more than he should. To say nothing of two glasses of Mondavi Cab. But he couldn't resist sticking it to Nate. No doubt the taxpayers anted up for the meal anyway. He wanted to get out of the newsroom as quickly as possible after deadline as he needed to get over to Cedars for a story. But Jessica was still screwing around with her jogging feature so, by the time she filed, they had little time left for that drink.

As they crossed the alley to the American Legion, Jessica was working herself into a lather about the next day's banner. "SPLIT!" the headline would scream. And the kicker would proclaim: "Jack's a Sex Dynamo."

It seemed that film star Jack Connelly had moved out of the Holmby Hills mansion he shared with his supermodel-wife Carrie Chute. Too many indiscretions with too many other women were the alleged problems. Big Bob had been highly pleased with the headline. Not only had he come up with it, he felt it was libel-proof. He couldn't imagine Jack Connelly's lawyer filing a brief to prove his client was *not* a sex dynamo. Nevertheless, Jessica was incensed.

"What kind of a fucked-up banner is that?" she demanded as the two reporters barged through the door of the Legion. "I wouldn't even put that story on Page One! It belongs in Darlene Temple's gossip column."

"Jack Connelly's number-three at the domestic box office," said Bill.

"I can think of several things that happened in the world today that were more important than Jack Connelly busting up with his bimbo wife," retorted Jessica.

"Maybe you can but not our readers," said Bill. The two sat at the bar since service would be painstakingly slow anywhere else. Bill signaled to the aging bartender: "Two Rolling Rocks, please."

The bartender pivoted in slow motion from Bill to fill the order while Jessica turned the most appealing shade of crimson. Bill loved it when her face flushed. It was a damn shame he had to get over to Cedars. If he could get a few lagers into Jessica, he stood half a chance of their making a night of it. Who knows where that would lead?

As it turned out, Jessica was so worked up over the banner Bill was unable to steer the conversation into more interesting avenues. Within twenty-five minutes Bill was heading west on Third, fighting a setting sun and rush hour traffic.

He stopped off briefly at Alphonse's Costumes and Props in East Hollywood. Mostly TV and movie companies utilized its services. Except for Halloween, the store was seldom patronized by citizens. Bill, however, was a fairly regular customer. Konstantine Theosophus, who ran the warehouse, never bothered to inquire why Bill so frequently needed costumes. Konstantine wasn't the curious sort.

Today Bill required a doctor's lab coat and stethoscope. Konstantine had him outfitted in a jiffy. All customers should be so easily satisfied. It wasn't as if he wanted a Roman Legion get-up. Now that would take a while.

Approaching Cedars-Sinai Medical Center, Bill turned on George Burns Road and then into one of the many parking structures for the hospital. Once parked, he slipped his Canon camera into a dark bag, then popped open the car's glove compartment and pulled out his treasured collection of passes and identification cards: Police and sheriff press cards, IDs from various security outfits, airlines and LAX, most entertainment venues and, vital at this moment, hospitals.

Locating his Cedars identification badge—he couldn't remember how he came by it—he got out of the car. He slipped into the lab coat and threw the stethoscope around his neck. Bill went through a public entrance but quickly veered down a corridor marked "Staff Only."

Dino Verilli would be on the fourth floor, his tipster told him. The rock star had collapsed in his suite at the Four Seasons a day earlier and rumors were it was a drug overdose. His manager attributed the collapse to exhaustion. An ex-lover said he tried to commit suicide—but ex-lovers were never reliable sources. Another source close to the rocker insisted his collapse was a result of taking an illegal recreational drug known a GHB. The Morning News was about to learn the truth.

After slipping into several rooms and having to act embarrassed by his "mistake," Bill soon was clueless. The fourth floor could mean anything in this vast medical complex. Which fourth floor? The key was to look for intense, hard-bodied men with steely stares. Those would be Verilli's bodyguards.

Bill wandered the corridors a while longer before encountering a pair of tough-looking types who clearly were not brain surgeons. He nodded as he passed between them, keenly aware of their unfriendly scrutiny but safe in the knowledge they would hesitate to challenge his uniform. The problem was they continued to monitor his progress along the corridor. This meant he had to walk more quickly than desired. He wanted to linger at each doorway. But this was not possible. Finally, he ducked into one room, where he came upon an elderly man hooked up to enough machines to look like something out of a 1930s Universal horror flick.

Bill debated what to do. Verilli must be nearby. But those guards detected something suspicious about him. Sweat dripped down his chest. He rechecked the microcassette tape recorder in his pocket, grabbed the chart from the old man's bed and carried it with him out the door.

Sure enough, the two rent-a-cops were staring at him when he emerged from the room. Pretending to be completely engrossed in the old guy's chart, Bill walked slowly toward them. The two must be standing very near their client's room, Bill reasoned. He stopped at an open door, glanced inside and decided the young woman on the bed was not Dino Verilli. Bill then remembered that a door just past the two guards had been shut. That must be the one. But how to get in?

Bill strolled directly toward the no-necks, totally concentrated on what the medical chart was telling him. He could almost feel the rising tension in the guards' bodies. In a few feet, he abruptly halted and stared at the chart.

"Oh no!" he exclaimed. "This can't be."

He looked up at the guards, looking at them in a manner he hoped was threatening. The two exchanged confused glances.

"When was the last time a nurse checked on Mr. Verilli's condition?" he demanded.

"Uh, 'bout an hour ago, I guess," said a guard with black hair and bad acne, who never realized he had just tipped his assignment.

"An hour?" Bill repeated the reply as if he had been told an earthquake was imminent. "I told my staff Mr. Verilli must be checked every twenty minutes. We must monitor his vital signs during this critical stage."

"Critical?" asked the other guard, who had long blond hair and looked like a surfer who had wiped out too many times.

"Maybe you rock 'n' rollers think something like this is just part of the music business," lectured Bill, "but Mr. Verilli's condition is damn serious, I want you to know."

"We're not rock 'n' rollers," sneered the dark-haired guard. "We're bodyguards."

"And who is threatening Mr. Verilli?" demanded Bill.

"Well, you know, fans and the press want to get at him," said the surfer.

"Do you see either in this corridor?"

The two again exchanged troubled glances. The blond said: "It's our job to keep it that way."

"And it's my job to keep Mr. Verilli alive so you can keep your jobs. I must look in on my patient at once."

As Bill anticipated, the two yielded ground with enough body language to indicate his target was indeed behind the closed door. Bill strode past the guards and flung open the door. He shut it with a purposeful slam.

It took a moment for Bill's eyes to adjust to the near dark. A shade had been pulled against the window and the overhead light was unusually dim. The patient, his face ashen and his long, tangled hair spread out on two pillows, barely glanced up as Bill came to the bed. Verilli's eyes were murky pools of self-pity. His pasty skin was unshaven. His hair looked like it hadn't been cleaned in weeks.

Bill gazed down at the sick man without an ounce of compassion. "How're we doing?" he asked. Bill knew few if any doctors call patients "we." But most patients, used to medical dramas on television, would figure this was hospital lingo.

"We're bustin' for a drink," rasped the singer from inside his web of IVs, a feeding tube and catheter. Bill mused that Verilli looked more wired than his cable television.

Bill slipped Verilli's chart from its bedside perch and glanced at it. He then fished inside his coat pocket from which pulled out a flask. He congratulated himself on his foresight.

"Will gin do?" queried the doctor to his startled patient. Suddenly, Dino's eyes lost their cloudiness.

"I prefer vodka," Dino replied in a husky voice.

"Oh, well then," said Bill, slipping the flask back inside his coat pocket.

"No, it's okay, mate!" said Dino anxiously. He sat up in bed. "Gin's great."

Bill smiled and pulled out the flask once more. "Let me get a couple of cups," he said.

As he moved to the sink, Bill adjusted the wires strapped to his chest that ran into the microcassette recorder in his other coat pocket. Inside that pocket, he depressed the Play button. After pulling two paper cups from the wall dispenser, he sauntered confidently back to the bed and filled both tiny cups to the brim.

The rocker hit a button on his bed's control panel and the top half of the bed jerked and groaned as it raised the patient into a sitting position. Dino eagerly reached for a cup. He was looking healthier already.

"Cheers," said Bill as he took a sip from his paper cup. No half measure for Dino, however, as he swallowed the entire contents of his cup in one gulp. This boy knows how to drink, thought Bill.

"Have another," said Bill.

"So it's okay to drink?" asked the singer.

"In moderation," replied Bill as he poured gin into Dino's cup.

"Good God, the other doctor was so upset when Bernie tried to give me some fuckin' wine," said Dino, shaking his head.

"Different doctors, different approaches," explained Bill. "So familiarize me more with your case. What's your explanation for this visit to Cedars?"

Dino jerked his head in Bill's direction and stared at him. This question seemed strange coming from a doctor treating him. Yet since in his hand the doctor clutched medicinal gin, he didn't want to insult his benefactor too soon.

"Ain't you supposed to know?" grunted the singer.

"I know what the admission sheet and your chart tell me. But I want to hear what you have to say. Liz Garbarkowitz told someone you tried to off yourself."

"That ho," spat Dino. "Liz Garbarkowitz ain't been with me in six months. She only wishes it was a suicide attempt. Fuckin' cunt."

Dino turned toward Bill. Yes, the color was coming back nicely to his patient's flesh. Maybe, Bill thought, I should go into medicine.

"I get millions to sing and play guitar," Dino continued. "I travel the world. Fans idolize me. Women scream they wanna have my baby. Why would I want to kill myself?"

Dino said this in a voice that sounded sweet and reasonable. The rock star looked away for a moment before Bill heard the man murmur: "Sometimes I party too hard, know wha I mean?"

"Drugs?"

"Well, you saw the admission sheet," rasped the rocker. "Sometimes you need a little blow to get it up, you know wha I mean?"

Bill smiled. What a scoop this was going to be.

"Tina Bonaventure has called to check on your condition a couple of times," said Bill. "Man to man and strictly off the record, you doing her?"

Dino grinned. "Hey, I won' lie to ya, mate. Tina digs my cock. Wha can I say?"

"And her girls?"

"She brings 'em along, mate. God, me an' my mates had a party goin' down at the Four Seasons. No wonder they kicked us out."

"They did? I thought paramedics came for you."

"Tha was after someone tripped the fire alarm. I told 'em not to free-base, know what I mean?"

"Could you do me a teeny-tiny favor?" asked Bill.

"Sure, wha?"

"My niece is such a big fan of yours. Would you mind if I took your picture?"

The flask floated in front of the singer's suddenly inflamed eyes. "Why the fuck not?" he replied. "You gotta camera?"

The Canon was out in Bill's hands before Verilli finished uttering the question.

***

At this exact moment, the broken melodies of a saxophone coming from her car speakers were carrying Jessica homeward. A surprising chill hung in the air as clouds drifted over the city, threatening but not delivering needed rain.

Jessica navigated through the exceptionally light evening traffic. For the first time this day, her mind relaxed. True, she was still occupied with upcoming stories. But to her this was relaxation. Occasionally her thoughts were interrupted by vague sexual fantasies. She couldn't decide why this was happening, but she certainly resented the intrusions.

Drive-time was her one opportunity to focus on the "big picture," to scrutinize the day's news events and conversations with sources and try to locate a trend that might vault her into the Page Three feature slot.

Yet erotic thoughts kept elbowing their way into her consciousness. She must remember to mention this to her therapist. She had not had sex in over eight months and preferred things that way. Unless she fell in love—and what were the odds of that in Los Angeles? Besides what was the point? At best, you get dumped and, at worst, you might contract a horrible disease. Fuck men anyway. At best, they were annoying and, at worst—she didn't want to dwell on the worst.

Refocusing her mind, she zeroed in on tomorrow's Metropolitan Transportation Authority press conference. She seldom got to cover anything to do with the city's subway. This story was the exclusive preserve of Dan Albright. But Dan was on vacation so she drew the assignment. A press conference was not sexy but the story stood a chance to land on Page One. She stifled a sniffle—she was fighting off another of her damn head colds— and pushed a button, switching from FM radio to cassette. Miles Davis' horn filled her with intense longings.

She drove into her underground parking garage. She was home. If a one-bedroom apartment on the Westside with cottage-cheese ceilings, drywalls and a tiny kitchenette can be called home. Here resided an extensive LP collection and cassette tapes, much of her mother's silver and a cat named Trixie. She slept here but otherwise, Jessica was a stranger in her dwelling.

She threw a frozen dinner from Trader Joe's into the microwave, then dumped her purse and coat in the bedroom. A "Chains Required" sign over the queen-sized bed made her smile. And people say she lacked a sense of humor.

She repaired to the kitchen's breakfast nook. Here she went to work with a phone and her Rolodex from work—she never left it there since she trusted no one. Her first phone call of the evening went to Peter Rivers, the assistant deputy mayor who was usually annoyed by her calls—his wife hated work calls at home—but generally would chat for a few minutes once he overcame his annoyance. This time she got only his answering machine.

Jacqueline Beller, who worked for Councilman Glenn Hawthorne, was in, however, and being a dateless single woman who loved to dish, Jackie was always excited by these surreptitious phone calls from the press. Jackie was in fine form this evening and before their fifteen-minute conversation concluded, Jessica had two leads for the following day. Jessica had no City Hall beat but if she came up with solid stories they usually were hers.

Trixie cried, purred and rubbed herself against her mistress as she chatted with Jackie. Only after Jessica hung up did she realize she had forgotten to feed the cat.

CHAPTER FIVE
BIG BOB

Big Bob Patterson slammed a meaty fist into his punching bag. God how he hated reporters!

Just as dogs hate cats and USC fans hate UCLA, he hated reporters. The moment he entered the newsroom in the morning, Big Bob would yell at a reporter. It was the way he woke up. A week into his regime at the Morning News, Big Bob had a large punching bag wheeled into his managing editor's corner office and rigged it to resemble a reporter.

Reporters were an untrustworthy lot. They fabricated their T&Es, took long lunches, went to bed with one another and never had enough sources to do a story properly. But what he hated most about reporters was that he was forced to rely on them. If a reporter got a fact wrong or misquoted somebody, who caught hell from the publisher? Big Bob did. Not the lunatic who fucked up.

On the wall of his office, only a short distance from his punching bag, Big Bob hung a framed sign with his favorite quote from Ambrose Bierce: "Nobody in the United States has ever been hanged for killing a journalist; public opinion will not permit it."

That was written in 1878 and as far as Big Bob was concerned nothing had changed in over one-hundred-and-ten years. His idea of heaven was a newsroom without reporters. There would be the wire services, photographers, assistants, artists, editorial writers, layout, copy and photo editors and maybe a columnist or two. But no fucking reporters.

The object of his wrath this morning was Bill Boyer. Secretly he was pleased by Bill's initiative. Big Bob was dying to splash the "exclusive" interview with Dino Verilli on Page One. But he had a major problem. Actually, he had two.

One, he was going to have to rely entirely on Bill's somewhat shaky memory of the previous night's interview. The sweat pouring down Bill's chest during the interview had shorted out the microcassette wires. So the damn recorder had picked up absolutely nothing from Bill's conversation with the rock star. And Big Bob had little faith in Bill's memory when he was drinking.

The second problem had to do with the rock star's serious setback late last night. Verilli, mysteriously drunk, had escaped his hospital room, fled his bodyguards, nearly raped a female patient, then believing himself to be in a concert hall fell down a flight of stairs while looking for the stage entrance. Big Bob feared someone might link these events with his reporter's exclusive interview with the star earlier in the evening.

"Jesus H. Christ!" fumed Big Bob as the punching bag swung back and forth from his last punch. "Reporters!"

"Sorry, Bob," said a contrite Bill Boyer, who was slightly hungover. "It's a nervous condition."

"What is?" thundered the ME.

"The sweat that shorted out the wires."

"Oh, damn your nervous condition. When I was a young reporter, we never even bothered to take notes. We remembered everything people told us and no one ever accused us of misquoting."

"I hardly think Dino Verilli will make that accusation," said Bill defensively.

"You mean if he regains consciousness. What kind of a stunt is that anyway—giving a man with a drug overdose a half-pint of vodka?"

"Gin," Bill corrected him.

"Gin. Like it matters."

"I always like to be accurate."

The ME took another swing at his punching bag but did so without properly planting his feet and nearly toppled over. Embarrassed, he righted his large frame, flushed to the roots of his thinning hair and decided to terminate this conversation.

"Get to work on the story. I want to read a draft by noon," snapped the ME. Bill slipped quietly and swiftly out of Big Bob's office.

Several minutes later, Big Bob emerged from his office and stalked the newsroom. He rummaged through his pockets from which he pulled scraps of paper—a napkin, matchbook, torn program— where he had jotted down story ideas. Big Bob knew reporters lacked self-motivation. They would come in and sit all day chatting to sources on the phone if he didn't light a fire beneath their collective asses.

Reporters who caught sight of Big Bob's morning patrol made hurried phone calls or abruptly hammered away at their keyboards. Deadlines hours away took on a sudden urgency. The ME's patrol brought him first to the desk of Howie Fulbright.

"Howie, cut that school board story of yours down to twelve inches, You're not getting paid by the word," he barked.

"Yes, sir," Howie murmured, his eyes glued to the monitor.

Big Bob fumbled with several scraps of paper. "Got an idea for a series of profiles on every member of the city council. Your councilman's lifestyle—and how he can afford it—that sort of thing. See me when you're off deadline."

"Okay," said Howie meekly.

Big Bob next stropped by the desk of Andy Reynolds.

"Jesus H. Christ, Andy, that news feature of yours is fifteen minutes past deadline. Get the finger out, will ya?"

"But, Bob, I'm waiting for a phone call from the mayor's press secretary," replied the young man, who had not yet learned to simply say yes to Big Bob. Since the ME invariably forgot his conversations with reporters moments after they transpired, most staffers developed the habit of yes-ing him, then ignoring his instructions.

"Ship the story," said Big Bob evenly. "You can add quotes later."

"Okay," said Andy. Big Bob moved on and Andy continued to wait for his phone call.

***

The Morning Snooze traced its lineage back to the turn of the century. That was when Oakleigh Benet, a hard-living, hard-drinking brute, married into Angeleno aristocracy and amassed a fortune by organizing the orange shipping industry. He founded the Morning Express to further his ambitions to rule California politically. Then he started a vice war.

It so happened that El Pueblo de la Reina de Los Angeles was at that time suffering from an invasion by Midwestern reformers. The invaders wished to strip the city of much of its colorful heritage of political corruption and to eliminate the red-light district flourishing in Chinatown. It came as a tremendous shock to old-timers to learn from these corn-belt intruders that horse racing was a creation of Satan and that controlled, medically regulated prostitution was a vice.

The Express jumped on this bandwagon by pushing for political reform. Editorials called for such measures as the initiative, the referendum and—most radical of all—the recall. Once installed, the recall was used to challenge the Southern Pacific Railroad's political machine, link vice to officials and shut down the red-light district.

The Express initiated the vice war by running a series of exposés called "Is Vice Protected in Los Angeles?" Ultimately the mayor was forced to resign rather than face a recall election, party rule ended and the forces of evil were routed. A haze of holiness hung over the city.

The reforms, of course, did little to increase the rule of the people. Bossism remained—but without the benefits of party responsibility. The reforms did, however, have the long-term effect of increasing the rule of a newspaper publisher who contributed heavily to various politicians' campaign funds.

Oakleigh Benet paid his reporters almost nothing, changed editorial stances to suit his whim and, ultimately, stood less for principles than self-aggrandizement. He nevertheless founded a dynasty that at one point owned radio stations, newspapers and a Pacific Coast League baseball team in the 1930s.

Despite an image nurtured by sunshine and Hollywood glamour, L.A. for most of the 20th century was a staid and proper cow town where a Midwesterner could feel at home. Restaurants closed at 10. Fans fled Dodgers' games early to avoid traffic. Unions were something that happened "back East." And its police force was tiny by standards of even a modest-sized town.

The Morning News — so named following a merger with the City News in the mid-Fifties — gave staid and proper L.A. its pizzazz. At its height, the News cranked out a million copies a day in a dozen frantic editions. It gave the startled city screaming headlines and blown-up photos of car crashes. Crime, violence, miracle diets, sex fiends and small-town boosterism ruled the day as a few sample banner headlines will attest: "Shrink's Son Commits Mayhem!" "Rams Fan Wins Nobel Prize!" "Guilty!" for any number of crime-of-the-century trials.

Whatever one thought of Benet — and newsroom opinions were never indifferent — printer's ink flowed through his veins. The same could not be said of the paper's current ownership.

The Morning News floundered badly after its purchase by the Chicago Chronicle in 1979. Consequently, Morning News Corp. had been recently acquired by Thornhill Corp., a New York-based media conglomerate with seven TV stations, three cable outfits, a New York publishing house and twenty medium-sized regional newspapers. The new owner vowed to reinvigorate the paper. There was talk of focus groups and marketing strategies and reaching out to readers. Sly could only shake his head over the nonsense.

Big Bob entered that newsroom only a month before. He was a hulking, deeply freckled, sandy-haired man with piercing green eyes, out-of-style sideburns and no hips. Winnie Yankovich was the first to notice the startling phenomenon of Big Bob's lack of hips. Others in the newsroom marveled when they recognized the accuracy of Winnie's observation: it was true. Big Bob's waist was somehow attached to his legs without any intermediary body part. His pants hung strangely too since he essentially had no ass. He lumbered when he walked which made his gait appear that of a Main Street wino. He also brought into the newsroom an air of pent-up fury. Perhaps he was engaged in an eternal search for his hips.

As was soon clear, Big Bob was heavily influenced by USA Today. He liked color photos (only the color in Morning News photos was often out of register). He liked brief, snappy items and capsule summaries. His preferences caused Sly to insist that Patterson was angling for the Morning News to win a Pulitzer Prize for the best investigative news paragraph.

On his first day at the Morning Snooze, Big Bob gave a lengthy pep talk about how he meant to spruce up the paper. Most of what Big Bob said does not bear repeating since Big Bob himself could not have done so five minutes after he finished. His main point though seemed to be that everyone was going to have to roll up his sleeves and buckle down to business and that every reporter would be expected to mind the store and keep his eyes peeled.

Sly winced visibly at each cliché. This, he thought to himself, was the kind of man who strung together bumper-sticker slogans as a kind of shorthand. In his hurry to get to his point, he tramples all that is fine and sensible in the English language. Indeed the conclusion of Big Bob's pep talk, which will be included here, nicely encapsulates his linguistic philosophy:

"What I dislike with a passion is loose ink, whether in thought or speech. Do you know what I mean? Unnecessary verbiage. When there's a job to be done, get to it, I say. Get to it. And never mind the foot-scraping and kowtowing."

Sly was amazed. He hadn't heard the phrase "kowtowing" since he was a child. And certainly never in a newsroom.

CHAPTER SIX
CORONER'S CASE 87-03694

"Bob?"

The ME turned to discover Jessica standing in front of him. Big Bob liked Jessica. Okay, she was a reporter. But she was a self-starter, quoted people accurately and had the body of a model. Big Bob was, after all, a reasonable man. Not *all* reporters were idiots.

"I heard on the scanner about a fire in mid-Wilshire," said Jessica. "Can I cover?"

Big Bob regarded her for a moment. He wanted to groom this one, but he meant to bring her along slowly. He knew she could handle a simple fire story. Hell, even Howie could manage that.

"Does this mean you're through with your MTA press conference story?" he asked.

"I've just got to polish it. You could have both by 4," she pleaded.

Big Bob shook his head. "Ron Mayfield can handle the fire. You concentrate on that press conference. I want it to lead the second section," he said and moved quickly on.

Back at her desk, Jessica slumped in her chair and stared at press releases and newspapers without really seeing them. The two leads Jacqueline Beller gave her the night before failed to pan out, and the morning's press conference about several technical reports was not going to produce scintillating copy. How is she ever going to land a major beat?

God knows, she tried every trick she could think of. On her way into work each day, she made sure she picked up L.A.'s four largest ethnic papers—La Opinion, the Sentinel, Jewish Journal and Korea Times—and with the help of co-workers, mostly in non-editorial positions, who spoke foreign languages, scoured these sources of neighborhood news ignored by her colleagues. She listened to the police scanner between stories. She volunteered for nighttime assignments. In short, she busted her balls. How else was she going to become a media superstar?

Jessica had grown up in Pasadena, attended Muir High, Pasadena City College, then UCLA. Her mom met her dad at the Pasadena Playhouse where she played Ophelia and he played an usher. Despite such class differences, Rose went with Josh during one particular rehearsal break around the corner to Colorado Boulevard for a soda and flirted outrageously—to the point his knees turned to rubber and his mouth went dry. Walking back with her to rehearsal, Josh told himself he would marry this woman.

Jessica's parents were good-hearted people, funny and neurotic; each lived in his or her world. Jessica often wondered how they got together enough times to produce her, two sisters and three brothers.

Her father was Jewish and her mother was raised Catholic but neither gave a damn about religion. Her dad did buy kosher meat, refused to mix meat and dairy and lit candles Friday nights—which were meatless in deference to her mom. At Hanukkah, they lit the menorah and dad handing out foil-wrapped chocolate coins as *gelt*. At Christmas, they opened presents underneath a fake Christmas tree, always two for each child.

Her parents visited their frustrations on each other and funneled their affections elsewhere: her mother into a series of ill-tempered terriers and spaniels and her father into actresses and business deals.

When she attended UCLA for her last two years of college, Jessica worked on the Daily Bruin largely because she was going with the editor. She could write, had a good liberal arts background and wasn't likely to libel anyone in the administration. So her boyfriend brought her aboard. Almost immediately, she knew this was what she wanted to do with her life.

After college and a trip to Europe, the only paper that would hire her was the Morning News. She began in the Valley bureau doing grunt assignments such as the events calendar and spot news reporting. It had taken her fourteen mouths to get out of the Valley and into the downtown newsroom. And she was still stuck with grunt work.

Jessica was a loner. She felt no need to have anyone around constantly. She rarely bought clothes that zip up in the back and never boots, which virtually require someone else to help extricate the feet. Even Trixie, her cat, tied her down to a certain extent. This caused Jessica to resent Trixie at times. She didn't lack for friends or an occasional lover, but they could be such nuisances. Since she was a kind person, she tolerated them. But if any showed signs of dependence or made demands, she froze them out.

Journalism was the perfect career for her. You were on your own—you had only yourself to blame if you got beaten on a story or screwed up the facts. A story was your baby and no one else's.

Jessica finished her MTA press conference story by 12:40 and told the receptionist she was headed for a long lunch. Where she was headed, though, was the coroner's office. For her, it was often the liveliest place in town.

***

The envelope read " Coroner's Case 87-03694." A man upended the envelope and out tumbled a silver ring, a braided black cross on a cord and two gold earrings. The man, Ken Tokunaga, sobbed and shook his head.

"I'm sorry," said Ken Tokunaga, his voice quavering.

"Don't be," said Jessica, who stood beside the grief-stricken man. "She was your daughter."

"Sara was so beautiful…and this is all that's left of her 14 years of life," said Tokunaga. "It's so unfair…so unfair. I don't even know if she was…molested. They won't tell me."

"When did you first report Sara missing, Mr. Tokunaga?" asked Jessica.

She was careful in posing this first question. A grieving relative is tricky to handle. Some want to spill their guts about their loss. Others retreat into a shell of privacy and fiercely resent any intrusion into that protective casing. Tokunaga seemed like he wanted to talk, though, from the moment Jessica spoke to him. But his emotional state was fragile.

"Monday," the man said. He hesitated, as the memory of the last few days was too painful to recall in rapid words. Tokunaga was about fifty, Jessica reckoned — she'd have to find out exactly once she got her interview — was almost completely bald and stood about five feet-four. His body trembled as he spoke.

"We went to file missing person report," he was saying. "Police say they won't start looking for forty-eight hours. Someone say, 'Runaway.'" I say, "Runaway! She not runaway. She missing!'"

He slipped the items back into the envelope and put it inside his jacket pocket. A tear trickled from his left eye and moved down through his beard stubble.

"Tell me about Sara," urged Jessica. "I mean, I hope you don't mind."

'No, I want talk about her," said Tokunaga.

Good, thought Jessica. She was home free.

"Sweet, frail girl with braces and…" A sob passed through his body like a bolt of lightning. Then he straightened his body, arching his back as if he were a soldier called to attention,

"She had long dark hair and beautiful brown eyes. She never talk back to her mother or me. Was always obedient and good student. She spoke Japanese and English. We very proud of her."

Jessica eased a notebook into her left hand and with a pen in the right started making notes. Three-quarter of an hour later, she was writing furiously at her terminal.

***

In America, which suffers under the burden of the Judeo-Christian ethic, one is taught that good deeds are rewarded and bad ones punished; that leading an exemplary life pays off down the road while leading a soiled one results in calamity. Reporters soon learn otherwise.

They realize that maiden aunts get uterine cancer, men leave faithful wives, five-year-olds get murdered in drive-bys and street punks get away with murder. The reporter does not try to explain this for there is no explanation.

So there is an inherent conflict between reporters and their readers. The crux of the matter is that the media deny the existence of moral justice daily. Tragedy is visited, seemingly, on those who least deserve it. On any given day on the police blotter alone, there are enough stories to embarrass the "Good is Rewarded" school of thought. Readers resent these stories and that resentment often turns into a kind of denial: the reporter didn't get all the facts. The reporter is biased, stupid or has an agenda. You can't trust the damn media.

There exist several ways to write such stories to make them acceptable to readers. Among the more time-honored is the "sob sister" route where tragedy is turned into a poignant there-but-for-the-grace-of-God-go-I tale. The advantage of this is the reader feels better for having confronted his worst fears and cried. It is usually written in such a manner to emphasize its uniqueness and not its ordinariness.

The incomprehensibility of the tragedy is what makes it news. Can you believe this happened? Where was God when this went down?

Jessica bit a fingernail and stared intently at her monitor. She typed a sentence, sat back to look at this latest creation, shook her head, highlighted the sentence and hit the delete key.

Bill came over to her desk and looked over her shoulder. After a moment, he spoke: "For your lead, how about 'At the morgue, she was a number, but to her father she was everything.'"

Jessica turned around. "Shouldn't you be going through celebrities' trash cans?" she asked with a sweet smile. This passed for newsroom humor so Bill took no offense.

"'Scuse me," he snapped and headed for more unwanted coffee. "You try to help somebody," he muttered in a voice loud enough to be heard across the newsroom.

An hour later, Big Bob called Jessica into his office. He was highly annoyed at her, he blustered, for going to the coroner's looking for a story on her lunch break. That's what we have assignment editors for, he said in a tone that indicated he minded less than his words would indicate.

"But I like your initiative," he told her. "Frankly, we don't have enough reporters at the Morning News who have the kind of drive you have.

"Thank you," she said. "And I am sorry about going to the morgue without an assignment. Call it desperation."

"We need more desperation around here," said Big Bob. He swiveled his VDT monitor around so Jessica could see her story which appeared on the screen. "I did punch up your lead."

Jessica leaned forward slightly and read the new lead: "At the morgue, Sara was a number. But to her father she was everything."

"That sounds much better," she said. "You're a genius."

Big Bob flushed. He knew that, of course. But it was nice to have it acknowledged by a reporter.

"Yes, it does sound better," he agreed. "You know, I think it's about time you had a regular beat. How does police blotter sound?"

"It sounds wonderful," she replied, unwilling to believe her ears.

"You married, Jessie?"

Jessica started. No one ever called her Jessie. "No," she managed.

"Just as well. Spouses don't understand the demands of this business."

"Yes, sir." She added quickly: "Bob, I want to thank you for your vote of confidence. I know I'll do a great job."

"I know you will too," said Big Bob, letting his voice fall into a lower register he reserved for fatherly-yet-virile-male chats with female subordinates.

"Now all I need is a good murder," said Jessica brightly.

CHAPTER SEVEN
TEMPLE OF DOOM

For Jasmine Ledoux's wedding day, her mother chose her sister Lorraine's backyard. It was the only space large enough to hold all the guests without renting a hall. Cash was tight enough after all the expenses on dresses and caterers and Rev. Charles Hillborough, who demanded money not only for his services and the rental of the church but for his benevolent fund. Diedre Ledoux wondered whom this benevolent fund benefitted, but didn't want to question the Reverend too closely before such a joyous occasion.

Of course, Dierdre Ledouox was feeling anything but joyous when the happy day came. She had definite qualms about her daughter's intended. Robert "Fat Boy" Wilkerson, a longtime resident of the Jordan Downs project, had been released sixteen months ago from a juvenile facility after serving over four years in a gang-related murder. He was only sixteen when, after a messed-up drug deal, he shot four people including a kid on a bike who died. But since his release, he didn't hang with his homies as far as she could tell and rarely carried a gun. She did worry about his insistence on being called Fat Boy, a name acquired long before the Youth Authority made him lean. At least he held several jobs over the last six months and seemed relatively stable.

So when the shooting started, astonishment and horror overwhelmed the mother of the bride. The shooters couldn't have been more than fourteen or fifteen. They belonged to a smaller, younger gang "set" based outside the projects, police later said.

Aunt Maisie was the first to be hit, taking a bullet in her left shoulder that would pretty much leave her a cripple for life. Little Eddie Watkins had no business lurking around the wedding party anyway since he had no real invitation. So when a bullet tore through his brainpan he certainly learned his lesson the hard way. Several bullets exploded into the four-tier cake, showering the ladies in waiting with vanilla fudge mingled with the blood of Perlee Watson, who was related to Dierdre's side of the family by way of marriage.

Lorraine's backyard was a mess by the time cops from Southeast Division showed up—none too quickly, guests would later say. Only two died, which was a true miracle given the fact that Jessica was able to report twenty-four rounds went off in under sixty seconds.

Big Bob cut this "fact" from her story. He never trusted statistics since his days as a reporter in D.C. where another Bob with the last name of McNamara would recite a litany of body counts to prove the U.S. was winning the war in Vietnam. The joke around the Press Club was that if anyone bothered to total up the Defense Secretary's body counts, he would discover that no enemy would be left alive.

Big Bob also buried Jessica's story on page six of Metro.

"If two grandmothers get into a catfight at a wedding in the Pacific Palisades, you got Page One of Metro," he quietly explained to Jessica the next day. "But blacks shooting each other in the Southeast Division is a back-pager."

Big Bob was in a surly mood so there was no questioning his judgment on this particular day. A typo in an important obit had suggested donations to an association to assist the "helpless" had utterly ruined his morning.

Which was why he picked a fight with Don Hazel. Don was a man about half Bob's size and Bob was in the habit of equating brains with bulk. When he fought with his city editor, though, Big Bob desperately wanted to educate Don about his thinking process. On days when Big Bob was not around, he wanted to feel secure in the knowledge the place would not go to hell in a handbasket under Don.

"I tell everyone I'm right one hundred percent of the time," he explained to Don. "Actually, I'm right about seventy percent of the time. But if I don't say I'm right one hundred percent of the time—if I had to think about whether I'm right or wrong—I'd be right only sixty percent of the time."

Don's eyes glazed over for a second, then snapped back into focus. He frowned. He wasn't certain he followed the math. "Which makes you right only seventy percent of the time?" Don ventured.

Big Bob peered at his subordinate with his steady green eyes. 'No, Don," he said impatiently. "I'm right one hundred percent of the time."

Big Bob turned on his heels—no easy task when you have no hips—and rumbled back to his office.

Don retreated to his desk, mulling over percentages and the mysterious ways in which the mind of a managing editor works. As far as he could tell, the ME was right about fifty percent of the time at best. He shook his head like a dog shaking off bathwater and turned to more important things. Thus, he was soon occupied with wire reports and lascivious thoughts about Darlene Temple.

Don had been married for over twenty years. He couldn't recall the exact number but he definitely knew they had passed the double decade mark a while ago. Every New Year's Eve, before he left work, Don would mark on his calendar his June 12th wedding anniversary. This way he wouldn't forget when that date rolled around. As a consequence of his remarkable ability to always remember their anniversary, his wife Bertha never suspected he couldn't remember the exact number of years they had been married.

Don had four or five children with Bertha, which was far too many. They held him back in his career. He would easily have gone on to journalistic glory in New York or Washington D.C. or who knows where if he hadn't been tied down by kids and schools and summer vacations. He long ago gave up his dream about the Pulitzer and a name-dropping memoir. All that would have been his if it weren't for those four or five damn kids. Instead of the Pulitzer, he daydreamed about Darlene Temple.

Don didn't particularly like the Morning News' gossip columnist. For one thing, he thought her writing sucked. He once complained there were more "..." in her copy than actual words. If you took out those three-dot ellipses, he insisted, it wouldn't be a column; it would be news brief.

He also disliked her choice of clothing—pants suits that emphasized the masculine lines of her figure. He preferred his women to be voluptuous. He was repelled by her flat breasts and narrow hips. Her hair was the wrong color, her skin pasty and sallow and, thanks to cigarettes, her breath was unbelievably foul.

He was desperate to fuck her.

To Don, Darlene epitomized the kind of girl who has done everything once and much of it twice. She moved in circles Don knew little about. She drank and laughed and shared cigarettes with the beautiful people Don only read about when looking over her copy, which the Morning Snooze's lawyers insisted he is to do every day.

His daydreams usually began with Darlene's sudden desire to take a long lunch with him to discuss problems she was experiencing with her writing. He would patiently coach her in prose style over a French dip and pickled egg at Philippe's. Then Darlene would slyly bring up the idea of a motel on Beverly. Don would, of course, vigorously protest. When you have a wife and four or five kids, you stick to the straight and narrow, he would gently explain. Darlene would then make a lewd joke about the "straight and narrow," Don would laugh heartily and finally, yes, he would acquiesce.

They would sneak back into the newsroom hours late, staggering their entrances to avoid office gossip. And for weeks they would smile or wink at one another whenever their eyes would meet. How many months this would continue depended on when the daydreams were interrupted by nagging questions from reporters or copy editors.

On this particular day, he had scarcely left the motel room following their initial tryst when someone was demanding his undivided attention. That someone — annoyingly — turned out to be Darlene herself.

"Who the fuck edited my copy yesterday?" she shouted. "My column is an embarrassment!"

Darlene had a way of drawing out the word "embarrassment" so that it hung in the air like a vulgar oath.

"What's wrong?" sighed Don.

"What's wrong?" she fumed. "I'll tell you what's wrong. Everything! Someone took out the item about Brad Townsell, changed Reed — r, e, e, d — to read — r, e, a, d — simply because the R was lower case — so I'm not allowed a typo every now and then? — and assumed when I said Liz I meant Elizabeth Taylor. I never call Elizabeth Taylor 'Liz'! What numb nuts did the reads on this?"

"I dunno, Darlene. I'll have to check."

"You fucking well better check!" she screamed. "I can't take much more of this shit. I have a reputation to protect."

"I am well aware of your reputation," he said.

Darlene's eyes narrowed. "What is that supposed to mean?" she demanded.

"I'm agreeing you have a reputation to protect," he replied blandly.

"It sounds insidious when you say it."

"It's a trick in my voice. I've always had the problem," he replied.

She glared at him, but swiftly returned to her office cubbyhole. For Don, the day was ruined. For Darlene, it was off to a fabulous start. After her first temper tantrum, she was aroused for the entire day. She never needed caffeine. The only better beginning in recent weeks was when the male head of programming for ABC made the mistake of calling her "Hon."

Her new assistant—Andy Reynolds—already knew to stay out of her way when she was in such a good mood. To placate Andy, who had taken to wondering out loud if his assignments to cover car wrecks had something to do with his race, Big Bob had given him to Darlene. Andy had quickly adapted to her unique style. He let nothing throw him. She initially took this as a challenge. But after a few days, she had grown comfortable with the notion that her assistant would treat her ideas and behavior as normal.

One of the first things she had explained to Andy was her method of cutting egotistical male celebrities down to size. One of her first questions to a male "star" would concern his cock size. If he measures up, she explained, he will be only too happy to tell her and the interview would be off to a terrific start. If a star doesn't measure up, then his overdeveloped ego shrinks and he's putty in her hands. Either way, she wins.

Andy didn't let this unorthodox approach to journalism— one certainly never taught at USC—throw him. He merely nodded, then speculated that she might consider writing a book entitled "Great Hollywood Pricks I Have Known." Darlene thought the suggestion an excellent one and was a little startled she hadn't thought of it herself.

On this day, the telephone rang early and often. The initial morning calls came from restaurateurs or their flacks, who rang up in a search for free PR whenever someone even marginally celebrated stopped by to eat. These were followed by those from ex-wives, still stung by grievances real or imagined, who were always a rich vein of information.

Tipsters rang up for all kinds of reasons. Darlene was especially fond of political tipsters. She adored California politicians; they made actors seem downright rational. There was, for example, the gubernatorial candidate whose fear of AIDS was so strong that on a recent trip to San Francisco he wore shower caps on his feet in the hotel bathtub. The poor guy never could figure out Darlene's source on that item.

The cosmology Darlene portrayed—where celebs were taken down a peg and readers felt right at home in Bel-Air—was a world apart from one the Times presented. The Times' editors could never understand how the celebrities they flattered tolerated—and at times even cooperated with—Darlene Temple's column in the rival publication. But Darlene understood that one's existence was validated through celebrityhood and celebrityhood was attained through fame rather than achievement. A mere mention in her column meant one was among the exalted. Anonymity was death.

Darlene fell into the gossip biz by accident. As a Metro reporter, she was nearly ruined by a cop who gave her the lowdown on a city department head being investigated for drug use, then denied ever speaking to her after the story ran. The Morning News was sued. The paper's lawyers settled at a fairly low sum since the plaintive had no real interest in letting his personal life become the subject of a court trial.

Nevertheless, Darlene was sent into purgatory, She was handed a back-page column that was essentially a round-up of wire items and press releases. Gradually though, Darlene turned the gig into a nasty, deadly accurate column that readers either loathed or loved.

Darlene Temple's column—eventually renamed for its author—now ran on the back page of the front section and was the first thing most Morning Snooze readers turned to when they picked up the paper. It was, in fact, so well-read and quoted by everyone from drive-time disc jockeys to the man in the street that celebs and power brokers began referring to it as the "Temple of Doom."

Darlene's major coup this morning was the marriage between two television stars in Mexico that was being kept out of the press. Darlene herself didn't believe in the story's veracity until both their publicists heatedly denied it.

Late in the afternoon, after putting the column to bed, Darlene asked Andy if he would mind driving her to a reception at the Beverly Wilshire. Andy didn't mind so long as

Darlene didn't mind arriving in his beaten-up Chevy. Darlene rarely drove, as she was much too nervous for L.A. traffic. Once safely inside Andy's car and out of the Snooze's three-tiered parking lot, she took out a pack of menthols and lit up without asking, blowing blue smoke through a rolled-down window. Andy said nothing, despite his intolerance for cigarette smoke.

The reception was for a charity and nothing brings out Hollywood guilt money like a noble cause. Darlene was in gossip-columnist heaven amid the mix of film and television celebs and business and political leaders. So it turned out she needed Andy for a full-court press.

Andy worked the room for a solid forty-five minutes while Darlene stood near the bar, drinking gin fizzes and chatting like a society matron. Andy was more than a little peeved. He was working his butt off while his boss seemed indifferent to the whole thing. Worse, he was getting very little dirt. Perhaps he was ill-suited for this job. All these very white white folks weren't going to open up to a young black guy.

As he drove her home, Andy was startled to hear Darlene rattle off two columns' worth of dirt. The items came faster and faster as Darlene's enthusiasm increased, each sharper than the last. How had she done it? When had she picked up all this stuff? Andy only remembered seeing her drinking gin fizzes at the bar.

He glanced over at her. Her eyes glistened with excitement. She talked about these people and their foibles in a manner that made them seem like laboratory rats in some grand experiment gone completely mad. He grinned. Then a laugh escaped.

"What?" she asked, the newsroom edge suddenly back in her voice.

"It's funny, that's all. The way you describe these people," said Andy.

"What's funny?"

"Your descriptions."

"What are you talking about?"

He looked over at her. He could see she didn't know what he was talking about.

"You have a knack for describing celebrities so that the person listening to you—or reading you—gets a kick out of hearing about these people, but is also very glad to not be one of them."

She was silent for what seemed to Andy like an eternity.

"I do?" she said in a voice Andy never heard before. It belonged to a shy little girl, who was awkward about hearing praise concerning her. That voice made Andy feel strange. Silence followed.

"Yeah," he nervously blurted out to quash the silence. "Maybe you should be on the radio. Or, better yet, TV. Your delivery is as funny as your prose."

"I was on a Valley radio station for a few months about three years ago," said Darlene. Again the little-girl voice. "I got the impression management thought I was too much of a bitch."

"Bitchy maybe, but not a bitch."

"Oh, trust me, Hon, I'm a bitch."

"You may think you are but you're not."

"You haven't seen me on one of my bad days yet," she murmured.

Andy chuckled and immediately wished he hadn't. She looked at him sharply.

"What?" Her voice reverted to newsroom-speak.

"Oh, nothing," he quickly said. Too quickly.

"What," she said. It was no longer a question.

"Oh, I was just thinking that my mama and sister could out-bitch you any day of the week, and I mean no disrespect to either one of them."

He was relieved to hear Darlene's full-throated laugh.

As they neared Darlene's Santa Monica condo, Darlene experienced a mild bellyache. Too many gin fizzes, she said. Andy stopped off at a Thrifty's to pick up what he called his "mama's miracle cure" for upset tummies. Darlene was none too pleased when Andy returned to the car with a package of baking soda.

"Trust me," said Andy.

He parked on the street and accompanied her in the elevator up to her second-floor condo. He mixed a teaspoon of baking soda with Pellegrino—she refused to drink tap water—and insisted she down the mixture in one gulp. She managed it in two. Darlene's nose and forehead wrinkled as the salty, chalky taste hit the back of her mouth.

"I may puke," she said angrily and retreated to her bathroom. A while later, a couple of slammed doors indicated she had quit her bathroom for her bedroom. Andy heard no puking.

As was his habit, Andy looked over the woman's living room in search of books. He always wanted to see what other people read. Darlene apparently didn't. Other than People, Newsweek, the National Enquirer, Vanity Fair, GQ, Interview and New York Magazine, that is.

Darlene emerged from her bedroom five minutes later. She had changed into a white blouse and patched blue jeans. Andy realized he had never seen her when she was not dressed up. The change was dramatic. The homey appearance softened her features yet, conversely, made her look more vigorous. She crossed the living room in six strides and went into the kitchenette where she grabbed a glass off the sink and poured a glass of Pellegrino. After gulping the water down, she finally acknowledged Andy's presence.

"That stuff worked," she said with faint disgust. "I'm surprised."

"I enjoy practicing medicine without a license."

She looked at him with piercing eyes and a faint smile. If before this moment someone had asked her to describe her assistant, she probably would have done a poor job. Black, average height, decent looks, short hair, medium build would be as much as she would have managed. Now she noticed the dimple in his cheek, the grayish tinge of his skin, the surprisingly thin eyebrows, the downturn of his mouth and the twinkle in his eye. The latter bothered Darlene. It was too self-satisfied for her liking.

"You wanna drink?" she asked. She knew he didn't but she was suddenly at a loss for words.

"No, thanks," he replied cheerfully.

She hated that cheerfulness too. She could use a drink right about now, but if she did tomorrow would be a lost cause. She didn't handle alcohol well; for that matter, she handled few things in life well. Including moments like this.

"Well, thanks for driving me home," she said with studied diffidence.

"No sweat," he replied and continued to gaze at her. Darlene's face flushed. This was becoming impossible. He's an assistant, for Christ's sake. She poured another glass of water because she needed something to do. Why the hell didn't he leave? She took a sip, then set the glass down hard on the Formica counter. It was time to establish a few ground rules.

"I see the way you're looking at me, Andrew Reynolds, and it's not going to happen," she said with all the authority she could muster. "I was married for three years and in analysis for four. I failed at both. I don't drink well—as you found out tonight—I'm lousy at computers, money, driving, keeping friends or sustaining relationships. All I'm good at is my work. So forget about any illusions you may harbor about you and me."

The smile never left Andy's face. He simply walked over to her, slipped an arm around her waist and kissed her. She responded immediately.

"Damn you," she murmured between passionate kisses.

Later she did insist he leave by 2 a.m. Darlene didn't like men to spend the night. She liked to sleep alone and wanted to maintain that distance. It was far too intimate to sleep with a man after having sex with him.

After Andy left, Darlene lay awake for an hour. She didn't like this. Her rule was to never get involved with anybody from work. She would talk to him tomorrow. First thing in the morning, she would close the door and make it clear to Andy that last night would never happen again. It was just one of those things. Well, to be accurate, it was just *three* of those things.

She smiled to herself. Three times. Better to reconsider that morning chat. But she needed to make it clear somehow that this was a short-term relationship. Short. Like a month or so. And how would they now work together? She sighed. What had she gotten herself into?

CHAPTER EIGHT
THE MAD BOMBER

The blast sent a red-orange fireball into the smudged Los Angeles sky and rocked the entire downtown business district. It threw a dirty black cloud of smoke and debris high into the air and hurled shards of glass and metal in every direction in a four-block circle. Cars in the area burst into flames and exploded. Everyone ran for his life.

Rescuers, their faces ashen, climbed through the rubble with bloody bodies and took many victims to County-USC Hospital. Wearing kneepads, protective masks and rubber boots, they squeezed into tiny spaces or sent search dogs into structurally unsafe areas to sniff out victims that might still be alive. The death toll mounted to thirteen.

It proved to be a low-order explosion, meaning one that causes the most damage at its ignition site rather than exploding throughout a large area. Authorities reached this conclusion partly because of the fifteen-foot-wide crater in the street where the truck had exploded. The police determined the damage was caused by a C-4 bomb, made of cyclotrimethylene and plastic bonding. It was detonated by dynamite and left small undetonated particles of plastique.

The media was in a tizzy since the city yearned for somebody to hate. Yet no one came forward to claim responsibility. Unfortunately, the Mad Bomber—the Morning Snooze's choice sobriquet—had parked his truck so injudiciously that the media began to quarrel over his true target. The damn bomb took down much of a federal government building, partially destroyed an abortion clinic, made a mess of an office building with several international firms and, for good measure, a Salvadoran nightclub.

Since the bomb went off near a government building, the media was quick to link the blast to international terrorism. While a State Department spokeswoman and an analyst at the Center for National Security Studies cautioned that it was a mistake to assume the bomber or bombers were foreign, the Morning News nevertheless was the first to insist on a link to international Arab terrorism. The paper's initial stories and lead editorial pointed out that the bombing occurred two days after an International Conference on Hamas was held in Santa Monica, an event, in the paper's words, "designed to promote Islamic revolution and hatred for Israel and America."

The Times favored right-wing hate groups. So many had sprung up in the wake of anti-immigrant hysteria fanned by the election-year politics of the current Republican governor. Three TV channels opted for an anti-abortionist—that played better in Hollywood and could immediately be turned into a Movie of the Week. Most hate crime experts speculated this could have been an example of "leaderless resistance," in which an anti-government or right-wing extremist loosely affiliated with a hate group acted alone.

La Opinion and the Daily News in the Valley insisted the bomber was a gang member bent on retaliation for being barred from the Salvadoran club a night earlier. La Opinion quoted the club's bouncer at length on this theory.

The real loose cannon was Channel 13 who tied the semi-destruction of the office building to a janitors' strike nine months earlier.

All of which left radio talk-show hosts in a bind. Under normal circumstances, where suspects are easily identified, they would unleash their fury against the foreign scum who blew up innocent women and children. However, since the bombing might be the work of an anti-abortionist or militia member—whom talk-show hosts naturally would never completely condemn since those causes were righteous—they were choked not with rage but impotence: they were uncertain how to react. And the media with so many different theories were of no help. So they settled for condemning the media.

Most talk-show hosts devoted hours defending arch-conservatives against accusations that their rhetoric had created any monsters and shifted the blame where it belonged — on the liberals who caused this tragedy. Besides, citing the Morning News, they saw the shadowy hand of Islamic extremists in the fiery deaths.

To boost the Snooze's choice — arrived at on the basis of no evidence whatsoever — Big Bob demanded that Bill get an interview with Hussein Nabhan, a guest at the International Conference on Hamas, who happened still to be in town after last week's "Hate-In at the Beach," the headline the News used for the Santa Monica gathering.

Nabhan, a radical Palestinian who broke with Yasser Arafat years before, was a leading rhetorician for the Palestinian cause. Yet for all his fiery speeches, no charge of violence had ever been laid at his feet. Which nevertheless failed to prevent the Morning Snooze from labeling him Sheik Satan.

Bill was ambivalent about this assignment. The likelihood of his securing an interview with Nabhan, the man his newspaper dubbed "the nincompoop of genocidal annihilation," was nil. Indeed all phone calls to his suite at the Century Plaza Hotel went unreturned. The whole thing was a grand waste of time. On the other hand, it would get him out of the office.

He dropped by the American Legion for a gin and tonic to clear his head. He sat by himself, away from the television and barroom chat, as he considered his assignment. Nabhan was staying at the Century Plaza, a hotel designed to be secure enough to bed American presidents. Gaining access to the politician would be virtually impossible and certainly couldn't be done through normal channels.

Perhaps with enough time and thought, Bill could have mapped out an intricate strategy to gain Nabhan's attention. A combination of phone calls and faxes to soften him up, say, followed by several days of cooling his heels in the hotel lobby. Or, better yet, thought Bill as he slowly sipped his drink, something fairly straightforward such as ringing Nabhan's hotel room and claiming to be a reporter for the New York Times. That had worked on several occasions. Foreigners were especially gullible on that score.

But Bill didn't have the time. Nabhan was leaving that night for Hong Kong. Besides Nabhan gave a lengthy interview to the New York Times only a week before. No, the best approach under the circumstances was simply to gamble: to get close enough to win him over.

Surely, Mr. Nabhan, you don't want to pass up the opportunity to plead your case to the people of Los Angeles? I'm sure your people didn't plant that bomb which destroyed so many innocent lives. Here's your chance to set the record straight, to explain why Hamas would never do such a thing on American soil. That sort of thing.

Bill was convinced that sincerity was the best strategy. And sincerity demanded a proper costume.

Bill stopped off at Alphonse's Costumes. The desert Bedouin costume that Konstantine Theosophus gave Bill hadn't been used since a four-hour miniseries on NBC ten years prior so Bill asked Konstantine to give the *jalabiyah* a quick press. Konstantine wanted Bill to wear an *abaya*—an open-fronted loose gown—over the *jalabiyah*, but Bill insisted this made him look too much like a peasant so they settled on a Western-style jacket. For the head, Konstantine gave him a *keffiyeh*, which was held by a ropelike *agal.* Bill decided against wearing the outfit until he arrived at the Century Plaza. He didn't want the *jalabiyah* to get mussed.

He parked in the structure at the rear of the hotel and entered the building by walking around to the front lobby, a floor above the banquet halls. After changing in the men's rooms downstairs off the Los Angeles Room banquet hall and checking a bag jammed with his clothes with a startled woman at the cloakroom, he rode the escalator up to the lobby. Bill tried to look more confident than he felt. He never liked impersonating foreigners. He knew he would get the accent wrong and would more likely mess up a key element of the culture that would give him away. He glanced down at his shoes. They not only needed a polish but felt out of place with the flowing *jalabiyah*. They looked, well, American.

He strode through the lobby, attracting stares, which he ignored. He wanted as little contact with people as possible. He pushed an elevator button and stared idly at the carpet as a middle-aged woman gaped at him with wonder. He was distressed when she and her husband got on the same elevator as he did. He thought momentarily of waiting for another car but decided it might be a while before he got a car of his own.

He got on the elevator and waited.

"Excuse me," said the woman, her voice the very essence of frost. "Are you with Mr. Nabhan's party?" she inquired.

Bill shrugged and pointed to his mouth to indicate he didn't speak the woman's language. This seemed to irritate her further.

"You don't speak English?" she accused him. Again he shrugged, then added in what he hoped was a good desert accent: "No English."

The woman glared at her bored husband, "They can set off bombs here but can't learn the language," she huffed.

The couple got off on the fourth floor to Bill's enormous relief. Jesus, he thought to himself. Such prejudice.

He rode the elevator to the penthouse. As the doors opened, his blood froze.

Several burly Arabs, who stood in the hallway directly in front of the elevator, stared at him contemptuously. They wore European suits and ties. One, who seemed the largest, immediately strode over to Bill as he sought to exit the elevator. A hand of steel was thrust into Bill's chest. Even more alarming, Bill's peripheral vision caught the glint of metal reflected from guns, which materialized in the hands of several other guards.

"What you do?" asked the man with his hand on Bill's chest.

Bill started to reply but words caught in his throat. He was aware of guns pointing at him, something that had never happened to him before in his life. Sweat poured from his body.

Gasping for air, all he could manage was: "I'm a journalist."

His interlocutor's eyes never left him. Was it Bill's imagination or did the contempt he saw in those eyes triple in magnitude? A man off to the side snickered. Otherwise, there was silence. Bill took a step back into the elevator. The man blocking his path grabbed his gown and pulled him back.

"You wait," said the Arab.

A door opened down the corridor and Bill was aware of muffled footsteps growing nearer. He allowed his head to turn ever so slightly in the direction of the footsteps.

An eternity passed. A man came into view. He was surprisingly short and his features were finely chiseled. The skin was lighter than those of the bodyguards and his suit, made of fine linen, probably came from Bond Street. He stopped several feet from Bill and stared at him as one would an animal in the circus. Bill recognized the man to be Hussein Nabhan.

Bill's minder addressed Nabhan in Arabic. Nabhan replied in kind, his eyes never leaving Bill. Suddenly, the guard let Bill go and moved away.

"And who do you think you are — Lawrence of Arabia?" Nabhan asked Bill in an accent that was more Oxford than West Bank.

Bill swallowed hard before answering: "I...yes, I'm sorry about the costume. I thought—"

"You thought?" interrupted the impatient Palestinian. He turned to the men gathered around him and addressed them in English. "You see how the American sees all Arabs—as desert sheiks in a silly Hollywood melodrama."

Bill saw his opening.

"But, sir," he began cautiously, "I am a reporter for the Morning News and if I could have a few minutes of your valuable time, I'm sure my understanding of your people and their troubles will greatly increase. My editor wants me to write a comprehensive, in-depth piece about the recently completed conference in Santa Monica."

Nabhan appeared not to hear him as he broke into Arabic once more and spoke directly to his bodyguards. In time, he turned back to Bill.

"The Morning News, you say?"

"Yes, I —"

"This is the journal that referred to our conference as the 'Hate-In at the Beach,' is it not?"

"Well, yes, but we reporters don't write the headlines, you see, and —"

"Quiet," Nabhan demanded. Several seconds went by as the Palestinian looked at Bill. When he spoke, his voice for the first time contained anger: "I sincerely doubt if a reporter from your newspaper would be interested in anything other than sensationalism."

Nabhan turned and spoke a few quick words in Arabic to his head bodyguard. The elevator opened and a young man in a business suit with the badge of a hotel employee stepped off. The man addressed Nabhan directly.

"Mr. Nabhan, would you mind leaving the hotel through an underground passage?" he asked politely. "A demonstration has begun outside."

"Against me?" asked Nabhan.

"Yes, sir. We believe it would be safer if the protestors were unaware of your departure."

"Very well," said Nabhan.

Bill found himself being shoved aside as the Palestinian leader, several bodyguards and the hotel employee boarded a private elevator. The door closed, leaving Bill to ponder his sins. Two remaining bodyguards stared at him indifferently. After approximately a minute had passed, one glanced at his wristwatch and nodded to his compatriot. This one turned to Bill: "You go."

The two men walked down the corridor back into the suite, closing the door behind them. Bill, who only now realized he had been holding his breath, sighed deeply. He punched the down button.

In the lobby, Bill found a payphone to call Don to tell him not to hold space for him on Page One. There was going to be no exclusive interview with Hussein Nabhan. He did not go into detail about his failure and hung up quickly.

Discouraged, Bill went to the cloakroom to retrieve his clothes bag. He tipped the woman four dollars—he was unusually generous whenever he was professionally frustrated. Returning to the lobby, he headed for the exit, this time ignoring the curious glances of those in the area.

Only when he stepped outside did he become aware of the noise. Helicopters droned overhead. Angry shouts punctuated the night. The demonstrators clogged Avenue of the Stars immediately outside the hotel's semi-circular drive. Police lines contained a surging crowd that filled the street back to the ABC Entertainment Center across the way. Homemade signs jutted above the seething sea of humanity. Television news crew vans with their microwave dishes ringed the perimeter.

"There he is!" someone screamed.

Bill looked around. Then a horrible thought dawned on him: He was the "he."

No, this was too silly. Bill reached up, pulled off his flowing headcloth and shouted, "I'm an American!" But even Bill couldn't hear his own words above the din.

He looked to his left and right. Demonstrators ringed the drive and spilled out onto the fringes. Several in the crowd angrily pointed at him. More shouts. Bill stumbled as he retreated toward the hotel entrance. Someone threw an object that landed on his right. On the left flank, several infuriated demonstrators broke through the police barricade and raced toward Bill. A roar of bloodlust went up from the throng. There was no time to be lost.

Bill turned and bolted through the entrance, nearly knocking over two businessmen bewildered by the commotion. He scrambled to the escalator and plunged down to the Plaza level.

He had to get into the men's room and out of this damn costume.

Couples in formal dress stood like so many bowling pins on the moving stairs. Bill politely squeezed past the first few couples but as shouts filled the upstairs lobby, all civility deserted the frantic journalist.

Jostling past one elderly woman who addressed him as "You fuck," he pushed and shoved his way down the remaining stairs. At the bottom, a man who had witnessed Bill's progress stepped off the escalator and stood to one side, leaving the passage open for Bill. As Bill followed him off the moving stairs, the man stuck out a leg and calmly tripped Bill, which sent him sprawling forward.

Clothes spilled out of his bag. Camera flashes went off from news photographers gathered behind ropes at the foot of the escalator. The crowd was arriving to pay tribute to a film star, which explained all the photographers. Bill momentarily wondered if the Morning Snooze was covering the event.

Quickly, he grabbed his clothes and stuffed them back into the bag. Leaping to his feet, Bill dashed across the reception area, nearly colliding with startled guests, and turned left down a corridor lined with smaller conference rooms. Somewhere there must be a vacant room where he could quickly change his clothes. Shouts from the reception area told him he had no time to change. The only hope was to somehow get to the parking lot in one piece. He would drive out naked if need be.

He slammed through an exit door and climbed the interior stairs back to the street level. He heard no more sounds, only ringing of blood as it pounded through his neck and head.

Bill peered out of the hotel's northern side entrance. Since Constellation Boulevard was blocked several yards to the east, there were no cars and little foot traffic. Clutching his clothes bag, Bill slipped through the doorway and made his way through a restaurant valet parking area. He headed gratefully down the drive leading to the parking structure.

Then he stopped. At the end of the driveway, he glanced up at the mob gathered on the top of Constellation Boulevard.

"There he is!" someone shouted.

Demonstrators took off in his direction at a gallop. Bill had no choice but to run again. He headed across the street where he might lose himself in a large shopping complex or possibly its underground parking structure. But with a backward glance, he could see that several determined demonstrators on the other side of the wide street had a better angle and would reach him before he reached the shopping center.

Abruptly changing course, Bill ran down the street's center in the desperate hope that a black-and-white might cruise by and rescue him. Were all the cops on Constellation? He ran and ran, his body feeling surprisingly light. Fear had taken control of his senses. Fatigue abandoned him. He felt neither heat nor cold. He could run all night if he had to. He no longer heard shouts or screams. As his running brought him to the Century Park West cross street, a black limousine materialized in front of him and came to a halt. Bill stopped dead in his tracks.

The back door swung open. Bill walked over and peered inside. The first person he saw, a person wearing what can only be described as a sly grin, was Hussein Nabhan.

"Get in," Nabhan told him.

Bill obliged. The car jerked forward, throwing Bill back into a soft, inviting seat. Before he could speak two loud bangs came from the rear of the car. Bill glanced back. Several demonstrators were hurling objects at the limo. Nabhan continued to gaze at Bill, the grin never leaving his face.

"So," he finally said, "how does it feel being a Palestinian, if only for a few minutes?"

Bill looked at him and let his breath slowly return to his body. He was not going to let this guy get the better of him.

"Nothing like *really* being one in Gaza, I'd imagine," he replied.

The smile left Nabhan's face.

"Sir," Bill began, "if you would grant me an interview to clarify your point of view, perhaps we'd all make fewer mistakes."

The Palestinian glanced down at his day planner for a few moments, then said, "I will answer your questions on the way to the airport."

***

Nearly an hour later, having finally changed his clothes, Bill stood inside the Tom Bradley Building at LAX and dialed Hazel on a payphone. The editor had gone out for a quick bite so he got deputy city editor Angela Perkins instead. She cut him off before he could finish what he had to say.

"Forget Nabhan," she told him.

"What are you talking about?" Bill all but shouted as he tried to maintain his cool. "This is a top priority for Big Bob!"

"Bill," she said sharply, "the LAPD arrested an anti-abortionist trying to leave on a bus for Salt Lake an hour ago. He fits KNBC's description of a man seen around the truck downtown minutes before the blast. The police are holding a press conference in a few minutes to announce they caught the bomber. And I can tell you Duke Whitcomb is furious. He doesn't like it when the News guesses wrong about its Mad Bomber."

Bill fought valiantly the following morning in Big Bob's office behind closed doors to get the ME to run his Nabhan interview. The editor had lost interest though. Flipping through his reporter's notebook he ran one startling quote after another past the editor until Big Bob finally relinquished and granted him a Q&A in the Opinion section on Sunday.

Big Bob was heard to mutter all week that one of his ace reporters had "gone soft." And he made sure to run a response by the American Israel Public Affairs Committee on the page opposite Bill's Q&A. This is what happens when the Morning

News strays from his mission, Big Bob told Bill. Its readers did not want blowjob stories about terrorists.

CHAPTER NINE
SLY

"One-year-old Larry Schatz should be bright-eyed and happy, learning to babble and crawl," Sly wrote. "He is not. When he was two-months-old, Larry was shaken violently by his father. Now the boy is blind, quadriplegic, severely brain-damaged and prone to uncontrollable seizures."

Sly pushed away from his keyboard and wished like hell he could smoke his pipe. He silently bestowed a highly original—though theologically doubtful—curse on Duke Whitcomb relating to the publisher's experiences in the afterlife, a curse directly linked to the Duke's decree the Morning Snooze would henceforth be a smoke-free environment. What the hell did the Duker care about smoke in the plant? Or for that matter, his employees' health? The publisher seldom came to the wretched, sick building and the Snooze's health plan was constructed in such a manner that Sly was more likely to collect death benefits before he ever saw any health care payments.

Of course, the more angry and frustrated Sly became the better a writer he was. For Sly needed to be thoroughly pissed off to compose his column. Moving back to the keyboard, Sly resumed typing.

"On Wednesday, little Larry was brought to court so a judge could see his condition before sentencing David Schatz, 23, for his guilty plea to child abuse charges. After seeing the boy, Municipal Court Judge Harold Chetwynd rejected a Probation Department recommendation that Schatz, a city clerk, be given probation. Instead, Chetwynd sentenced Schatz to a maximum of seven years in prison.

""I think this should send a message to others who might be tempted to shake their babies to stop their crying," Chetwynd said.

Fuck, thought Sly as he paused in his writing. This is no good. It's sob sister stuff. Unworthy of Sly's Life. The whole thing would have to be junked. Then inspiration came to him: Better to start the damn story in the hospital rather than the courtroom. Plays better. Sly moved his copy into another file, just in case he changed his mind, and opened a new file.

He began again:

"An emergency room physician initially believed the Schatzs' story. Their son's injuries were the result of a fall, the couple said. Only on a follow-up visit did a hospital doctor spot what she believed were signs of shaken-baby syndrome.

"'When a parent loses his temper, the first reaction is often to shake the child out of frustration,' said Pete Gribbin, a child abuse investigator for the Los Angeles Police Department. 'When a baby gets shaken, the brain rocks back and forth in the skull, causing bleeding and scarring. The brain can swell and retinal bleeding is common,' he went on. Mary Pollack, the foster mother who cared for Larry in recent months, said doctors have told her the child will never be able to walk, talk, feed or care for himself."

Sly again stopped. He shoved his cramped body away from the VDT as if to remove himself from the stench of his copy. This was even worse, he thought to himself. I might as well be Gary Parker, writing some goddam medical story. Maybe the focus should be on the mother. It's her story, isn't it? The asshole she married gets free room and board for seven years and she gets a vegetable baby.

Opening a third file, Sly thought for a moment, then typed:

"Maria Schatz, little Larry's mother, cried during Wednesday's sentencing hearing. She faced no criminal charges. But Larry and his two-year-old sister, Bobbi, were taken from the couple by authorities after his dad's arrest."

Sly smiled. This was a much better lead. You don't know what's going on at first and want to read more. Sly continued writing, having forgotten about his cravings for tobacco.

The secret to Sly's success as a columnist lay in his eye for telling details. A few months earlier, Sly had followed up on a tragic fire in an East L.A. bar where four people died only to discover that the bar a year later was still in violation of many fire regulations. The back door was locked after 9 p.m. and there was no fire extinguisher. "But the bartender does have a bottle that can very accurately squirt seltzer," he wrote.

That last detail was what lifted the story out of the quotidian. On another occasion, in a column devoted to the various defensive devices women carry to protect themselves in the city, Sly pointed out that while women in L.A. often carried pepper spray, the preference in Orange County was for "a light curry spray with a hint of fennel."

Sly was frequently mistaken for a humorist, which he was not. He was, in fact, an angry man—"bitter and twisted" in Bill's phrase—a man seething with rage at his fellow human beings. Yet his sagacity and cynicism would not allow him to indulge fully in that rage. Rather it forced him to peer into his own black heart and sigh: he too was culpable.

Sly would quote Camus that "we should like, at the same time, to cease being guilty and yet not to make the effort of cleansing ourselves. Not enough cynicism and not enough virtue. We lack the energy of evil as well as the energy of good."

However, some of his readers had bundles of energy. Angry minority leaders were always calling his publisher or editor, trying to get Sly fired. For the columnist had little use for what he called the softheaded notions of multiculturalism. Letters and phone calls would rain down whenever Sly railed against activists seeking to protect minority cultures in Southern California.

"Culture is far more durable than people will admit," he wrote recently. "Culture is a living thing that is never really killed. The idea of enshrining, say, the Latino culture in

California is stupid. Our internal culture, whether ethnic, religious or familial, is a closed system; it survives within you. One of the worst things to do to a 'culture' is to ghettoize it — to classify it as a political cause and separate it from mainstream culture."

Like most Southern Californians, Sly was a transplant. Born and bred in New England, he grew up amid the faintly bohemian literary set that still dominates certain elements of that Yankee society. Its gods are Robert Frost, Sylvia Plath and Robert Lowell. Its denizens voted for the Kennedys but would never dream of socializing with them.

Sly's first cousin was a minor poet and a major pain. His mother was very pretty and exceptionally normal, which made her the family eccentric. Holiday gatherings had at their very core a mixture of the Pilgrim's First Thanksgiving and a Broadway opening night. They were full-scale productions, beautifully stage-managed but with enough plot twists and in-fighting to rescue any gathering from the most dreaded of possible contingencies — boredom.

His was a large family that would marry each other and produce manic-depressives. There were at last count, three suicide attempts — two successful — and any number of mysterious demises. There was also a not insignificant shelf of his father's library taken up with volumes written either by relatives or by the "shirt-tail" variety, those that married into the family and, once published, received as one of its own.

Everyone was Catholic though not necessarily practicing ones. Some were, in fact, lapsed Catholics but no one saw much difference between the two kinds. After all, divorce was accepted family practice. Indeed the suicide rate would have climbed much higher were divorce truly forbidden.

So Sly was raised Catholic. The Confraternity of Christian Doctrine was the official name for Sly's Sunday School sessions in the catechism. The instructor was a young man named Hugo Higgins, only ten years their senior, who also taught religion in Catholic high schools. He wore seminary black suits and ties and thin white cotton socks. His hairline was already receding shockingly for one so young.

Sly and his buddies went to Mass and then to Sunday School together. Held in the church basement, Sunday School found boys and girls grouped separately in opposite corners like warring camps on the eve of battle. To make certain class would be entertaining, a couple of guys would ask questions of poor Hugo about sex and girls and French kissing. The boys had swiftly learned that Hugo was incapable of exploring the nuances of Catholic teaching in these areas without explicit details and graphic language, the kind that caused young heads to swim with impure thoughts.

Sly toyed for a while with the notion of becoming a priest. He greatly admired Father Acosta. And he cherished the magic of the church building itself. He adored the dark wood and expanses of stained glass, the towering arches and shafts of sunlight pouring through the stained glass, catching the incense and charcoal from the censer during the procession as they lingered in the air. He fell in love with the Monsignor's purple regalia and dramatic manner. He revered the rituals, pageantry and ceremonies.

The first time he committed mortal sin was with Donna Goldoni. By then a high school senior, Sly nevertheless felt socially inept. He never dated, seldom attended football games and preferred driving the back roads of Massachusetts, tracing Revolutionary War maneuvers, to going to movies with friends. He had no real buddies as such, although he spent time with Eddie Dougherty. But Donna, for some unknown reason, was determined to get him out on a date.

She had persisted for several weeks about his taking her to see "The Sound of Music." Sly hated musicals. But he hated, even more, the idea of going out with Donna Goldoni. It wasn't a matter of her being unattractive—although her hair never quite seemed washed and her skin was bad. The truth was Donna terrified him.

He had forced himself to go out with a couple of girls his junior year, but they at least had the common decency to treat him with indifference. However, Donna did not attempt to disguise her aggressive pursuit of him. And Sly had no idea what to do with Donna Goldoni's ardor.

He skillfully avoided her entreaties for the better part of a month. But the Oscar nominations "The Sound of Music" earned somehow triggered an increased urgency in her need to see the movie. The pressure on Sly proved too great. He gave in. He told himself: what could happen while watching the sentimental adventures of the Von Trapp Family Singers? It's not as if Donna wanted to see "I Am Curious (Yellow)."

So on the fateful Friday night, Sly took Donna to the movie theater. A fair number of moviegoers were on hand. Donna chose to sit on the far left toward the rear where no one else was seated. Julie Andrews had no sooner finished serenading the hills above Salzburg when Donna grabbed Sly's hand.

Sweat broke out on his forehead. What the hell was he supposed to do with her hand? As he seldom went to movies, Sly had never been educated by Jimmy Stewart or Rock Hudson on what one does with a girl's hand. This was an alien thing that wiggled in his palm. He could scarcely follow the movie. He wanted to remove his heavy coat but didn't know how to extricate himself from this handholding girl.

About the time the Von Trapp's eldest daughter was singing about her being sixteen going on seventeen, Donna sighed and pulled Sly awkwardly toward her so she could lean her head against his shoulder. Sly was now in a complete panic. He tilted rigidly toward Donna, like a human Leaning Tower of Pisa, as she strained to rest her head against his stiff shoulder. He could no longer stand it.

"I want to take my coat off," he murmured, closer to her ear than he cared to be.

"Oh, sure," she said sweetly, and her misinterpretation of this action could not have been more profound.

He shifted entirely away from her and removed his coat, thinking that he was now free from Donna. Settling back into this seat, fully determined to focus on the coming of World War II, Sly was horrified as Donna draped herself around his coatless body. He could feel her lipstick on his lips, which tasted terrible. Worse, her wet tongue wormed its way into his mouth and was pushing coarsely against his. He felt like throwing up. Sensing his surprise at her brazen behavior, Donna jerked her body away. She studied Sly for a moment.

"There," she said. "I'm glad I did it."

"I'm glad too," he said bravely.

"You'd never know it."

Sly shrunk in his seat, but his serenity lasted only a few minutes. During a musical interlude, she grabbed Sly and kissed him for all he was worth, the grease of her lipstick somehow penetrating to the bottom of his throat. Sly said several silent Hail Marys.

Somehow the unimaginable then happened. Her hand drifted down to his lap toward his genitals. Horror arose in his throat. Should she discover his penis in any state other than a full-blown, red-blooded American erection, his manhood would be forever in doub. Without thinking he seized her hand and yanked it around his neck. Startled, Donna pulled away.

"What's the matter?" she whispered.

"I'm not feeling well," he declared. Which was the truth.

" What's wrong?" she asked, concerned.

"I'm a little dizzy," he replied. "I need air."

He leaped from his seat and stumbled up the aisle, leaving behind his bewildered companion. The fresh, cold air outside soothed him as the marquee lights played upon the puddles of rainwater on the sidewalk and street. Donna was by his side all too quickly and this time her tone of concern was absent.

"Have you been drinking?" she challenged him.

Instantly, he saw his redemption and seized upon it with alacrity.

"Yes," he admitted sheepishly—or what he hoped would sound sheepish.

She laughed. It was all right then. This had nothing to do with her.

"You naughty boy," she chided him. "Boozing and not sharing with your best friend."

"I am bad," Sly readily conceded. "You shouldn't go out with a reprobate such as I."

"I adore reprobates," she said, threateningly.

"Let me take you home," he suggested and, fortunately, she agreed.

Fearing another scene at her home, Sly succeeded in knocking over a metal trash can in her driveway, which alerted the Goldoni household—indeed much of the neighborhood—that Donna had arrived home. She regretfully said her goodnights to Sly under the watchful scrutiny of her doting parents.

The following Tuesday, Sly went to Father Acosta for confession. They went round and round, the priest and his penitent. Sly tried to build this incident into a moral crisis but Father Acosta would have none of it.

Finally, the priest sighed: "Oh, Francis, what am I to do with you?"

"I am a sinner and know not God's mercy," said Sly.

The priest chuckled. "The whole Gospel is full of declarations from heaven of God's mercy, and his readiness to receive penitents and forgive them," he said softly. "Does not God complain, 'Ye will not come to Me that ye might have life?' His Gospel is the Gospel of Peace and the Gospel of Grace."

Sly grew concerned. "Donna tempted me," he declared. "She made me"—he had to be careful here—"want her."

The priest thought for a moment.

"We are all searching for the light," said Father Acosta. "But without the darkness of temptation, we can never know or appreciate the Light of Divine Guidance. God guides us through the darkness so we may know its power. Offer your torment as a constant prayer and He will never forsake you."

This wasn't what Sly was bargaining for. But by the time he made an Act of Contrition, he was nonetheless in tears.

Having escaped the seminary, Sly spent four years instead at Harvard where he studied modern history and made Phi Beta Kappa. He gloried in his university years. He lived in Cambridge, just across the Charles River from Boston.

Boston. The city of the Tea Party, of old money on Beacon Hill and in Back Bay, of colleges and universities, of the classical architecture of Charles Bulfinch, of Irish politics and the glory of the Celtics and the curse of the Red Sox.

By his second year, he acknowledged his homosexuality to himself. By his junior year, no one who knew him had any doubts. Yet to this day, he had never come out of the closet as such. Management at the Morning Snooze was conservative and its health policy carrier rigorously hunted down any evidence it might be insuring someone with a high AIDS risk. It was simply best to keep quiet.

After Harvard, Sly drifted for a time. His draft lottery number was high enough that there was no chance he'd wind up in Vietnam. He joked to his Harvard roommate, a straight guy named Samuel Pierce who claimed to be related to the fourteenth President of the United States, that his number, 239, meant "women and children first." So he could afford to take time off to find himself.

He knocked around New York City, where he wrote occasional pieces for the Village Voice, then turned to the Post and Daily News. He discovered he preferred the tabs to the more circumspect broadsheets. In the Post's old building, he felt like a character out of "The Front Page." In fact, he tried hard to make himself into a character out of "The Front Page," adopting for the first time his red bow tie and pinstriped suits. A city editor had to explain to Sly that "Stop the presses" was a phrase that had no meaning in modern-day journalism. Nobody stopped the presses. You may re-plate for later editions, but you never stopped the presses.

Sly came to New York several years after the Stonewall riots in1969. He felt estranged from the gay rights movement. He was all for gay freedom, but it played no real part in his life. He disliked the gay community. For one thing, he objected vehemently to the misemployment of the word "gay." Gay? What was gay about it? Sly wondered. Even the frivolity of the limp-wristed queers came off as forced and unconvincing to him.

He was not the kind of man who would pick up youngsters on the streets. Most of those who cruised the streets were, in Sly's opinion, closeted victims of repression, often married with children, leading otherwise straight lives.

Hanging around gay bars and parks was equally distasteful. Sly found the emphasis on youth and appearances nauseating. He despised all the slender, decorated young men who flocked to the dance bars as much as he did the surly masculine types with their leather. Sly never felt young or attractive. He made friends but felt little desire for a committed relationship.

In Los Angeles, thank God, things were freer. He maintained many friendships with both men and women, gay and straight, and took comfort in the community of journalists. He hung out with news people; they were his "gang." He didn't believe in falling in love but he still wanted to. Whenever it did happen, he would explain over the many beers he stood friends at the American Legion, you have the best several months of your life.

"Longing is one of the most compelling human emotions," Sly would say. "But being loved, having someone in your life, isn't nearly as hot as the longing for someone."

Sly preferred the thrill of the chase. He adored the torments of desire, the gnawing hunger he felt when he yearned for another. Too often when that desire was satisfied, something died inside him.

Sly was essentially a loner. He steered clear of the after-hours clubs, bathhouses, all-night coffee shops, West

Hollywood gyms and the Silverlake and Hollywood transvestite bars. He attended St. Monica's Church in Santa Monica, where a mixed congregation of Latinos, Anglo Westsiders and Hollywood hipsters turned out for the rock bands and sermons that never truly dealt with the notion of repentance.

Father José, new to the parish a few months back, was heavy into repentance until several colleagues took him aside and explained the parish's demographics. His ratings — attendance at his services and, more importantly, the collection box — improved once he switched to other topics.

Sly particularly liked Palm Sunday with its emphasis on the Passion of Jesus Christ. His plea on the cross to the God that had forsaken him struck a resonant cord with Sly. For his relationship with God was a strange and troubling one. He felt God was doing a bad job, that He had more or less forsaken His creation.

Sly did not think God had died — as was fashionable in mid-century. Rather he believed God was on an extended sabbatical, a master chemist too long absent from his laboratory where experiments were running amok. As a columnist, of course, Sly was grateful for this state of affairs. The whole messy business of mankind never let Sly down: he never feared he might lose his sense of moral outrage or material for a column.

"When you consider His power and omniscience, God has bungled things," Sly insisted to Jessica one day. She pondered this for a moment. Like anyone raised in Southern California, she was seldom encouraged to think about theological matters.

"I think there's a purpose behind everything, but we simply can't always see it," she said.

"What's the purpose of hemorrhoids and tooth decay?" demanded Sly.

"Maybe those things remind us to take better care of our bodies so we don't fall ill from a more serious disease," she speculated.

"What's the purpose of AIDS?"

"I don't know. Maybe when we conquer AIDS, we'll discover a new super-vaccine that will cause everyone to live longer and better than ever," she said brightly.

"We'll never conquer AIDS, but let's say your conjecture is correct," said Sly. "Since there are more people alive today than have previously died in the short history of mankind, people living longer would mean overpopulation, increased poverty, massive starvation, increased infant mortality and social chaos."

"And that could lead to the exploration of new modes of living—on the ocean or in outer space," Jessica retorted.

"No, such chaos always leads to a Thermidorian Reaction, right-wing rule and a potential dictatorship."

"You're a very strange Catholic," Jessica told him.

"I'm a newspaperman," he explained.

CHAPTER TEN
IT'S MURDER

A La Puente man of nineteen was shot to death in what authorities said was a gang-related homicide in the unincorporated neighborhood of West Valinda.

"He was shot three times in the upper body as he stood on a street corner," said Sheriff's Deputy Angie Schlossman.

News of this tragic event ran as a back page item in the Morning Snooze, but the following day the paper played a killing in Mid-Wilshire on the front page of Metro. In that story, police said they believed gang retaliation was the motive for the killing of a twenty-four-year-old city employee who was chased into a hardware store and executed by two gunmen. The killing of gangbanger Michael Sevilla, slain near Belmont High School two nights earlier, may have triggered the slaying, police speculated.

The Morning Snooze staff was having a hard time keeping track of all the recent slayings and editors had to make value judgments as to which ones actually constituted news. Guns were blazing again on the home turf of the city's largest Latino gangs. Gang-related killings were soaring in the Rampart Division—with eighteen murders in the previous month along—after a year-and-a-half decline. The rise in killings meant a gang truce might be over.

The division is home to the 18th Street and Mara Salvatucha gangs. The latest round of killings signaled a breakdown of the Mexican Mafia's control over heroin sales in the area. The prison gang had ordered a truce nearly two years before, demanding that L.A. gangs stop drive-by shootings and turf warfare as such activities were hurting street sales of drugs.

Known as La Eme—Spanish for the letter M—the Mexican Mafia had divided Rampart among different gangs, each assigned a specific zone for drug sales for which they were taxed. But the recent imprisonment and deaths of La Eme's truce enforcers had given rise to increased violence. With one hundred and five homicides through October, Rampart was already on a pace to pass the record total of one hundred and forty-nine set three years before. And with each murder, the Snooze was confronted with decisions. Decisions as to which ones to report and how to write those stories.

The latter was the most important element. The difference between a back page item and a screaming Page One headline had more to do with style than substance. And the Snooze, in its battle with the Times for the hearts and minds and advertising dollars of Southland readers, needed screaming headlines. The newspaper needed to portray a different Los Angeles than the one Times readers were acquainted with. The Snooze needed a rough-edged, nerve-jarring town that jumped off the Front Page, gave fits to its editorial writers and caused Sly to wax eloquently about mayhem and madness.

Murders committed in Southern California are not, of course, any more gruesome or spectacular than those committed elsewhere. Any notion to the contrary is mostly the result of a convergence of highly volatile urban jungle of displaced souls with a disproportional number of seekers of literary fame. In short, Southern California is always full of writers—writers weaned on Hollywood melodramas and thus prone to latch onto the sensational.

The Southland, after all, nurtured Raymond Chandler, James M. Cain, Alfred Hitchcock, Ross Macdonald, James Ellroy, Joseph Wambaugh and Robert Towne to name a few who dabbled in literary or cinematic bloodletting. Los Angeles may be one of the few cities defined largely by detective writers and genre filmmakers. These fictional masters invented its sun-blasted, existential landscape where a man can lose his soul and lonely white knights drift through the haze of corruption in moral isolation They also created its killers — tough, dishonest, cynical creatures whose greed and bloodlust know no bounds.

True, serial killers do seem to thrive in L.A.'s temperate climate. There was Charles Manson with his mangy hair, Rasputin eyes and weak-minded female followers and Kenneth Bianchi and Angelo Buono, who raped and murdered young women in Silverlake and Glendale and got tagged the Hillside Stranglers. Next came Richard Ramirez, whom the Times dubbed the Night Stalker, crawling through open windows and killing people in their beds, and William Bonin, the Freeway Killer, prowling in his van, seeking young male hitchhikers.

Death is somehow more attractive in Los Angeles, murder more experimental. The glare of the media rather than of sunlight turns California crimes into celebrated cases. L.A. is full of brutality and the writers ready to turn its best crimes into instant horrors. From the William Desmond Taylor slaying in the Twenties to Winnie Ruth Judd, the trunk murderess of the Thirties, to the Tate-LaBianca murder cases of more recent vintage, Los Angeles print and television newsrooms, even more than its mean streets, echo with such cautionary lore.

Spectacularly violent crime has always been good copy for L.A.'s newspapers. Really good murders can turn into juicy meals on which the public may dine for months. The public expects its journalists to deliver all the tantalizing clues, blind alleys and side issues that any spectacularly violent crime provides. Public appetite drives editors who drive reporters who drive the "news."

Ultimately, the great crimes of Los Angeles somehow become litmus tests of new directions in American society. The Black Dahlia murder in 1947 — in which a young, struggling actress named Elizabeth Short was cut in half and left to rot on a vacant lot near Crenshaw and Exposition Boulevards — spoke to all kinds of paranoid fantasies about Hollywood and young women and the price of fame. The murder of RFK at the

Ambassador Hotel spoke to the death of Camelot and the end of hope for disenfranchised voices in American society.

If a reporter other than Jessica Tannenbaum had covered the initial crime scene near Washington and Vermont, it's doubtful if Dr. Death would ever have made his appearance on the Los Angeles stage. It would have been just another statistic buried at the back of the Metro section, one of the seven homicides in the county that weekend alone.

***

Jessica had taken to the police beat so readily that in no time Big Bob considered her his ace police reporter. Most of his crime beat reporters were content to come into the office and get hold of Chauncey Jervey's "overnight notes." This was an impressionistic memo written in the early morning hours by Jervey, the paper's oldest crime reporter, now somewhat incapacitated by age, who spent his nights listening to several police and fire department scanners in which he recorded the murders, holdups, carjackings, rapes and fires that plagued the City of Angels the previous night. These were the crime reporter tips for the day.

Jessica chose, however, to develop sources inside the department. Generally speaking, LAPD detectives are real closed-mouth when it comes to journalists. But Jessica knew how to joke around with them. The older ones tended to see a woman reporter differently. Or to put it another way, it never hurt with these guys to play the damsel in distress: "Gee, my editor really wants to get this. Can you help me?" No, that sort of thing never hurt.

Jessica developed the art of cajoling people into helping her via a unique alloy of neediness, likability and—when she chose to turn it on—kittenish seductiveness. Suddenly, a detective was made to feel as if he had to help her. Suddenly, her big problem was his big problem. But behind the poor-little-me façade lurked a tough and talented journalist.

Jessica developed a casual manner of speaking about death and mayhem to her best police sources. "Promise me no big murders will take place this weekend while I'm off," she said to one guy at Wilshire Division, who laughed and agreed to prevent this from happening.

When an illegal alien mysteriously fell from the fourth floor of an apartment building, she queried the Rampart watch commander about "your Salvadorian skydiver."

Jessica also noticed that homicide detectives loved the mystique that surrounds them as they cruise the city or strut through the squad room. Homicide guys live and die homicide. It's in their blood. And they all put in a lot of overtime.

"Police work is a lifestyle and homicide is a complete subculture," a detective told her on one of her first days on the beat. The guy mentioned this when she wondered about the presence of five investigators at a crime scene where nobody wanted to go home.

"It's like trying to throttle a bloodhound. They all want to stay on the case," he told her.

Homicide guys were also really sensitive as to how they got quoted in the press. They read all the newspapers every day and most were highly articulate. They knew their business and expected Jessica to know hers.

For the most part, the job was routine. A boyfriend shoots his girlfriend in a jealous rage. Every week that went on. Just fill in the blanks. Even gang killings were absurdly unimaginative and called for no stylistic flourishes in her prose. Only their sheer numbers made them newsworthy.

The Dr. Death story certainly started as one of these routine assignments. The man's body was found in an alleyway off Vermont Avenue that ran parallel to Washington Boulevard. It lay on the ground that rainy Monday morning under a white sheet. A beer can and some objects Jessica couldn't make out were circled in chalk. The drizzle had stopped, but the skies refuse to clear. Because of the rain, the air smelled fresh and clean. Shallow puddles of water filled holes in the cracked and broken asphalt.

A detective she didn't know stood near the body. He was diagramming the crime scene, recording the location of the evidence with a measuring tool that looked like a golf club with wheels. He called out the location of each item while his partner, a young kid who appeared fresh out of the Academy, jotted them down.

The detective was a good-looking guy with a dark complexion, dressed in slacks, a sports coat and tie, seemingly unaffected by the early morning chill. His eyes roamed the ground in the immediate area. She wanted to go up to him but he was concentrating. Bits of grit and gravel were inside her shoes. Why the hell hadn't she worn loafers?

A coroner's technician named Reuben, whom she recognized from a previous story, pulled the sheet off the body and knelt next to the victim who was face up. Jessica instinctively moved in to take a closer look.

Death does funny things to a body. Even a 25-year-old man can look much older when rigor mortis sets in. The victim was a Latino, possibly in his late twenties, with his skin already turning gunmetal gray. His hair was completely shaved and his eyes stared vacantly. Reuben seemed disinclined to shut them until his work was done.

Reuben wore white rubber gloves. A fishing-tackle box lay open on the ground next to him. He emptied the victim's pockets. He pulled out a wallet, which contained nearly one hundred dollars, and noted that his driver's license said his name was Hector Escobar. Reuben removed the victim's shirt and lowered his pants.

He then removed a scalpel from the box and cut into the side of the body above the left hip. He took a thermometer from the box, attached it to the end of a curved probe and stuck it into the incision, driving it into the liver. This would help establish the time of death.

The detective walked over to Reuben. He ignored Jessica. The technician was working the dead man's legs and ankles. Then he pressed his hands down on the abdomen and, lastly, tried to turn the corpse's head. It didn't move.

"Neck locked and stomach getting there," he told the detective. "Extremities still have good movement."

The detective nodded. Reuben pressed the eraser end of a pencil against the skin on the side of the torso. There was purplish blotching on half of the body closest to the ground, which was post-mortem lividity. The pencil pressed against the dark skin did not blanch white. That meant the blood had fully clotted.

"This guy's been dead four, maybe five hours," Reuben said.

The cop checked the plastic evidence bag, which contained a hypodermic needle, a small vial that was half filled with some liquid, a wad of cotton and a pack of matches.

"Reuben, would you roll up his sleeve, please?" It was the first time Jessica heard the detective speak and she liked the way his voice sounded—strong and forceful with a gentle hint of East L.A.

Reuben rolled up the victim's left sleeve to reveal scar tissue left by abscesses and infections from old needle marks—and one very recent mark where a tiny bit of blood had dried. The detective nodded and abruptly turned away. He walked up the alley littered with old sofas and rusting bedsprings. He stopped dead in his tracks and looked down.

"Manny," he called out. That was all he needed to say. Manny, the crime photographer, was beside him in a moment. The detective pointed down to a trail of fresh shoe imprints. Many took several pictures.

Now was as good a time as any. Jessica made her way over to the detective. "Excuse me," she began. "My name is Jessica Tannenbaum. I write for—"

"The Morning News," he said softly. "My name is Alex Valesquez."

Jessica was startled. Had they already met? God, she hoped not. That would be too embarrassing not to have remembered him. Especially such a good-looking guy.

As if reading her thoughts, the detective smiled. "You wrote the story about little Sara Tokunaga. I liked it and remembered your byline."

"Well, thank you," Jessica responded, flustered. Then to change the subject quickly: "What do we have here?"

Alex Valesquez shrugged. "Looks like some poor hype overdosed." He gazed away for a moment before continuing. "I don't know though. We've had a rash of ODs like this one lately. I'm thinking there's some kind of killer junk going around."

"Like what?" asked Jessica.

"The lab's checking it out. It's a mix of heroin and I don't know what else, some kind of amino acid maybe. The stuff is so strong you don't even have to shoot it. You can snort it or even mix it with grain alcohol."

"You think this victim may have done that?"

"No, he definitely received a shot. I'm just trying to figure out if this is an OD or a homicide."

"A homicide?" Jessica was surprised. Nothing she could see pointed to that conclusion. "You've got a hype kit and a dead junkie. How could that be a homicide?"

"Well, that hype kit looks new. Could be a plant. And other than the pop that killed this guy, he hasn't used his arms in years. Those scars are all old."

Jessica swallowed. He was right. She hadn't noticed any of this. Detective Valesquez shrugged with an air of studied casualness.

"It's just a theory," he said.

"I'd like to hear it," she said.

His left arm wrapped around his stomach and the right elbow came down to rest on the left hand. His right hand reached for his face with the index finger massaging the jawline next to his ear as if this action would help induce the theory to spring from his brow.

"Well," he began with some reluctance, "all the ODs I'm talking about had a lethal dosage of heroin injected with a hypodermic, almost as if the victim had been stabbed."

"Stabbed?"

"Some corpses have shown signs of violence as if the guy had been beaten. Others, like this one, show none."

"How many victims are we talking about?"

"Five in the space of a month. Oh, well, with today make that six," he said.

"Could they all be pushers?"

He glanced at her. She had picked up on it right away. He nodded: "It's a distinct possibility," he said softly.

"Did you happen to mention any of this to Hank Deitz?" she asked, glancing over at her competition from the Times who appeared to be bored out of his mind.

"Deitz is an ass-wipe," snorted Alex. "I talk to him only when I have to."

"Good. I'd like this to be my exclusive," said Jessica.

"Hey, wait a sec," said Alex, a note of alarm in his voice. "Don't print anything about what I said. This is on deep background."

"But it's a great story — police speculating that maybe a serial killer —"

"What serial killer? What police? This is you an' me talking is all. Can't I trust you?"

Jessica stopped cold. This guy could turn out to be a good source. Sure, he should've established that everything he told her was off the record right from the start. But no need to blow a source over a minor point.

"Okay, just tell what's on the record," she said, determined to get some story out of him.

"Only that we have an apparent drug overdose —"

"And you've had a rash of them lately causing you to speculate that … what?"

"I can't speculate. That's for Commander Fairchild to do," he said, referring to the LAPD's main press contact. "Look, all I can confirm to you is a possible drug overdose. It's not even a story. If you want to say police sources are concerned about a rash of such overdoses, which might indicate a more potent form of heroin, I guess that's okay but leave my name out of it. There's not nearly enough circumstantial evidence."

"Okay, okay," said Jessica, nodding her head. "That's all I'll do then. But promise you'll call me when you get another victim like this one."

"You got it, Jessica," he said, a smile returning to his face.

CHAPTER ELEVEN

SOPHIE

Jessica dutifully filed her overdose story — a backpager if ever there were one—but she did mention her conversation with Alex to Big Bob. He shrugged, a common enough gesture by the ME but the significance of this gesture divided the newsroom. A majority of reporters interpreted his shrugs to mean "Don't fucking bother me," and there was ample evidence to suggest this was a valid explanation. Yet others, a minority to be sure, were included to read a deeper meaning into Big Bob's body language.

Since the ME suffered from no shyness in regard to expressing his displeasure with reporters, no internal mechanism to short circuit the urge to utter a phrase such as "Don't fucking bother me" to a staffer, this minority opinion held that a shrug contained a more complicated meaning, a noncommittal neutrality toward the subject under discussion that might be roughly translated as "Interesting. Get harder information next time."

Consequently, Jessica, who was predisposed to this latter viewpoint, was highly encouraged by his shrug. She took it as a definite sign, a green light, a "Good work, kid," an encouraging pat on the back coupled with a swift kick in the fanny to nail this story and see her career blossom.

Big Bob, on the other hand, had other matters on his mind. Moments after his mysterious shrug, he was closeted with Sidney Wersching behind a closed door in his office. Wersching fully intended to camp in that office until something was done about Sly's next column.

"How am I going to get anything out of City Hall if we let this run?" Wersching demanded.

"I don't see—" began Big Bob before his political editor cut him off.

"He's calling the Mayor of Los Angeles 'a hypocrite' and 'a voracious leech on the body politic'."

Big Bob held up his right hand. "Sid, are you objecting to these descriptions on grounds of accuracy or taste?"

Sidney was genuinely stumped. "Well, taste I guess," he replied weakly. "We all know it's accurate."

"Then it runs," said Big Bob with finality.

The defeated political editor trudged back through a newsroom that featured a bemused Andy Reynolds listening to a torrent of abuse over his headset from a victim of the Temple of Doom and Danny Evans shouting into his telephone.

Danny hung up and stared at a nearby reporter as if he were the perpetrator of the Lindbergh kidnapping. "Hey, Martin, where's that story ya'll were supposed to hand in *yesterday*?"

The reporter interrupted his intense concentration to glance over at Danny. "You'll get it. Don't get your shorts in a twist," he said.

"Wouldn't dream of it, lad, since you may have to eat them in a few minutes," replied Danny. Within moments, however, his tone of voice abruptly changed: "How ya'll doing, Miss Lillian?"

Lillian Campbell, the Morning News' society editor, hovered over Danny's desk. She clutched several color photos in a hand that always seemed to shake unless it held a pen and reporter's notebook. In those instances, nothing could be steadier. A woman of indeterminate age, she began her journalism career in Southeast Asia following World War II. So nothing in the world of society ever caused her to lose a moment's sleep.

"Just fine, Mr. Evans," replied Lillian. "How are you, sir?" The formal address she reserved for Danny and Danny alone in the newsroom.

"Well, I tell ya, Miss Lillian, I feel like I've been rode hard and put away wet."

"Yes, I've had days like that too," she sympathized as she thrust out her hand. "Photos for Tuesday's column."

The editor took the photos from her and glanced through them. The rest of the copy desk ceased work for a moment to hear Danny's commentary. It was immediately forthcoming.

"Who's this old bag?" he inquired. "She looks like a dried-up creek bed in late summer."

"Mrs. Harriet Wellington, a leading figure in Los Angeles society, who indeed looks as you so succinctly described her," responded Lillian Campbell. "But her photo absolutely has to run. Didn't your mother ever teach you to speak well of your elders, Mr. Evans?"

"I didn't get to see much of my mother when I was a kid," he allowed. "She was always away on maneuvers with the Army."

"I have no reason to doubt you, Mr. Evans," said Lillian as she turned to leave.

"Bye now, Miss Lillian. Have a nice week and try to stay sober and out of jail. But if you don't, it's okay to call. I'm used to it by now."

Lillian Campbell had long ago learned to let Danny have the final word unless she was prepared to give up the better part of her afternoon on such give-and-take.

Over in his cubicle, Bill wore an undisguised grin. Bill didn't drink during work as a general rule. On this afternoon though, he made the mistake of joining Larry Conrad, the paper's restaurant critic and wine writer, in a tasting of young and tannic Napa Valley Cabernets in the paper's test kitchen, a tasting in which he had failed to spit out little of the inky red wines. He had, as he liked to say, "spit inside." Consequently, he was fifty-five minutes past deadline.

After a dressing down by Big Bob for this situation, Bill took a sip of the Snooze's stomach-churning coffee and glanced at Jessica. She had slipped her headphones on and was already dialing a number. He went back to teasing a paragraph about a psychic who was advising local politicians. A few minutes later, when she momentarily yanked off her headphones, he seized his chance. Bill came to her desk wearing what he hoped was his most sympathetic face.

"Big Bob giving you a hard time?" he inquired. She slumped in her seat and pulled on the ends of her long hair thoughtfully.

"No, it's nothing," she said.

"You need to relax a little. Terry Meehan"—this was the newspaper's film critic—"give me his press invite to see the new Al Pacino flick tonight. Why don't we catch it in Westwood, then grab dinner?"

"Thanks, but I've got plans tonight. Give me a rain check."

At that point, her phone rang and Bill had no reason to lurk around her desk. He retreated once more to his political psychic and Jessica took a call from Commander Oates of Southeast Division. Even though Oates had little to tell her, she was frankly glad for the excuse not to continue talking with Bill. She, in fact, had nothing to do that night and her brain was too tired to come up with what those "plans" she alluded to might entail were he to ask.

Bill's clumsy attempts at initiating a relationship with her were growing increasingly difficult to evade. The truth was she couldn't go out with him because she liked him. The only men she would go out with—if she went out at all—were guys she didn't care for. It was vital to limit her dating to men of no consequence to her. Then she would be in control. A serious relationship would distract her from her goal of getting a major beat at the Times.

The Morning Snooze was a stepping-stone for Jessica. The way she figured it, she would establish herself with a beat, build up those clips, then land a job on a real newspaper or a TV station. She certainly felt she was pretty enough to go on the air, and certainly a lot brighter than those bubbleheads on television. Imagine a real newswoman on the air.

So Bill was out. She was way too fond of him. She realized this when she learned about that ax in his trunk. When he told her about his future ex-wife and the ax, she thought the story endearing. Too bad she couldn't meet him in five years after establishing herself with the Old Lady or, better yet, Channel 4. Then things would be great.

As it turned out, Bill was destined to fall in love that evening.

***

Bill drove to the Women of Color Bar with low-heat anger simmering in his belly. The anger wasn't directed at any one person or thing. Rather it shifted from moment to moment from Big Bob for bawling him out to Jessica for not going out with him to his wife for dumping him to Larry Conrad for sampling all that wine.

Mostly he was angry at the fates which had failed to deliver a juicy story in over a week. The Palestinian fiasco also pissed him off. The interview had gone great—Nabhan had explained his hatred of the American government in no way affected how he felt about the American people among whom he had lived for over a dozen years when he taught at Yale. So he wasn't the Mad Bomber. Why should that make his views any less important to the Morning Snooze?

Bill parked his car on Third Street. Traipsing through sidewalk trash, he shoved aside a dirty burgundy curtain to enter the Windsor Arms. He occupied a stool that faced a mirror, which ran the length of the bar, and ordered a Miller Draft. Looking around, he couldn't help noticing all the tattoos. Somehow he had never realized that most of the dancers had them. There were tattoos on thighs, arms, buttocks and even breasts. June, who had a butterfly on her shoulder, latched onto him. She kissed his neck and explored his lap as he bought her a shot of tequila. She did all this while using her body to shield her activity from the closed-circuit TV cameras the bar's owner, whom the dancers referred to as Miss Lily, had recently installed for security—and surveillance of her girls.

Her turn to dance soon came up, freeing Bill to fall into a conversation with a black guy who was bitching about closing a shop he owned downtown in the garment district. Cal/OSHA had conspired to ruin his business, the guy, who said his name was Ernie, told Bill. Ernie was packing up and moving to San Jose.

"One fella worked for me said he had a pain in his back, and went and told Cal/OSHA he'd lifted a 300-pound piece of equipment. That's a goddam, bald-faced lie! I don't got a 300-pound piece of equipment in my shop! My insurance rates went up to where I can't afford them."

"That's a shame," Bill was saying as Ernie detailed his plans for selling off equipment and getting the hell out of L.A. As Ernie started exploring the nuances of Cal/OSHA and the damage it was doing to the garment business, Bill saw in the mirror an Asian woman he had never seen before had climbed onto the runway and was slipping her cassette into the player at the edge of the stage. He turned the moment the Rolling Stones blasted onto the sound system.

Her dancing was like velvet. She had a bored look on her face but her body was alive to the inner rhythms of her sensuality. She enjoyed the voluptuousness of her body and its ability to send shock waves through the sinew and viscera of every man who looked on. The muscles of her back pulsated to the music.

A transparent cape worked its way off her shoulders to reveal smooth creamy skin. The skin gave off an animal charge that would send a warrior cheerfully to his death and weaken the resolve of the strongest of men.

Bill soon excused himself from Ernie, probably too abruptly but then Ernie would find somebody else to complain to about the government's conspiracy against him, and moved to an empty chair at the tip of the runaway. The dancer, sensing new meat, worked her way toward him. He pushed his chair away and pulled out his wallet. He needed to make a major statement.

Her eyes flickered for a moment, taking in the bill he draped over the rail. But she refused to flinch. If he had thrown down a couple of dollars, then she would have pranced over and waved her bottom in his face for a half minute. But twenty dollars declared a serious interest. And no rush.

She spent Mick Jagger's best efforts grinding in front of a young, tongue-wagging Latino. She fixed Bill with a stare, then turned and arched her back, letting her body drape over the Latino before hoisting herself back on her feet. Suddenly she hit the floor and did the splits, her legs kicking out in opposite directions, the flesh of her hips bulging ever so slightly.

Bill slipped another twenty on the rail, then pushed his chair away from the runway. She gyrated toward him without fully acknowledging his presence. Then she looked at him squarely in the face. And smiled.

All her hard facial featured softened; her body relaxed. She swung her bottom over the rail and wiggled it. Bill nonchalantly glanced in that direction for a brief moment but looked quickly away. She moved her butt lower and, in so doing dragged the two twenties down to the runway.

She backed away, her eyes fixed on Bill as she slowly rolled her top down her breasts to the nipples. She pulled the elastic top away from her body for a swift moment, her nipples almost coming into view. She flattened her hand against her breasts, gently massaging the nipples as she gave Bill a look. Abruptly she turned away from him and, hips swaying, danced back toward the Latino who performed more nasty tricks with his tongue. She pretended to laugh and wiggled her index finger back and forth as if to say, "No, no, you naughty boy."

The music ended. She gathered up her cape and loose dollar bills tossed on the runway, especially Bill's tribute — she flashed a smile at him as she stooped to pick this up — then serenely departed the stage.

A couple of minutes later, she strolled along the side of the runway, giving each donor an obligatory peck on the cheek and "thank you." Finally, she came to Bill. She smiled and leaned down. He asked, "What is your name?" at the exact moment she asked him the same question. She laughed and sat in his lap.

"My name is Bill," he told her.

"I'm Sophie," she said. "I come from Thailand."

"How are you?" he asked.

"Not so good," she declared. "I sign my divorce papers today. I be better tomorrow."

Sizing him up, Sophie launched into a tale about coming to America two years before to visit a friend and how she fell in love with an American who insisted on marrying her and how five months into the marriage he left her for another woman. The woman would call her at all hours and call her "bitch" and she would never know whether her husband would come home that night or not. She was separated from him a year—Saturday was her "anniversary." She was sad and drank a lot, but she was happy not to have to worry about him anymore.

"I have no one here and I not speak good English," she told Bill after her drink came. "I take ESL at L.A.C.C. but people laugh at my English. I can't get no job except this one. I worked at Cameo Club, but it closed and now I work here. At home, in Thailand, I never dance in bar."

***

Sophie or Siranee Jaebkratoke had been born a few miles from the ancient abandoned capital of Ayutthaya, a place of ghosts and stone pagodas. She was born into a world where women were conditioned to endure suffering, to accept it as their fate. If you suffer in this life, perhaps in the next you might come back as landowner or merchant. But at least as a man.

When she was sixteen, her father, a rice farmer, sent her away from the two-room hut with a high pitched roof that was her home to Bangkok with a distinguished visitor who offered the young women in her village an opportunity to enter the fashion and movie industries. In exchange for the loss of his daughter's services, her father received compensation of twelve thousand baht and five hundred a month. Of course, the monthly payment was never received once Sophie departed.

The morning following her departure, Sophie's mother and grandmother got up early to prepare food for the monks, a custom that brought them merit points for their next lives. Armed with lighted joss sticks and lotus buds they knelt on the floor of the temple to thank Buddha for their good fortune.

In a way, Buddha did well by Siranee, who soon called herself Sophie, a name easier to pronounce for the Germans, Australians and Japanese she encountered in the sex tourism trade. It took her several years before she could escape this trade, scrape together enough money to get a real job and a white boy to marry her and bring her to America.

It took over a year to convince the American authorities that theirs was a real marriage, though, one built on love rather than convenience for an alien who wished to come to America and needed papers. By the time that year was over, it was the parties themselves that needed convincing. The separation—he visited Bangkok twice from L.A. but only for a week each time—gave them time enough to drift apart and to reconsider their hasty marriage.

Also, the white boy wanted a subservient Asian woman who would fetch his beer and massage his back. Sophie rebelled against all her conditioning, all that bowing to a man who wanted to lord over his woman. Thus, she sat in Bill's lap in the Women of Color bar on Third Street in Los Angeles and explained her story in highly edited terms she thought he could understand. If there was one thing she had learned in the bars of Bangkok, it was how to tell a sad story well.

"I can see you don't belong here," Bill was saying in earnest.

"I don't," she replied with equal earnestness.

"I don't want to talk to you here where men paw you and stick their tongues out at you. Let me take you to dinner. When do you get off?"

"I no eat tonight. I dance so I can't put on weight. If I eat at night, I get fat and work no more."

"Then I'll take you for coffee or a drink. I want to know you better and talk to you."

"I know you do," she said. "We talk again. Maybe next time you come. This time I want go slow. I must do things on my terms. I still love my husband but I divorce him."

Her body swayed and her eyes swam. She was slightly drunk and the cessation of dancing and this chat with a customer was sobering her up too quickly. She didn't like the feeling or the empty throbbing inside her stomach.

She leaned close to him, kissing his cheek and murmuring, "I come back" into his ear, her soft, warm breath giving Bill the chills. She leaped off his lap, squeezed his hand and headed to the bathroom. He watched her go, her hips swaying gently beneath the diaphanous cape. He was in love.

CHAPTER TWELVE
BODIES

Police found the dozen dead bodies, arranged in a star formation around a campfire, on a remote plateau in the Angeles National Forest. The bodies were discovered after a massive hunt that followed the disappearance of twelve members of the Solar Life Force sect. They also discovered several of their cars parked a two-mile hike downhill. Although police said identification could take some time, the dead were believed to include Jack and Jeri Whalley, the husband-and-wife architects who founded the sun cult in the early 1980s.

"It looks like some kind of collective suicide," Commander Fairchild told the gathered media in a nearby staging area. No reporters were allowed to go up to the site, although helicopters jockeyed overhead for good angles for the Five O' Clock News.

"The bodies are in a site that is fairly inaccessible and in positions that suggest some bizarre ritual," Fairchild went on to say. The victims appeared to have died elaborately planned deaths—by stabbing, asphyxiation, shooting and poisoning. Authorities did recover several handwritten notes suggesting mass suicide.

"Death does not exist. It is an illusion," said one of the notes. "We look forward to seeing each other in another world."

Over a year before, in a lifestyle interview with the Morning News, the Walleys said they hoped one day to "leave the Earth, to find a new dimension of truth and beauty, far from the hypocrisies of this world."

A police helicopter had spotted the bodies Saturday morning on a plateau that apparently had been cleared by the group.

Commander Fairchild said the bodies were arranged in a star pattern with feet facing the campfire. The group attached great importance to the sun, and the cult experts said the star formation suggested a desire to die in the shape of the sun.

The following day, Sly's column stirred a more angry reaction than any column since he suggested the Dodgers return to Brooklyn. As it happened, Sly had tracked down a guy named Gary Grable who ran a business that sent messages to the dead. Gary called his outfit Paradise's Gate.

Gary charged $200 for fifty words or $350 for a hundred. He delivered these messages via "messengers"—terminally ill hospital patients who, as Gary delicately phrased it, "through an unfortunate act of nature will soon be joining those no longer with us."

These patients read the messages and promised to pass them along after they died. When the "messenger" did die, Gary notified his customers of the "time and place of departure." Many of his customers wanted to contact celebrities, particularly Marilyn Monroe, Natalie Wood and John Lennon.

Of course, terminally ill patients could not always be relied upon to die as scheduled. So customers had the option to renew the service or receive a full refund if the message had not been dispatched by a Paradise's Gate messenger within one year from date of acceptance. For Priority Service, the message was placed with three "messengers," thus greatly increasing the chances of early departure.

While the appearance of his Paradise's Gate column on the same day as the Page One story concerning these dozen early departures by members of the Solar Life Force sect was coincidental, Sly couldn't resist speculating that Gary and surviving members of the Solar Life Force cult might join forces to create an Express Service. No deputy editor had questioned the propriety of this remark nor had Big Bob given it any thought when he read the column before it was paginated.

When the shit hit the fan the following morning, Big Bob claimed never to have read Sly's Life. With the other newspaper's Op-Ed columnists and several TV commentators and self-appointed community leaders frothing at the mouth over the next couple of days, Duke Whitcomb took the unprecedented action of giving Sly, and therefore Sly's Life, a week off with pay.

Sly was astonished. Never before had he gone on the journalistic disabled list. Worse yet, he was depressed. Since the Morning Snooze was not a union shop, he had no guild to appeal to over this "suspension," as he termed it. Nor did any editor jump to his defense. Only fellow journalists. Big Bob failed to return a single phone call and for once the ME was not seen roaming the newsroom.

To cheer his friend up, Bill took Sly to the Water Grill, the clubby, newly opened seafood joint where they consumed several dozen raw oysters and tender, delicious clams before settling into a dark wood upholstered booth for vast quantities of Hawaiian long-tail snapper, skate wing and plump patties of Alaskan Dungeness crab cakes. They washed this down with Alsatian wines — flowery Rieslings and citrus-like Gewürztraminers. None of which did much to cheer up the disconsolate columnist.

The silky lobster which followed did at least bring a slight smile to Sly's coarsened face and the peach tart and vanilla bean ice cream took the edge off his fury. A Château Climens Sauternes played its role as well.

But no real cheer came to the sullen though increasingly loquacious columnist until their bill arrived. News about Sly's "week off" had by this time spread throughout the restaurant staff. Thus alerted to the dire sadness of his client in booth 39, maître d' Charles Moller presented the check himself along with a complimentary cognac.

Sly was charmed by Charles' solicitous smile but truly dazzled by his baby-blue eyes and shockingly blond hair. Sly had never cared much for blonds — too Beach Boys for him — so he was genuinely surprised by the surge of emotions he felt as Charles fussed over his wounded client and demanded to know what else he and his staff might do to ease his pain. Sly fought the impulse to take the question literally. Instead, he inquired as to the maître d's health and how long the restaurant had been open.

In an intense conversation which followed, a conversation covering Los Angeles area restaurants, their mutual careers in the city, places of abode and favorite dishes, the two men managed to make a date for the following day without Bill ever catching on.

Sly's week vacation turned out to be the most thrilling he had ever experienced. Charles was too good to be true. As skilled in bed as he was overseeing the restaurant, Charles was — in keeping with the two men's general tendency to evoke seafood terminology — the catch of the season.

When Sly did return to work, few could not help noticing his uncharacteristic yet unmistakable good cheer. The tone of his column subtlety shifted as well. It took notice of good deeds among the citizenry of Los Angeles and failed to take a pot shot at the Mayor for over ten days. The latter was believed to be a record for Sly's Life.

***

Darlene was as good at managing her affair with Andy as she was her column. No one inside the company was aware of the blossoming relationship. And she kept Andy in a tizzy with her deliberate mood swings. When she feigned aloofness, he would become all puppy dog-like in his clamoring for attention. When she turned on the heat, he swiftly melted.

Andy redoubled his efforts to collect dirt for his lover. He hit the phones harder — "dialing for dollars" he liked to call it — and wore himself out on the party circuit. When he got a good scoop, he got into the habit of trotting into Darlene's glass-enclosed office. The newsroom soon became used to the sight of Andy slamming down his phone receiver in triumph, leaping from his swivel chair and, like Rocky climbing those steps in

Philadelphia, loping into Darlene's inner sanctum. The two would then become quite giddy over the latest tidbit from Tinseltown.

Before becoming lovers, Darlene would closely question Andy's sources on a story and reject at least two out of three. Now she loved every one of his items. Of course, the lead item in each column was always hers, no matter what the strength of an Andy Reynolds item.

What disturbed her though was a dramatic change in the quality of Andy's items. They were not only more biting than hers they were often better. It became harder and harder to keep his items out of the lead. She made a few casual comments, fishing around for an explanation, but none was forthcoming. He was getting too damn good.

Andy had picked up a few key sources. He had managed to plug himself into the "gay mafia" among the town's talent agents, nearly all of whom possessed an insatiable appetite for gossip. Like animals devouring their own, these agents loved to dish and somehow Andy, for all his heterosexuality, became part of the inner circle. This circle alone was good for several items on most days.

Another key source came about when the manager of the Viper Room tipped him off about Sharon Morgan. The sex video superstar had a history of dating rock performers. When Andy ran an item bout the porn queen and a rock star engaging in "full-scale whoopee" in the crowded club, Andy received an angry call from Miss Morgan herself. He had no business running items like that without checking first with her publicist, she told him. Nor did she appreciate the fact that the item was more about the fading rock star than about her. And, finally, it was inaccurate. She had not engaged in full-scale whoopee with the rock star. She had given him head. If you're going to run items like that, she told him, you might at least get it right.

Once she got over her anger, the two hit it off. Andy made a joke or two and Sharon revealed a wicked sense of humor herself. A day later, she called Andy with a tip about a rocker with a "chemical imbalance" being kicked out of the Beverly Hilton, which Andy thoroughly checked before he ran with it. Darlene was thrilled to break the story—which the wires and major newspapers picked up the next day—and Sharon "got off"—her phrase—on being Andy's tipster.

When sex is your profession, Andy mused, perhaps something else must substitute for the thrill of sexual encounters. Did being Andy's "Deep Throat"—again her phrase—fill that void? She certainly knew most of the dirty secrets of the music world. And more than a few TV stars, film directors and others in the entertainment industry loved to hang out with a genuine porn queen so she picked up dirt from all over.

What Andy enjoyed most about his lengthy, three-times-a-week conversations with Sharon was her vivid descriptions of all those she encountered. Sharon was obsessed with physical details, from the way a man's eyebrows moved around the forehead to the erratic patterns of excitement the male member displays when exposed to her charms. Tales of her rock-star lovers were replete with hilarious descriptions of failed performances, unwanted drug reactions, poor hygiene, embarrassing bowel movements and hairpieces that refused to stay in place.

Her depictions of female physiology were no less sharply observed. She could tell within moments of meeting another woman the kinds of medical procedures, diets, hair dyes and false adornments she endured to achieve her looks. She was no less unsparing when it came to her own body, which she tended to refer to in the third person. To Sharon, her body was simply the instrument through which she made her money.

A writer uses his brain, a poet his soul and she her body. Mother Nature had done well by her. Nevertheless, she gave Mom a hand by having one rib removed on each side and enhancing her breasts slightly so the nipples pointed out like a pair of pistols. Peroxide turned her long, murky blond hair a luminescent near-white so that when it tumbled down her back against naked pink skin, men broke into a cold sweat. Her body was a work-in-progress that she was constantly studying and refining, but seldom if ever thought of in conjunction with herself. It was simply her place of business.

In that business though, Sharon was a troubled star. She more than once walked out on a shoot when one of her paramour rockers came to town. She demanded extravagances unheard of on a porn set and enjoyed humiliating male co-stars. But the sex video industry indulged her tantrums. She was its biggest star. At least for the moment.

Sharon herself made no bones about the fact she hoped to make a transition from sex star to legitimate actress like Traci Lords. No one said much to her on this embarrassing topic: it was easier to humor her and her fantasies than to challenge them. Sharon had a six-figure income yet owed money to the IRS. Nude dancing engagements helped cover some of her expenses. She could pull in $5,000 a night as a featured performer at clubs around the country. That's where the real money was, she explained. Andy once made the mistake of kidding that he could come to see her perform when she appeared at a club near the airport. Sharon flew into a fury and said if he ever came to see her dance, she would never speak to him again. But that was their only quarrel and Andy made sure the connection between him and Sharon remained telephonic. He did rent one of her videos though.

***

Bill dropped by the *Women of Color* bar every night to see Sophie dance for a week. He made certain to never again tip her as much as he did the first night. He was determined this was not going to be a relationship built around money. She was impressed by his persistence. And as much as he was dying to touch her, their only contact was brief kisses hello.

She finally agreed to go to dinner with him on Friday. She met him at the bar and he took her to Taylor's on Eighth Street.

Hidden away in the heart of what had become a mixed Korean and Salvadorian neighborhood, the steak joint with its long dark bar, horseracing motif and red leather booths was a restaurant locked in a time warp. The place was never new; it was old-fashioned the day it opened. But it served great martinis and prime rib, which made Bill happy and Sophie perplexed.

She had never gotten used to the American penchant for having a huge slab of meat for a meal. Meat cut up in a nice beef *massaman* or Panang chicken curry or for barbecue as the Koreans liked it was one thing. But to simply consume a hunk of meat? She swallowed two martinis—an Americanism she took to readily—and picked at her ice-cold green salad and hot steak. Most of the meat she would later take with her in what Americans called for some incomprehensible reason a "doggy bag."

Bill talked to her with such earnestness that she knew he had fallen for her. Too bad he didn't have more money. It was every Thai bar girl's solemn duty to take as much money off a wealthy *farang* as possible. But while Bill was spending cash, he was far from rich. She thought he was sweet, which gave her an unusual sensation. Men were many things to Sophie but sweet was never one of them.

He also drank a lot, although she didn't mind that so much. He went through a bottle of red wine all by himself since she stuck with her martinis. She let her hand rest on his thigh as she picked at her steak. She was afraid after dinner that he would want to take her home but he merely took her back to the bar, had a beer, watched her dance one more time, tipped her ten dollars and left.

Now she was really puzzled. Five nights watching her dance and then dinner together and he hadn't once tried to fuck her. When he didn't come in the following night, she was surprised to find that she was not only disappointed but alarmed. Had she done something wrong the night before? Was taking the steak home in a doggy bag not done unless one had a dog?

Should she have not put her hand on his thigh? Or maybe her hand should've been more active under the table?

She missed him all the more the second night she danced without any sight of Bill. Where was he?

When he showed up the following Wednesday, her heart leaped. She was dancing as he came in. He smiled hello, sat at the bar and ordered a Miller's Draft. Once her routine was over, she hastily collected her dollars—not nearly enough—and went to sit with him. Her lips held his in a long kiss.

"I miss you, honey," she said. "Where you go?"

"Had to go out of town," he lied. He had, in fact, withdrawn himself from the Women of Color bar to see how she would react. He was madly in love with her but there needed to be reciprocity on her part he felt.

"I glad you're back," she said with real conviction and kissed him again. "Buy me a drink?"

He bought her a drink and chatted with her until the next time she went dancing. As she left for the runway, he stopped her for a moment and asked when she got off.

"One a.m.," she replied.

"I'll take you home," he said.

"Okay," she was startled to hear herself say.

It turned out to be the first night she ever slept with a customer since coming to America.

***

"We got another victim."

Alex was on the phone with Jessica.

"Talk to me," she purred.

"It's another hypodermic stab and, I'm willing to bet, the same type of heroin."

"Where was the body found?"

"Pico-Union area. We have an autopsy and brain procurement. You wanna come?"

She knew this was a challenge so she said yes immediately. She had talked to Alex on the telephone three times since their first encounter over the body of Hector Escobar. Anxious to follow up on the junkie-murders story, Jessica had been disappointed at the slowness with which potential homicides get treated by the LAPD. Alex still had no word yet about the tests on Escobar's body. The lab was backed up by over 600 slayings, robberies, rapes and other crimes.

"Sometimes it takes an impending start of a trial to get evidence analyzed by the lab," Alex warned her. But she called anyway and tried to convince herself that she was only interested in her story.

Alex met her in the front lobby of the medical examiner's office at County-USC Hospital. They marched down the green corridor where an omnipresent sweet smell lingered in the cold air.

"Understand," Alex was saying to her, "you can't do anything with this until I say so because it might screw up the investigation."

"What if I get independent corroboration?" she asked.

Alex shot a glance at the woman marching by his side. He recognized her as a fellow bloodhound, one that would not give up until the quarry was captured.

"Let's just say you'll check with me before you run anything, okay?'

"Okay," she agreed, an agreement she would later regret.

They put on paper gowns, paper masks and booties in the scrub room and went down another hall to the autopsy suite. Gurneys lined the corridor with the city's wretched waste — bodies under white sheets, their protruding legs with ID tags looped over big toes. Alex pushed through double doors.

The odor hit her immediately. It was the odor of sweaty socks and rancid fish, of human feces and vomit smeared over decomposing meat swarming with maggots. It was the smell of rotting eggs, filthy toilets and homeless men who never bathed.

It was a bouquet that made the throat close up and the stomach roil with indignation.

Inside the suite were six stainless steel tables. Each had gutters running alongside their edges and drain holes in the corners. Four had tenants. The nearest cadaver was of an eighty-year-old man found in his apartment four-days dead. It was not a pretty sight.

Alex strode swiftly past the tables to the last one where an intact body lay on its back, naked. A man greeted the police officer and Alex, in turn, introduced Jessica to deputy medical examiner Samuel Michaelson, who Alex explained was known as "Bones" for his uncanny knack for getting bodies to reveal their deepest secrets.

Jessica attempted a weak joke about the stench in the room. "That's the smell of job security," said Bones brightly. The slight, unprepossessing forensic pathologist grinned at this, then turned his attention to the body. In his rubber-gloved hand, the medical examiner held a plug of flesh.

"I'm going to need slides of this," he said to an assistant. He explained to Alex that he had removed a one-inch square section of the chest where the unusual needle puncture wound was located. He then turned to the cart that held his cutting tools and rolled it next to the autopsy table. He switched on a sound-activated tape recorder, picked up his scalpel and began:

"The body is that of a Hispanic male measuring sixty-seven inches, weighing one hundred and fifty-five pounds and appearing to be around thirty-six years..."

Jessica all but held her breath as she watched. When the smell of urine invaded her nostrils, she thought surely she would vomit. Then she remembered she hadn't eaten since last night—this new diet was the pits—so what was there to throw up?

Bones opened up Jesus Melendez Saura with shears and went on to describe the hypodermic puncture, the condition of his spleen, gallbladder and genitalia. With the decedent's chin resting on his chest, Bones pulled down the face and opened the skull with a small, high-speed circular saw. Now that the skullcap was removed, Bones lifted the brain from its home, producing a sucking sound.

Jessica had a sudden flash of a dead frog in her high school biology class with various bits of its insides strewn about her working bench. She threw up that day, was endlessly teased by male classmates and wound up with a C- in biology. She remembered her biology teacher's name was Mr. Small.

When the autopsy was complete, Bone sewed the chest closed with thick twine, then checked the slide of the deep wound.

"The slide," Bones was saying to Alex, "shows a straight perforation through the skin into the pectoral muscle. I couldn't testify this is a homicide based on the totality of the medical evidence so far. We'll have to wait for the tox studies to be completed.

"Thanks, Bones," said Alex, who seemed perplexed by this news. His face turned to a scowl. He turned to Jessica: "Let's go," he said quickly.

They walked back past bodies. Alex held the door open for Jessica. She smiled weakly and brushed past him. She had taken no more than two steps when she heard a strange noise and turned to see Alex Valesquez lying unconscious on the floor.

CHAPTER THIRTEEN
ALEX

At that moment, Jessica Tannenbaum fell in love. Seeing this ruggedly handsome cop lying on the hallway floor in a dead faint stirred something within her heart she had never before felt. The sight was erotic, maternal and highly emotional. It made her stomach muscles tighten and her nipples tingle.

The corridor was empty save for the bodies lying on gurneys. It was pleasantly cool and she no longer noticed the sick-sweet smell. She bent over Alex and pulled off his paper mask. He looked so peaceful in this repose she hated to disturb him. Her hand brushed his hair back from his forehead.

She got up and went to a water cooler. Filling a paper cup with water, she returned to the unconscious police detective. After removing her mask, Jessica got down on her knees and splashed the water on Alex's face. He came to slowly, as if unwilling to awaken from a pleasant dream. Such luscious dark brown eyes, she thought, as the orbs fluttered to life. The tingling sensation returned to her nipples.

Alex stared up at Jessica in momentary confusion. Where was he? Before his mind could fully account for this strange predicament, she leaned over him so that her hair fell like a curtain around his face. He felt her warm breath on his face.

"You fainted, my dear," she said and before she could help herself she lightly kissed him. A look of utter astonishment came over his flushed face.

"I thought it was the handsome prince that was supposed to awaken Sleeping Beauty with a kiss, not the other way around," she said gently.

The memory of where he was then hit Alex. "Christ..." he moaned. "I fainted? It's not possible. I've seen brains blown all over walls and guys with their guts spilling out and—"

"Hush," demanded Jessica. "I think it's adorable that you fainted." Her hand moved to his chest, which she rubbed through his paper gown and shirt. Her other arm, the one taking all her weight as she leaned over him, trembled slightly. Alex reached up and pulled the woman down to him for a lingering kiss. His hand massaged her neck through her paper gown. They finally pulled apart and gazed silently into one another's eyes.

"Someone may come," she said almost gaily and pulled herself to her feet. Alex got up too. They looked silently at each other. She looked around and spotted an unmarked door. "Come," she said, grabbing his hand and pulling him not unwillingly toward the unknown destination.

The door led to a dark room that when Jessica turned the light on proved to be a small lab. She turned the light back off and the two people fell into an immediate embrace. Their hands, mouths and tongues hungrily worked each other over, searching always for flesh. The paper gowns came off first followed by shirts and pants such was the aching demands of their bodies. Neither was able to completely undress, the urge being too strong. They made love leaning against a cool tile wall with quick intensity.

Afterward, as they gulped for the air they had denied themselves in the frenzy of intercourse, Jessica stifled a giggle.

"What is it?" asked Alex.

"What a place to practice unsafe sex," she said.

***

Alex took her to a bar on Figueroa for a drink. Jessica said she didn't think cops drank on duty and Alex told her she watched too much television.

So far they were managing to avoid the topic foremost in their minds. Instead, Alex went into detail about his dilemma in putting together a probable scenario that would link the deaths of these junkies.

"The problem is," he said, "we have no central file — no single LAPD computerized database — to look at for clues about similar crimes in other parts of the city. There's no way to look for patterns across the city. You gotta rely on what people remember."

"Sounds like the library database at the Morning Snooze," Jessica said with what she hoped was the right note of sympathy. "We're so far removed from cutting-edge computer technology that most reporters keep back issues of the paper at their desks."

He nodded and sipped his vodka. "I'm assuming you're not married," he said.

"No. And you?"

"Divorced. It's an occupational hazard."

Jessica glanced down at her iced tea and suddenly wished she had ordered vodka too.

"I'm not sure what the journalistic ethics are in this situation," she said, feeling her way as each sentence came out of her. "Does a reporter go out with a news source?"

"Cops aren't supposed to fraternize with the enemy either."

"Is a journalist the enemy?"

"It's an antagonistic relationship — cops and reporters," he said softly, then added: "But when a reporter looks like you..."

"You're a pretty good looking news source yourself," she said. "Tell me about yourself."

He looked at her, a twisted smile on his face. After an embarrassed cough, he said," Well, you understand, this won't be anything out of Joseph Wambaugh?"

"Got it," she assured him.

Alex Valesquez had been on the force for a decade. He had been promoted quickly: from patrol to a gang task force to vice, then to an elite burglary unit and finally bunco forgery before landing in Wilshire's homicide bureau.

He came from Lincoln Heights, an area east and somewhat north of downtown that was almost entirely Latino when he was young. Known simply as East Los Angeles when first settled in the late 1800s, the neighborhood adopted its current name about 1920 after the construction of Abraham Lincoln High School on North Broadway. Alex attended that school and wasn't a bad halfback in football. The 1980s brought a new wave of immigrants — to Alex's family's distress — mostly Chinese and Vietnamese families.

It never occurred to Alex not to be a cop. His dad worked for the Department of Water and Power and one uncle had been a sheriff's deputy. His mom worked for a while at the Glass House, which is what everyone called LAPD's Parker Center. Government and police work were simply part of family life.

His ex-wife, Marguerita, never fully understood that. When they married, she was nineteen and he was twenty. He got a B.A. in history at Cal State, and she eventually earned a master's degree in art at UCLA and opened a ceramics shop near Olvera Street frequented by tourists. By the second year of their marriage, he was in the Academy learning law, police procedures and traditions.

Veteran officers would drop by in the afternoons for sessions with the recruits. At these informal get-togethers, Alex would absorb the wisdom of the trade: things such as never stand in front of a closed door and when responding to a stick-up keep in mind that the bad guy may have a backup nearby and don't get separated from your partner in a crowd and that a woman or child can kill you just as dead as a man.

After he graduated, he and Marguerita fell into a routine when he returned to her after his shift for long dinners (or breakfasts) where they debriefed one another about the day's adventures, made love and fell asleep in each other's arms. But Alex was one of those cops who was never content to pull eight hours and go home. As his arrest records soared, so did the time he had to spend in court. And he and Marguerita spent less and less time together.

He also began hanging out at the bar at the Academy, especially after a four-to-twelve tour, unwinding from the job and listening to the older cops and detectives complain about "the life." He would hear about the high suicide and divorce rates among cops; about girlfriends and hookers who rat on cops; about cops who shitcan their cases to keep their desks clear. Sometimes these sessions would last until early morning.

Being in this job was something a civilian would never understand. You had to see the face of a real victim. You had to go to a murder scene and see the face of death.

A case a couple of years back still haunted him. Betty Ellen Meyers, an old lady who never hurt a fly all her life, was found in her living room. Some goon got inside her apartment and maybe she heard him so he picked up a candelabra. Alex would drive by her apartment every few weeks, walk up the backstair, listening for something—anything that might offer a clue. He would stare at the door, looking for something—anything that might have been overlooked. The guy that killed her got maybe fifty bucks. Why'd he kill her? Why'd he have to do the whole number?

Alex came home one night to find Marguerita in tears. "What is happening to us?" she sobbed. "What is it about this job that takes up so much of our time? I'm losing you to the fucking police department!"

He tried to explain that he was not the kind of cop that could shitcan a murder or rape, but he never found a way to talk to her about this job.

A new routine developed, one that consisted of longer and longer stretches of the day apart, passionless lovemaking and only an occasional movie. They divorced after eight years, six months and nineteen days. She told him she had never been unfaithful to him and he believed her.

***

"There's no real evidence," Big Bob muttered to Jessica as he stared at his terminal screen.

"But we have a series of mysterious, possibly related deaths, a police source speculating there may be a connection and Commander Fairchild issuing a denial so weak that it virtually confirms a possible connection," Jessica pleaded.

"Do you hear the words you're using?" groused Big Bob. "'Possible.' 'Mysterious.' 'Speculating.' You need *hard* facts."

"Just remember how the Freeway Killer stories began — with mysterious murders and loose connections."

Big Bob caught the subtext. He certainly didn't want the Morning News to miss the boat on the next big serial killer.

"At least those were mysterious murders," he grumbled. "These are simply mysterious deaths. Your cop pal won't go on the record?"

"No, he won't. Nor do I blame him."

"Don't fuckin' sympathize with a cop," Big Bob snapped. "You're doing him a favor in this case. Okay, we run a speculation story about a potentially lethal strain of heroin on the streets of L.A. on Page Six in Metro with no mention of murder."

"That buries it!" she protested.

"I'm late for the budget meeting. Be sure to log the story."

Big Bob leaped from his chair with surprising agility for a man carrying forty more pounds than he should and possessing no hips. Secretly, Jessica was pleased. Front Page or even Page Three would give her story too much prominence. After all, Alex could be wrong.

***

"A series of recent drug overdose deaths in the Los Angeles area has caused LAPD investigators to fear that a potentially lethal strain of heroin has entered the local drug scene," began Jessica's story. The statement was attributed to no one. Neither was the next paragraph. It summarized seven "mysterious" deaths—Alex on deep background had added one more to the ones Jessica already knew about—and some curious coincidence of circumstances among at least four. The only on-the-record quote was attributed to a drug counselor and Commander Fairchild, who said: "Naturally we're concerned about these unfortunate deaths. At present, the LAPD feels they are simply that—drug overdoses—and not an indication of a new and virulent type of heroin. But we are waiting for lab results to be certain."

Alex took the Page Six story well enough. He wasn't quoted and speculation in the press might even help his investigation. He even called Jessica to suggest they use his upcoming comp time for a trip to Palm Springs.

"I'd like to take you to the Spa Resort for five days and never let you out of bed."

"That would be kidnapping, false imprisonment and molestation," she pointed out.

"For starters," he replied.

"I've got the weekend off," she said. "Can you perform all those crimes in two days?"

CHAPTER FOURTEEN

THE GOOD DOCTOR

Sly was genuinely concerned. The affair with Charles Moller was going great guns and this kind of thing wasn't supposed to happen to him. Worse yet, it showed no signs of burning out. There seemed to be no bittersweet light at the end of this particularly long tunnel of love.

Sly, of course, was a loner. A gregarious loner but a loner nonetheless. But the continual companionship of Charlie wasn't the real source of his alarm. No, what worried Sly was the almost instantly settled nature of the relationship. They got along fabulously, rarely quarreled, made allowances for one another's foibles, shared similar tastes and belief systems, genuinely cared for each other and hated the Dodgers with undisguised glee.

When it was discovered each had the same obscure LP of Noel Coward performing his songs in Las Vegas, the look that passed between them was one of astonishment and delight mixed with a kind of horror at such a remarkable kinship. Sly wasn't all too certain he wished to share his life with another soul so closely attuned to his own.

Sly then did the unthinkable. He cruised a West Hollywood bar to see if another man might stir his libido. None did. Not that a glance or two weren't thrown his direction. But he felt impervious to any blandishments and weirdly disconnected from the whole scene.

He always adored the chase—that unexpected moment when two pairs of eyes lock together, when hands accidentally brush against each other as someone subtly suggests his attraction to you. That was a thrill Sly was not certain he could live without. But there can be no chase when the catch of the season awaits you each night.

Sly tried to pick a fight but Charlie only laughed and soon Sly laughed too. He tried to stay away from Charlie for two consecutive nights but broke down midway through the second day and telephoned the Water Grill to make a date for that night.

By then Charlie knew something was wrong.

"What's bothering you, Francis?" he asked as the two worked their way through a pitcher of margaritas in a cozy alcove at Charlie's Brentwood condo off San Vicente during unseasonably hot weather.

Sly drained the glass and fished out a slice of fresh orange from which he pulled the fruit off from the skin and thoroughly chewed it as if to illustrate the intensity with which his mind was chewing over Charlie's question.

"Nothing's bothering me, per se," he said softly, his voice barely audible above the hum of the air conditioner. "I do sometimes wonder when we're headed. You and me, I mean. It's probably foolish to even ponder the future when the present is so bloody wonderful. You're *almost* too good for me. So maybe I'm afraid it won't last."

"Maybe you're afraid it will," said Charlie, a silky smooth purr in his voice that Sly found ever so appealing.

"That too," Sly agreed, a grin tugging momentarily at his mouth.

Charlie's right hand reached for a canister of pipe tobacco on the glass table next to the margarita pitcher and shoved it directly in front of Sly.

"You see, that's what I mean," said Sly with fake irritation. He pulled his pipe from the pocket of his coat draped over the sofa. "You knew I was dying for a smoke. You can bloody read my mind. It's damn disconcerting."

"Years in the service industry do that to you."

"Bullshit. Nothing to do with the service industry. You know me. Too well."

"Too well?"

"Don't get me wrong: it's flattering for someone to know you and to concern himself with your bad habits and creature comforts. We've just grown so close so fast."

"And that bothers you."

"A little. What about you?"

Charlie poured margaritas from the ice-cold pitcher, first into Sly's glass and then into his own. Setting the pitcher back on the table, he let a bemused smile break out on his face.

"No, it doesn't bother me. Rude patrons bother me. Road rage bothers me. Homophobic assholes bother me. But nothing about the man I love can bother me."

Sly felt certain a gasp escaped from his throat. His heart thumped in his chest. The man I love? Did he say that? Was it even right that he should say that?

The smile on Charlie's face grew larger. "Put that in your pipe and smoke it," he said quietly.

"You took me by surprise."

"I know. It's the devil in me."

Sly couldn't help himself. He reached over to Charlie, grabbed him by the neck and pulled the man toward him. He kissed him with passion. After several moments, he pulled slightly away and said, "The devil indeed."

"Don't let it throw you. I ask nothing of you. And I too sometimes wonder where we're headed. Don't let's worry about it now. Have another margarita and let's go to bed."

Sly poured another glass-full. It was going to be a good night.

***

A few days later, Bill showed up for work rather the worse for wear. He had spirited Larry Conrad, the paper's restaurant critic and wine writer, off to Arizona the previous weekend to do peyote with the Indians. From a source in the drug community, he had heard that the hallucinogen named ayahuasca could induce ecstatic states of mind. Not only did he and Larry fail to locate this nirvana, but Bill's car also had a flat tire and they lost a lot of money playing blackjack at an Indian casino.

Returning to town in this sorry mood, he holed up in the Women of Color bar. Sophie hadn't worked there in several days, he learned, and she was not answering her phone. He worried that maybe her husband was back in the picture.

He had then left the Windsor Arms and driven by his wife's apartment building with the full knowledge his ax still took up space in his trunk. For once though, he didn't get out to see if she was in. He drove home basking in this moral victory.

Returning to his messy Hollywood house — an excellent purchase he and his wife made during a downturn in the economy — he poured a cold beer and for the first time in weeks went back to writing his novel about a Los Angeles reporter who nailed the town's crime bosses. After several more brews, his typing was shit. He finally gave up and passed out on the couch. No wonder he was grumpy in the morning.

Nor did the mob scene in the Morning Snooze lobby improve his disposition. Somehow there was always some kind of scene going on in that damn lobby. The congestion was often caused by security guards who backed things up with endless security checks and demands for identification These procedures were an exercise in the absurd since the building's rear entrances were always unguarded and there was little rhyme or reason to the guards' demands. One infamous day, the British consul-general came to visit and the guard made him show countless IDs before going in. Moments later, a man dressed in a bear costume, who was part of a circus passing through town, arrived in the lobby and the same guard waved him through right away.

On this particular occasion, both Bill and Lillian Campbell entered simultaneously to discover the lobby jammed with a mob of men.

"What on earth's happening?" Lillian demanded of the harried guard.

The guard rolled his eyes. "Sly's Life is searching for a spouse for a very pretty illegal alien about to be deported," he responded wearily. "These are the applicants." Then he added: "Today."

Lillian shook her head and bulled her way to the elevator as she clutched her huge bag. Bill wisely stayed close behind her much as a football running back would behind a pulling guard on an end sweep. Two minutes later, she deposited the bag on her desk in the newsroom, a desk she seldom used but demanded to be kept free and clear at all times. Here she unloaded from the bag a series of notebooks, a microcassette tape recorder, an assortment of prescription medications and several rolls of film. Only then did she pick up a stack of photos from her box and glance through them quickly, eliminating several shots that included individuals with whom she was feuding or people too trivial for her column.

Bill slumped into his chair and glanced over at Jessica who was chewing on a fingernail and staring at her terminal screen. Damn, she looked fine, he told himself. To blot out her beauty, he tried to conjure up an image of Sophie naked. Tiring of this, he climbed wearily to his feet and headed for the coffee machine, passing by Danny's desk where Lillian was now depositing the approved photos.

"I need that art pronto," Danny barked into his phone. "You speak Mexican, don't ya'll? 'Pronto' means pretty fuckin' quick!"

He banged down the receiver in its cradle and turned his attention to Lillian, "Hi there, Miss Lillian," he greeted her. "Say, I waited for you in that motel for three hours and you never did show up."

"Dear man, I don't know what you've got in that thermos of yours, but it's playing havoc with your fantasy life," she responded sweetly.

Ignoring her comment, Danny squinted at the photos thoughtfully. "Shit, you wan' me to use this photo? Why if I looked that ugly, I'd shave my ass and walk backward."

"You of all people shouldn't cast aspersions," she noted.

"Okay, Miss Lillian. It's your column. I'll dummy this one in. But I still say this woman's as ugly as a three-fingered puke."

'You're most gracious, sir," said Miss Lillian.

At that moment, Jessica's phone rang. She slipped on her headphones. "This is Jessica," she answered in her usual flat monotone.

The male voice on the other end had a dry rasp that sent electricity shooting down her spine and a cool, steady tone that made her instantly uneasy.

"Jessica Tannenbaum?" the voice asked.

"That's right."

"You wrote that article about the dead pushers?" the man demanded.

"I wrote a story about seven overdoses in the L.A. area," she said. "I said nothing about pushers."

"They're all pushers," he rasped. "I was wondering when some rocket scientist in the media would figure it out."

"What do you mean?"

"Those pushers. They got what they deserved."

"You mean they were killed?"

"You got it, Miss Tannenbaum. They were killed."

"Are you implying that you killed them?" she asked.

"I'm implying nothing. I'm flat out saying I killed them."

"Why?"

"Think of it as performing a public service — ridding the city of its scum."

Jessica immediately started typing his comments into her computer, right in the middle of a story about a police chase along the Harbor Freeway the previous night.

"Murder is a public service?" she asked.

"Make L.A. clean again is my motto."

"Who are you?"

"Oh, c'mon. You know I'm not going to tell you that. But I do think you should alert the pushers of L.A. that they're going to get stuck with their own medicine."

"Stuck?"

"Yeah, stuck…as in with a stab of a hypodermic needle. They then get to enjoy a particularly stimulating cocktail of heroin and amino acid. Boy, what a rush they'll get out of that. Quite a send-off."

"How do you select your victims?"

"My little secret. But you can alert the pushers of this town that your next customer may be death."

The line went dead. Jessica slowly took off her headphone. She then saved her notes.

***

Chaos reigned in the newsroom for the next few hours. Big Bob called the brain trust—Hazel and Wersching along with Bill—into his office to chew over Jessica's phone call. Jessica pushed hard for a Front Page story. Wersching wanted nothing to do with it.

"It's a hoax, Jesus Christ!" he screamed at one point, his forehead drenched with sweat.

"We can't ignore the LAPD's public relations officer," added Hazel, his tie even looser than its usual highly relaxed state.

"I'm not ignoring anything," replied Big Bob, who was the calmest as he munched on the peanuts he kept in a jar on his deck.

"Jessica, what did Commander Fairchild say again?" asked Hazel for the third or fourth time.

"Fairchild dismissed it as a sicko's prank. But," she added for the first time, "I don't think he gave my questions serious thought."

"Why is that?" inquired the managing editor, who stopped munching his peanuts and fixed her with an intense gaze.

"He didn't check with anybody in the high command," she replied. "He simply issued that statement—if you can call it a statement—off the top of his head."

"What's your relationship with Fairchild?" asked Big Bob.

"There isn't much of one. I've talked to him before but, remember, I am pretty new on the beat."

The editor's eyes held those of his reporter's for a moment. "We need to get a hold of Detective Valesquez," said Big Bob.

"I've been trying ever since the call came in. He's in the field or something and can't be reached."

"Keep trying," said Big Bob. "Meanwhile go ahead and write the story and check with every source you've got. Let Hollis and Bill help you make calls. I'll call Fairchild. Let's see where we are at five o'clock."

Jessica called Alex another twenty times between three p.m. and five p.m. without luck. Another detective, Irv Kinsolving, who was a pal of Alex's, told Jessica she was on to something but couldn't go on the record. Numerous other officers told reporters they trusted that it was common knowledge in the department that a serial killer was suspected in the deaths of several junkies over the past two months.

Throughout the afternoon what continued to encourage Big Bob was the caller's mention of a 'hypodermic stab." The ME had demanded that Jessica keep all mention of struggles, stabbings or murder out of her story. The caller had even correctly identified the mix that went into the "cocktail."

By 5:30 Jessica still had not reached Alex. A follow-up call by Big Bob to Fairchild elicited a more formal—but at the same time more tentative—denial. A Hollywood division detective speaking to Bill went so far as to speculate—off the record—that two unsolved "deaths by misadventure" in the Hollywood area sounded suspiciously like the deaths in Pico-Union.

By 5:45, Big Bob had ordered a Page One story but decided not to make it the banner. Big Bob was going to put the Morning

News solidly behind this serial killer but he wanted to leave himself wiggle room if the call were a prank.

This left only one more issue.

"We need a catchy moniker for this guy," mused Big Bob. He said this in his closed-door office in which stood Bill, Jessica, Hazel, Wersching, Ruth and Larry Beale.

"The Junkie Killer?" said Wersching.

"The Something Stalker or, no, wait—something to do with heroin," said Hazel. "The Heroin Assassin. Something like that."

"Maybe something that picks up on this guy's motto about keeping L.A. clean," suggested Ruth. "Mr. Clean…The Eradicator…The Exterminator." She looked around weakly. All heads were shaking.

"Something about hypodermics or needles or doctors?" ventured Jessica. "This killer seems intent on administering to pushers a dose of their own medicine."

"How 'about Dr. Death?" said Bill. Big Bob turned around quickly and looked at Bill as the skin on his face flushed hot pink.

"That's it," said Big Bob. "Dr. Death. He injects his victims with narcotic poison. He's all yours, Jessica. Make Dr. Death a star."

With that Big Bob dismissed everyone from his office.

***

"'Dr. Death' Terrorizes L.A.'s Drug Dealers" shouted the Page One headline. Underneath Jessica's byline, the story began: "Message to all Los Angeles drug dealers: Your next customer may be Death."

"A man claiming responsibility for the murders of at least seven Los Angeles-area drug dealers called The Morning News Tuesday afternoon with a warning to all pushers: Get out of business or you may 'get stuck with (your) own medicine.'

"Sources inside the Los Angeles Police Department told the Morning News this warning is legit. Police homicide detectives have speculated privately for weeks that the apparent overdose deaths of several local drug users may, in fact, have been murders. All these deaths featured a common MO: The wounds appeared to be caused by a stab of a hypodermic needle. The medical examiner said a lethal dosage of heroin may have been bolstered by an amino acid.

"The self-declared killer, who contacted The Morning News, verified both theories.

"Confirming that he stabbed seven victims, all drug dealers, with a hypodermic needle, he told a reporter that what he injected into their systems was 'a particularly stimulating cocktail of heroin and amino acid.' This gives the dying criminals 'quite a send-off,' he added.

"The deadly doctor then issued a warning. The Morning News 'should alert the pushers of L.A. that they're going to get stuck with their own medicine.'"

***

The initial Dr. Death story did not exactly tear the town up. In fact, save for Alex Valesquez's reaction, the response was tepid at best. Plucking the story off the Morning News, the AP ran a short item, which two local late morning news shows picked up and ran near the top of their newscasts. In each, the anchor attributed the story solely to the Morning News and added a brief police denial.

Commander Fairchild called Big Bob to advise him that he had scheduled a press conference that afternoon to deny the story much more firmly and to express regret that he had not been more emphatic the day before to prevent this "rookie mistake." He felt bad for Jessica: This could ruin her career.

Alex finally did return Jessica's many frantic phone calls of the day before. He had taken the day off to visit his mother in the hospital with pneumonia, and in his anxiety over his mother's health had left his beeper off. He was not pleasant to Jessica.

"What's this shit doing in that fucked-up rag of yours?" he demanded less than ten seconds into their conversation. "*Dr. Death*? Give me a break."

"Sorry about that," she said. "I didn't name him."

"I don't give a shit about the name. Why have you turned a crank phone call into this garbage?"

"The paper felt—"

"The paper!" he exploded. "What about you? You wrote this crap."

"My editor felt the story was solid."

"What solid? A crazy calls you and suddenly he's the perp! What evidence you got?" Alex was virtually shouting into the telephone.

"Alex, I couldn't reach you. And this guy knew stuff about the OD deaths we never printed."

"Okay, what did he say—word for word?"

She took a few moments to call up her notes on the VDT screen. Looking at them, she continued: "Okay, he first claimed to have killed all the junkies I wrote about in my earlier piece and he insisted they were all pushers—as you speculated to me more than once. Remember, I never wrote that. *And* he said he was performing a public service—ridding the city of its scum, quote-unquote. He said his motto was 'Make L.A. clean again.' Most importantly, he talked about sticking each victim with a hypodermic needle. 'Stab' was the word he used. My original piece never mentioned that common link. And he knew the heroin was mixed with an amino acid."

Alex sighed. "The call's a prank. And your story destroyed my investigation. I got no chance of being taken seriously now. 'Dr. Death' be fucked."

"I'm sorry you feel that way," she said.

"Yeah," he said. He hung up.

So much for that source, thought Jessica. To say nothing of the relationship. She looked over at Bill, who happened to glance her way. Noticing the misery etched in her face, Bill cocked his head, got up from his seat and came over to her.

"It just hit me," she told him. "I've become a tabloid journalist. Christ, what's a nice girl like me doing in a place like this?"

"Nice girl?" said Bill. "If I thought you were a nice girl, I wouldn't associate with you."

***

The press conference at the Glass House had an unstated agenda that would feed into the Dr. Death hysteria soon to erupt. This had to do with the state of war that existed between Mayor William Warren and police chief Ned Sinclair. In a nutshell, they hated each other's guts.

For the mayor, a businessman himself intent on luring tourism and new businesses to the city—to say nothing of clinging to local businesses poised for flight elsewhere—Los Angeles was a benign metropolis bathed in racial harmony, prosperity for all who wished to work and an enlightened government determined to reform its antiquated tax structure. Nothing was impossible in this town where business and labor were willing to roll up their collective sleeves and achieve greatness.

To the mayor, serial killers belonged to the city's colorful past. These were creatures to be celebrated by screenwriters, pulp novelists and historians and not by lowly, embittered journalists determined to wreck this picture of civic bliss and the mayor's campaign for re-election next year.

To the chief, battling for greater funding for his police force, Los Angeles was a feral urban jungle where human predators roamed, their dope-fried brains seething with race or class hatred, searching for things to steal, women to rape and men to kill. It was one big gang-bang where the police were outgunned and outmanned and no place was safe except Beverly Hills.

Chief Sinclair was also eyeing a possible run for the mayor's office himself. So the capture of a serial killer with the chief personally making the arrest was a wet dream that truly tantalized the chief. However, Chief Sinclair worried about the new poster boy being promoted by the Morning News, a newspaper he loathed. A guy who kills junkies and pushers was undoubtedly doing the city a service. Drug traffic in Los Angeles had long ago reached the stage of a pandemic. The chief knew no police force, even one triple in strength, could cope with the number of drugs flowing through its streets. So if someone was offing pushers, Sinclair needed to spin that situation.

This killer, he reasoned, if there was a killer at all, was undoubtedly a pusher himself, staking out his territory like a dog pissing its way around the block. So a hot news story that lasted several weeks about a pusher — better yet a drug lord — killing off rivals, a story capped with his capture or death at the hands of Sinclair's LAPD, would not only highlight the chief's continuing and noble struggle with the narcotics trade but give a tremendous boost to his chances in any mayoral contest.

Carefully watching this conflict between Chief Sinclair and Mayor Warren was the Los Angeles Police Protective League. The union's board was made up mostly of rednecks, old farts who came from military backgrounds unlike the younger, more educated officers coming onto the force these days. Its president, Bill Hardcastle — nicknamed "Hard Ass" — genuinely enjoyed irritating people. Hard Ass was currently working the corridors of City Hall to get a new and better union contract which, not incidentally, would bolster his media image as the real force behind the LAPD.

But his combative style was sending conflicting signals to council members. Even the most ardent supporters of the LAPD were tired of Hard Ass' "blue flu" sick-outs. Despite a court order barring such tactics, the League had secretly organized a series of mass boycotts on certain shifts and had planted more than a few stories in the media about the dangerous conditions on L.A.'s streets and the chief's indifference to the conditions under which his officers labored.

Thus, Commander Fairchild was forced to perform a delicate juggling act at his press conference. On one hand, the LAPD officially denied knowledge of any serial killer roaming the city streets; the proof simply wasn't there. On the other hand, the department would investigate any information from any legitimate source that might connect these deaths.

It's fair to say that the news stories on local television that evening and in newspapers the following day did little to refute the Morning News' original story about a serial killer. The Times and Daily News' refusal to give the story any real prominence had more to do with those papers' disdain for their rival than their editorial judgment. Indeed the managing editors of both papers ordered top beat reporters to look into "Dr. Death." But, as the Times' Lloyd Friedkin told his deputy editor, any killer would have to have a new nickname should his existence be verified.

CHAPTER FIFTEEN
GINA AND REGGIE

As the late afternoon sun burned through the ozone layer that blanketed the city, several limo drivers at LAX waited, their long, squeaky-clean cars idling in the limo rendezvous spot at the edge of a runway. About 200 yards away, dozens of cabbies schmoozed and joked. But the limo drivers sat in quiet solitude, each in his vehicle doing paperwork or reading with the air conditioning set at "glacial." They were waiting to pick up film stars, politicians or business executives at the airline gate. Just as they were the elite of the city's drivers, their clientele was the elite of airline travelers.

For the most part, a limo driver treated a journalist as he would a dirty carburetor. Limo firms required drivers to sign a pledge stating they will not divulge anything involving their work or the people they drive. Still, an extra $500 can't help but come in handy from time to time.

Bill had an arrangement with Big Bob and the paper's controller to maintain a T&E account that far exceeded those of the rest of the staff save for the restaurant critic's. Consequently, Eric of Luxury Limos Ltd. had tipped Bill that Reggie Wakefield, the slugging outfielder of the Chicago Cubs, was due in at 5:10 this evening. Reggie had no real reason to be coming to L.A. as this was the off-season. No reason, that is, unless those rumors about the married ballplayer and singer-actress Gina Malone were true.

Men were to Gina what worms were to a bird—she liked them in constant supply, a bit slimy and with an enticing wiggle when caught. According to Celebrity Service, Gina Malone was currently in town and residing at her pad in the Valley. The Morning Snooze had a duty to find out about Gina and Reggie.

Which explained why Bill Boyer had been circling the airport's lower level in his Honda since 4:30, watching for Eric's black stretch limo like a hawk.

At approximately 5:42 p.m., Reggie Wakefield, a six-foot-one, one hundred and eighty-nine-pound tribute to American manhood, conditioning and steroids strolled from the Southwest Airlines baggage claim area along with a guy who was clearly a bodyguard. The bodyguard, whom Bill decided to nickname Sluggo—it helps when you personalize these things—got into a blue Ford parked nearby. Eric's limo materialized immediately.

Sluggo pulled out first followed by the limo. He was riding point, looking for somebody just like Bill. Bill let three cars get between him and Eric on Century Boulevard, which led them out of LAX. Then a tourist bus abruptly pulled in front of Bill's Honda, causing him to brake. One too many vehicles were between him and his quarry. Eric and Sluggo were nearly two blocks away now.

Bill edged into the left lane and pushed down on the gas pedal. He swiftly made up the distance only for Sluggo and Eric to stop at the red light at Airport Boulevard in the left-hand turn lane. Eric was taking the LA Tijera shortcut all professional drivers take to the 405 Freeway. Bill fixed his eyes on the top of the limo.

He followed the limo as it turned right on La Tijera and eventually left at the entrance to the San Diego Freeway. Bill bore down slightly on the accelerator as the limo picked up speed entering the freeway. Eric had promised to keep Bill's car in his rear-view mirror at all times. Heavy traffic on the 405 made this an easy vow to keep. They were heading north, no doubt to Gina Malone's place in the Valley.

But Eric and Sluggo left the freeway in the Sepulveda Pass at the off-ramp for the University of Judaism, a course change that caused Bill's stomach to contract. If Reggie wasn't going to the Valley, where the hell was he going?

Tailing became harder work once the limo began navigating the curves of Mulholland Drive. There were few cars on the road and Bill found it difficult to keep more than one car between himself and Eric. With all the turns on Mulholland, he had to stay fairly close. However, he was comforted in the knowledge that Reggie would in all probability not be monitoring the cars behind him. On the field, he was known for missing signs from coaches and fellow players so he was unlikely to be more acutely aware of his environment off the diamond.

Eric and Sluggo turned left at a road heading to the Valley. In three blocks, the limo and blue Ford turned again at a residential street with a steep grade before coming to a stop in front of a white house set close to the street. The building was done in a strange architectural style that seemed like a cross between a Moorish dwelling and a mausoleum. Bill rolled to a stop half a block up the street and waited.

Sluggo got out of the Ford and looked around like a guy in a bad Mafia movie. Moments later, the back door of the limo swung open and Reggie pulled his hulking frame out the door. America's greatest baseball hero was not going to wait for a pansy limo driver to open the door for him, by God! The front door to the Moorish mausoleum now swung open and a blonde came briefly into view. Bill grinned. Bingo! He hit pay dirt.

Bill grabbed the Canon with a motor drive from his black nylon camera bag in the passenger's seat and stared through the viewing eyepiece. Almost as swiftly as she had appeared and waved, Gina Malone stepped back into the house. Eric popped open the trunk and got out. Bill continued to watch the scene through the camera's telephoto lens. Sluggo grabbed Reggie's bag from Eric and followed him into the house. The door shut.

Damn. Bill knew his story had to be accompanied by a photo of the two lovebirds together, indulging perhaps in a romantic kiss followed by a second shot of them gazing fondly into one another's lust-filled eyes.

Eric, who stood near the limo, glanced over at Bill and shrugged. He had done his part. Bill nodded glumly at Eric, who got inside the limo, started the car up and headed down the hill. Several minutes passed while Bill considered his situation. Clearly, Gina had borrowed a friend's house for her rendezvous with Reggie. With photogs camped out at her Valley lair when she was in town, Bill should've expected this.

This was an even better situation: Now he could guarantee his story — with photos — would really be exclusive. But he still lacked The Shot. Unless he got it, the best he could hope for would be an item in Darlene's column. No fucking way! He wanted Front Page with a photograph.

Shortly, the door opened and Sluggo slipped discreetly out of the house. He approached the Ford, took one last look around — Bill had already taken the precaution of ducking down — got inside and took off down the hill.

Bill righted himself in his seat and sighed deeply. It would have been so lovely if the lovebirds had climbed into the limo and speed off to an out-of-the-way romantic dinner. But now, more than likely, Reggie would be shagging Gina for hours. Which meant a stakeout.

He turned his ignition key and coasted down the hill past the Moorish mausoleum. He turned around in a driveway several houses away and drove back up the steep grade until the car was positioned directly opposite the house. He turned off the engine. All Bill could do now was wait.

He slipped a Learning Spanish cassette into the tape deck and went through the ninety-minute lesson twice before he grew bored. He was determined to know what the Latina dancers at the Women of Color bar were saying about him.

Next time, he thought, he must remember to get takeout chicken and a bottle of wine if there was even a possibility of an all-nighter.

As the evening hours wore on, Bill grew convinced this was all a conspiracy, that Gina and Reggie were deliberately keeping him waiting. Waiting to get The Shot. Okay, so he would wait.

By midnight, Bill let the driver's seat down and drifted off to sleep. Despite wearing a leather jacket and pullover sweater, he grew cold about 2:30 and never quite got back to sleep. He listened for a while to talk radio and the paranoid ramblings of anti-government fanatics. A rain drizzle began around 4. At 5, he took a leak behind a nearby shrub, which caused a dog to bark for nearly fifteen minutes. By dawn, he was munching on a Snickers and dying for a coffee.

The street was coming to life. Joggers in sweats and Walkmans hit the street. A couple of men, probably stockbrokers, piloted late model cars up the hill to offices downtown or in Beverly Hills. A woman in curlers walking a tiny dog was upset to see a man hunched over a candy bar in a car parked near her house. Would she telephone her Westec Security service? Bill vaguely wondered.

Then, at about 6:45, it happened.

He heard a murmur of voices and glanced at the Moorish mausoleum in time to see Reggie standing in the doorway clutching his bag. He wore a different sports jacket than the one he arrived in and Gina accompanied him from the house. She wore a bright pink jogging outfit, a big smile and carried a nearly spent wine bottle in her left hand.

Bill yanked the seat release button, causing the seat to pop back into an upright position, which nearly threw him against the steering wheel. He snatched the Canon off the seat and rolled down the window. Looking through the telephoto lens, he saw Gina pull the front door shut as Reggie headed for a BMW parked at the curb. Gina caught up with Reggie and as she hugged him, Bill depressed the shutter release button on top of the motor-drive handle.

Adrenaline pumped through his body. Every moment his camera was on Gina and Reggie was electric. He was getting The Shot. Several of them, in fact.

Bill had met many famous people before. He joked around with Bruce on the "Die Hard" set, shared a drink with Sly at a Sunset Strip eatery, shaken hands with Liz at a fundraiser and with Liza at a press reception. But this was different. This was fame focused by the camera lens. Everything was happening so fast that time blurred. He was in this strange moment with these two famous people. The three of them suddenly had a relationship that hadn't existed before this instant. All three shared The Shot and would continue to do so until the photos had all faded and the negatives crumbled to dust.

A rapid succession of shots caught Reggie and Gina in an embrace, an abrupt halt at the sound of a clicking lens shutter, a mutual turn toward the car and a final shot of two lovers with angrily contorted faces. When Bill noticed through the viewing piece that Reggie had started toward his car, he realized his continued presence at this location was no longer tenable. His hand shot to the ignition switch.

Only then did he remember the car keys were in his right trouser pocket. With a stunning lack of foresight, he had taken the keys out of the ignition switch and slipped them into his trousers when he had taken his 5 o'clock leak. What the hell was he thinking? Genuinely alarmed, he frantically locked the door and rolled up the window as he fumbled in his pocket. He fished out the AWOL key chain out along with a dirty handkerchief and jammed the car key into the ignition. It was at this moment that Reggie reached the Honda.

Reggie's enormous right hand slammed into the driver's side window. The Honda swayed and shuttered from the blow as if it had been broadsided by a much larger car. This was, after all, a sample of the power that had driven forty-three home runs out of National League ballparks last season.

Bill's car started instantly—thank God he had a tune-up two weeks earlier—and he jerked the gear stick into drive. Retaining his composure, Bill pulled the steering wheel sharply to the left. The Honda lurched forward, nearly clipping a car parked in front. By now, the dog was barking again and Gina was shrieking in what sounded almost like a foreign language. Words issued from her mouth that even Danny Evans never used.

Reggie's massive hand now chopped at the departing Honda, creating a significant dent in its roof. A wine bottle landed on the car's hood. The bottle did not shatter but left another gouge in Bill's rapidly aging Honda.

As his car pulled away from the infuriated celebrities, he glanced in his rearview mirror to see Reggie race toward the BMW. Gina was already opening the driver's side door. Bill's eyes widened. Good God! Did they mean to give chase? Well, never mind, he thought. By the time they turn the BMW around, I'll be long gone.

He hurried up the street and hung a right at the road leading to Mulholland. The Honda skidded slightly on the wet asphalt. It hadn't rained in the city for a while so water lying on a build-up of grease and crud meant dicey driving conditions.

Bill drove his car up to Mulholland and turned left. The street was fairly deserted so Bill depressed the accelerator and got the Honda up to about forty-five, which was as fast as he wanted to take the road's twists and turns.

He looked again in his rearview mirror and did a double-take. The BMW with Gina at the wheel hurtled onto Mulholland a quarter of a mile behind him, having taken the left-hand turn so violently that the car nearly spun around. These people meant business.

Bill further depressed the accelerator, pushing the car close to sixty. If he could get enough distance between him and the BMW, he would easily duck down a side street and hide. But the BMW was gaining on him! Above sixty, Bill wasn't certain he could control his car. Nevertheless, the speedometer needle edged past sixty.

One curve nearly triumphed over the Honda. But Bill fought the skid and got back into the right-hand lane just as a Mercedes sped by him in the opposite direction, its driver honking angrily. He glanced up at the mirror: the BMW kept coming.

What the hell is wrong with these idiots? Celebrities can be such a pain in the ass.

As he neared Benedict Canyon, he debated which way to turn. Left meant the Valley, a windier road but—should there be an incident—the LAPD. Right meant Beverly Hills, more gradual curves and a police force that would side with celebrities.

Bill turned left and plunged the Honda down the treacherous canyon road. A shriek of tires behind him told Bill the occupants of the BMW had not abandoned their pursuit. As the Honda charged around a sharp turn, the Canon flew off the passenger's seat and hit the floor. Bill silently swore; that camera had better be okay. He'd used the thing for years.

Despite the cold, sweat flowed from his body. Adrenaline pumped his heart at a terrific rate. That nervous tick in his left eye returned. But through it all, Bill remained as focused as a Formula One driver. Which only underscored the amazing driving skills of Gina Malone, a talent hitherto undiscovered by the press. Bill was now the first journalist to glean an insight into this ability when another look in the rearview mirror revealed the BMW rapidly closing the distance between it and the Honda.

Bill's eyes immediately snapped back to the road ahead. From this point on, his sole concentration would be on driving and not the car behind him. He gunned the car coming out of a turn and hit a steep grade at what was most definitely an unsafe speed. The Honda took off down the grade, nearly hydroplaning at the next turn.

Bill's emotions had ridden a rollercoaster from mild irritation and anxiety to tension and fear. A new sensation now overtook him: that of bitter anger. What right did these pampered, overpaid jerks have to chase a hard-working, underpaid working stiff?

He hadn't asked them to become famous or to indulge in adulterous activities. He didn't force them to flaunt their behavior in the open where The Shot might capture their actions. What mental or moral deficiencies led them to wish harm to a journalist merely doing his job? Who the hell did they think they were? Danny was right about celebrities: they were degenerates!

These were the thoughts flying through Bill's head as he hit a gentle grade that led to the Valley flatland. He floored the accelerator and the Honda took off. He glanced a final time at the rearview mirror and was disheartened to see the hated BMW closing in. A Honda's engine was no match for a BMW's

It was at this moment Bill hit upon the solution to his dilemma. Why hadn't he thought of it earlier? It certainly would have saved a lot of wear and tear, not only on him but his poor Honda and its tires. He pulled the steering wheel to the right and gradually depressed the brake pedal. The car slowed to a stop at a shady suburban curb. Bill reached down with his left hand and popped open the trunk lid.

With supreme calm, the journalist opened the car door and got out. He strolled back to the open trunk as the BMW skidded to a halt a few yards behind the Honda. Its occupants, Gina and Reggie, were out of the car almost before it stopped rolling. Bill reached inside the trunk and then whirled to face the two irate celebrities clutching in his hand an ax.

The look in Bill's blood-shot eyes as he strode toward Gina and Reggie was not pleasant. That look — and the ax — froze his two nemeses in place. As he neared the BMW, his right hand pulled the ax blade above his shoulder where it was more than ready for action.

"You fuck-head!" screamed Gina.

"Hey, guy, lemme talk to you," reasoned Reggie.

Bill said nothing but kept walking directly at them. Gina started to back toward the BMW first, a steady stream of expletives issuing from her mouth. Reggie, who by now was genuinely frightened since ax blows are not in the same league with pulled hamstrings and tendinitis, took two steps back, then abandoned all pretense at machismo: He turned and scurried back to the BMW.   At this juncture, Gina saw no point in damaging her life or career in a confrontation with an ax-wielding madman. After all, she wasn't the married party. And she swiftly remembered the old saying in show business that any publicity was good publicity. She too dashed back to the car.

The BMW jolted backward as Bill's final stride positioned him to take a stance with his ax modeled after that of an actor's he once saw on a poster for a movie called "Walking Tall." The BMW spun around, shuddered to a halt as Gina shifted from reverse into drive, then shot across the street and up Benedict Canyon. Moments later, it was gone.

Bill's heart hammered. His head pounded, His diaphragm pulled air in and out of his lungs. The ax head rested comfortably in his right hand. He wondered if this was how Dr. Death felt when he plunged his needle into pushers.

CHAPTER SIXTEEN
MURDERERS

Gary Parker loved secondhand smoke. He could write graph after graph rhapsodizing about its dangers. Even with heavy editing by Morning Snooze editors, the thrill of outrage permeated his prose like a pungent aroma.

Parker was the Snooze's medical/environmental reporter. But his real business was doom and gloom. How many times had he written that exciting phrase: "Everyone is at risk?" How many times had he lovingly extrapolated evil from a litany of statistics? How many times had he warned readers about the dangers that lurked in their everyday environment?

Parker loved carcinogens. He loved benzene in Perrier, Alar on apples and asbestos in buildings. Had he broken the story about cholesterol-raising fat in movie popcorn, he would have been happier than if he'd won a Pulitzer. He went after Mexican fat platters. He had the skinny on fettuccine. He knew the folly of foie gras. Once Parker sunk his journalistic chopsticks into Chinese food, no one could look at moo shu pork again without a tingling sensation in the chest. It was said that Parker wrote so often about cancer, caffeine, carcinogens and cholesterol he wore out the "C" key on several keyboards.

The Dr. Death story provoked no excitement in Parker. Human killers bored him. Only silent, invisible killers gave him a hard-on. The problem with human killers was the complete randomness of their attacks. There was no order, no real purpose to the deaths they caused. But a cup of coffee—now there was a sneaky assassin.

As Parker sipped his herb tea and glanced around the smoke-free newsroom, a perverse smile broke over his face. Nearly all his fellow reporters gulped dark poison as they hunched over their keyboards. Every single cup of coffee contained ten grams of natural carcinogens. Parker told these fools about this in the Morning Snooze six months before. Did any of his colleagues read their own damn paper? And what caffeine did to their blood pressure! Poor, deluded fools, he thought as he shook his head. They fuss over an idiot knocking off a few drug dealers and ignore a mass murderer such as dioxin. Now there was a real story!

Parker belonged to the Pleasure Police, a group that had reversed the countercultural imperative that if it feels good, do it. His rule was that if it feels good, it must be risky, immoral or dangerous to your health. Everything we eat, touch, drink or breathe might hurt us. In his determined march into anhedonic intolerance, Parker had gradually shunned much of what delighted him in his youth. He had withdrawn from coffee, cigarettes, hard liquor, gambling, promiscuous sex, fast cars and bowling. Nothing pleased him unless it contained the possibility of connoisseurship. He sampled fine wine—but never got drunk—became a health food fanatic and read mostly nineteenth-century literature.

Parker sighed. So many insidious villains to write about and so little time and space in which to do so. Terrified of Alzheimer's disease? Well, try to remember the words "aluminum" and "zinc." Does heart disease trouble you? Well, down those troubles in popcorn, margarine and red meat. Do you think antibiotics will cure what ails you? Sure, every time you get a cold, gobble down those antibiotic pills. Why not increase the biological odds that nastier pathogens will emerge?

Cancer got you down? Now there's a laugh. Go ahead and drink coffee, eat hot dogs, hang around high-power lines, punch holes in the ozone layer, get silicone breast implants and breathe in that lovely secondhand smoke!

He nearly laughed out loud in his happiness. He was basking in global warming. The Ford Pinto and the Dalkon Shield were his poster boys. He loved 'em all. Dr. Death, get fucked!

Meanwhile several desks away, Jessica Tannenbaum, who did have to worry about Dr. Death, was quietly dealing with a raging headache. She gulped her second round of aspirin with her third coffee—whatever would Parker make of that combination!—and pretended to be going through her reporter's notebook. She had desperately wanted to avoid Big Bob that morning. Moments earlier, though, she had no sooner dumped her purse in the top drawer of her desk then the ME was all over her.

"Jesus Christ, I've been looking for you," Big Bob stormed despite the fact Jessica was at work a good half-hour before her usual reporting time. "We need a new Dr. Death story today!"

"Well, is anything new?" she inquired.

"Good God, Jessie," he snorted. "Find out what's new. We've got to keep on top of this story. It's *our* story. Call around. We can't let this one die!"

There was absolutely no hint of irony in his last remark.

Big Bob wheeled from her and continued his morning patrol of the newsroom. More tired than she realized, she turned to Bill, who happened to be in the vicinity of her desk.

"What does he want me to do?" she asked Bill. "Kill a junkie?"

"Well, you could report that so far fifteen people have claimed to be Dr. Death," said Bill, who was having a tough time not looking at his Page One scoop about Gina Malone every few minutes.

"Yeah," I know," said Jessica. "I get dozens of calls every day from psychics and Tarot card readers with tips about the killer. My good buddies these days are ex-cons, ex-priests, psychics, forensic psychologists and clinical psychologists."

"Personally, I think the murderer is the chef at the American Legion," said Bill. "I had his new pub lunch on Friday and it damn near killed me."

Bill was definitely in a chipper mood. Photo editor Guy Rutledge, who once worked for the National Enquirer, said Bill's Gina Malone pictures were among the best *Gotcha* celeb photos ever taken. After seeing Bill's splendid photojournalism, Guy had immediately gone to Big Bob and secured a commitment to full color on Page One.

Jessica sighed. "I'd better call around," she said. "Let's hope something has happened."

She picked up her phone and, with a slight grimace, dialed Alex's direct line. He wasn't in, and she felt relieved.

The longer the glare of publicity rests on something, the harder it is for the makeup to stay fresh. On a story such as Dr. Death, a journalist is under pressure to find a new angle whether one exists or not. The tyrannical questions repeat themselves daily: What's new? What can be added? What can you say that you didn't say before?

The best she came up with by 12:30 was the number of man-hours being logged on the case by the LAPD. Weak, but at least it was something. Her phone rang and she picked up the receiver.

"This is Jessica."

"Jessica Tannenbaum?" asked a hesitant male voice.

"Speaking."

"This is your old pal, Dr. Death."

"Oh, really?" she said, the tone of exasperation unmistakable in her voice. Nevertheless, she pushed the start button on a tape recorder she had hooked up to her telephone to record each potential Dr. Death call.

The voice on the other end chuckled. "Miss Tannenbaum, I am shocked. Is there no trust left in the world?"

"Look," she told him, "if you are really Dr. Death, then you should turn yourself in."

"But don't you want my exclusive story?"

"Of you turning yourself in? Sure."

"But that wouldn't be an exclusive," he reasoned. "The whole world would be there. Remember, I'm a star now. Thanks to you."

"Why should I believe *you* are Dr. Death?" It was a struggle not to sound bored.

"I'll tell you where to find the next body. How's that?"

Jessica started, then grabbed her pen. "Go on," she said.

"Thirty-two fifty-nine and a half Marlboro Drive in Hollywood. The door's unlocked. Go right on in."

The line went dead.

This time she got through to Alex and gave him the information. He said he and his partner would meet her at the address, but not to go in if she got there first.

***

The apartment building was a drab, two-story structure on a street below Sunset Boulevard, not far from Hollywood High School. The lawn was burnt brown and trash littered the driveway. Expecting to see a scene bristling with police activity, Jessica was surprised to see only one prowl car from Hollywood division parked next to the curb facing the wrong direction, Alex's car and an ambulance.

She made her way up to the landing for the second floor. The door was open and a uniform stood in the doorway. He nodded as if she were an expected dinner guest. "Go on in," the uniform said.

The living room was in shambles with furniture knocked over and debris everywhere. Two paramedics, one standing and the other kneeling, worked on a slightly built man, who appeared to be Latino. Alex, his partner and another uniformed officer stood in a semicircle. Alex nodded slightly to Jessica who walked cautiously over to the paramedics.

The victim was still alive. Next to him laid a hypodermic needle. His body jerked spasmodically. Blood, seeping from a wound in the neck, was congealing at the collar line. The eyes, glassy and unfocused, rolled in his head. The lips trembled as if struggling to form words that would not come.

Suddenly, vomit gushed from the gullet and dribbled down the chin and onto a soiled T-shirt. A death rattle seized the man. He stared for a painful moment at Jessica, a helpless supplicant, and in another moment the eyes went blank. The body seized a final time. The noxious odor of excrement filled the room. Jessica left as swiftly as possible.

Alex came out about ten minutes later to tell her what she already knew: the man was dead, no doubt from a massive narcotic overdose. Jessica's body was still shaking.

She was also angry: "So this poor junkie dies to guarantee this creep his place on the One."

"Not exactly a 'poor junkie,'" said Alex. "I suspect this guy's a dealer. He has enough drugs in there to keep Hollywood stoned for a week."

"Doesn't fucking matter," she said bitterly. "He's dead — murdered."

"Aren't you glad your Dr. Death story stood up?"

"What troubles me," said Jessica, "is that voice on the phone today. Alex, I swear it was a different voice than the other day."

CHAPTER SEVENTEEN
REPERCUSSIONS

The Morning News headline read: "Dr. Death Strikes Again!" This time the town went crazy.

Over the next few days, you couldn't escape the story if you tried. Every news outlet searched for a competitive edge. There was an insatiable hunger for every scrap of information in this case. This was punctuated by various sideshows: the war between the mayor and chief of police; the scramble among detectives as the case was transferred to robbery-homicide downtown; the incessant chatter of talk radio; the moral debate over someone ridding the town of its drug pushers.

Two "eyewitnesses" to a Dr. Death murder demanded payment from reporters before they talked. A TV tabloid show did a dramatic re-enactment of Dr. Death's latest crime complete with moody background music. KNBC aired a tip that quoted knowledgeable sources inside the investigation that Dr. Death was a prominent West Side physician determined to put junkies out of their misery.

KCAL's Harry Harding, who throughout his career had many accused gang members insist on his presence when they turned themselves in to the police, landed what he thought was a great exclusive: Dr. Death would turn himself in to Harry to protect himself from reprisals by drug dealers and cops. Police released the mentally incompetent man three hours later into the custody of the VA hospital. Fortunately for Harry, the footage never aired.

The Times played its coverage straight while maintaining a wary distance from the case on its editorial pages. Meanwhile, the Daily News reported in a single-source story that police felt "Dr. Death" was tied into several murders over the past decade. Many journalists privately wondered if Dr. Death might not be responsible for the Hillside Strangler killings, Sleepy Lagoon murder, Robert Kennedy assassination and Black Dahlia slaying as well.

Then the national tabs started spreading money around and sources usually available to mainstream media dried up, forcing them to throw rumors on the air and into print. The Morning News was in serious jeopardy of being left behind on its own story. Pressure mounted on Jessica. But she was new on the police beat and had few sources to rely on. Worse, several had developed a hearty animosity toward her main source, Alex Valesquez.

***

The apartment building was off a dingy street and surrounded by a filthy courtyard. Here buildings huddled against one another without light or air. Inside this particular building were manifestations of a grander past, of an oak baluster exquisitely carved and walls that still had paneling. Units were thickly inhabited. Whole families occupied each room, and there was incessant noise of children playing in the courtyard. The walls were the breeding place of vermin. The air was so foul that several reporters lit cigarettes. The Latinos—nearly all undocumented immigrants—who dwelt here lived hand to mouth, picking up day work where they could, paint jobs or cleaning homes in West L.A.

Facing a phalanx of television news crews and reporters, the landlord at first refused to emerge from his 18-unit building to be outfitted with an electronic ankle monitor designed to keep track of his whereabouts. After Deputy City Attorney Gregory Rodriquez threatened to go back to court and seek additional sanctions, he stepped outside.

Three months earlier, Alan Blaché had been convicted of slum violations for the third time in eight years after pleading no contest to ten violations of fire, health and building and safety codes. On this day, Blaché was to begin serving sixty days of house arrest in his wretched apartment building after failing to comply fully with a court order to make repairs. A recent inspection had revealed broken fire doors, missing fire extinguishers and cockroach infestations in the five-story structure.

Confronted by reporters he could no longer ignore, Blaché responded to their queries about the city's allegations with a string of epithets that would never appear in newspapers or on the evening news. But he was growing angry enough that he finally responded with a sound bite that would make the news.

"You cannot hold me responsible for the lack of smoke detectors in certain bedrooms because how am I supposed to know children living in closets? How am I supposed to keep tenants from ripping out plumbing? You are making a mockery out of me. I can't change the lifestyles of certain tenants. I've helped the poor. I've helped the needless," he insisted, unaware of his slip of the tongue.

Blaché stared at the crowd of news people that surrounded him.

"What's the matter with you people?" he demanded. "You got a slow news day? Did Dr. Death not kill anyone today?"

***

Probably the only newsperson in L.A. who failed to respond to the Dr. Death story was Darlene Temple. Darlene was experiencing a moral crisis. She had created a monster in Andy Reynolds. He was no longer her "leg" man; he was now her eyes, ears, nose and arms as well.

Every day she found herself, as she liked to put it, "with ten pounds of shit but only a five-pound sack." When she did eliminate items, they were invariably her own. One day, she was forced to lead her column with one of Andy's items. He was getting too damn good.

But her real problem with Andy was not the profusion of his items or even their accuracy. Despite many a lawyer's threat, no lawsuit had yet to materialize because of anything Andy reported. No, her problem was the mean-spirited, even vicious tone of many of his items.

Andy seemed to have a knack for catching people at their most vulnerable. The overblown egos of celebs and politicians needed deflating, God only knew. But Darlene nevertheless caught herself sometimes feeling sorry for the bastards. The pleas over the telephone not to run items grew more and more poignant. Was she getting soft?

One day, she broached the subject to Hazel. Unaccountably, the city editor invited her out to lunch. Why? She couldn't stand Don. His toupee alone was ridiculous. But her lunch date had canceled and he was paying so she said okay. Of all places, he dragged her to Philippe's! This is just what she needed, she thought, as she munched her French dipped sandwich standing up—a fucking cafeteria with sawdust on the floor, tourists jostling her for the cheap coffee and delicacies such as pickled eggs. Christ, why had she agreed to this horrible lunch?

Meanwhile, Don was assuring her she was not getting soft, that she was one of the best journalists on the Morning News, that he always read her column first when he got to work. Darlene shook her head.

Sure, she wanted people to begin their day with a good hoot at the expense of pompous assholes. And Andy was certainly providing that. But he was providing something else too, something that she couldn't quite put her finger on.

Darkness had crept into her column. Corruption and vice ran rampant between the ellipses. The blackness of men's souls and the bleakness of the human condition cried out beneath her byline. Sin, humiliation and God's mercy were the subtext of many of the items. HarperCollins even offered her a book contract—to write a novel, for pity's sake. What was becoming of her gossip column?

Perhaps the News should reward Andy's industriousness by transferring him to Metro, she broadly hinted to Don. Dr. Death and his companions in evil-doing seemed more up Andy's alley than actors and politicos. Don promised to speak with Big Bob. He would always help Darlene, no matter what, he assured her. She thought this was an odd comment but let it go.

***

Sophie returned to the Windsor Arms without any explanation for her absence. She switched to working days Tuesdays and Thursdays so she could spend those nights with Bill. She refused to switch completely to the daytime because she lost too much money by not coming in at night. Men got drunk more easily at night and were more generous.

Bill would come by just after 7:30 and wait outside in his car. Sophie would come out minutes later in her sweats and they would grab Thai food at a joint on Sunset or Korean food on Western before going to his house. They never went to hers. Bill supposed it might have something to do with her ex-husband. Anyway, he preferred his place.

She would shower, then dance a little striptease for him. Sometimes they would play schoolmaster and schoolgirl or bold chauffeur and naughty princess or randy priest and worshipful penitent. Sophie had worked briefly at the Skool Girl bar in Patong Beach, Phuket—until the mama-san got rid of her when she started looking older than sixteen—so these games were quite familiar to her.

Whatever the scenario, they were soon quite naked and romping in Bill's king-sized bed. Bill adored running his hands over her taut smooth flesh. It was all wildly exciting. But once they finished screwing, they were finished indeed.

Sophie's ESL language skills were still rudimentary so there wasn't a helluva lot to talk about. Nor did she seem interested in much of anything besides acquiring money. Bill tried to get her to teach him some Thai, but his mind couldn't seem to retain those foreign-sounding words.

She taught him "sanuk," which meant having fun, and "wai," which meant the bringing together of the palms of the hands in front of one's face in the traditional Thai greeting.

Mostly, she wanted to watch American television, which Bill considered only slightly more exciting than watching wallpaper peel from bedroom walls. He would suggest a baseball game or a movie but she would only shrug. She did like horseracing at Hollywood Park but that was probably because she won over $250 playing an exacta.

It got to the point that Bill didn't even mind those evenings when she was tired and wanted simply to be driven home to her apartment. He welcomed the quiet and a chance to return to his novel for a couple of hours. It also bothered him that she usually managed to extract a "tip" from him. He refused to equate the money exchanged with what happened in his bedroom. Rather, he told himself, Sophie was a young girl with many unexpected expenses here in the New World. Since money was the basis for most relationships in her native land, Sophie would probably have agreed with Bill's assessment.

***

Meanwhile, Emma Mae Hoot, a "strawberry" who often hung out at Western and 54th, was having a damn hard time getting any rock cocaine in exchange for her skinny body. Downtown white-collar workers were having similar difficulties making buys from their cars. Rocks as small as a quarter aspirin were suddenly selling for $5 hits. And the number of customers desperately needing to use the restrooms at Denny's or Canter's or other all-night restaurants was declining precipitously. Dr. Death, whether real or imagined, was taking his toll.

The city's upscale drug users had no problems getting their hands on coke or for that matter on codeine, sleeping pills, Ecstasy, pot or heroin. Few Westside physicians hesitated to prescribe Librium, valium. Xanax or desyrel to a truly needy patient. But on the street, things were getting edgy. Dealers were looking over their shoulders or moving temporarily into other enterprises.

One day, Jessica filed a story that chronicled the dwindling drug trade in Los Angeles. For her story, she spent time with one distraught crack dealer. Life was getting tougher, the kid complained. Here he was trying to help his community. He was selling a new, cut-rate stimulant that was less hazardous than earlier free-base methods. And he sold this commodity in units everyone could afford. The cheapness of his product made it attractive. Was it his fault that crack's short-lived high forces a user's frequent return to the supplier?

Now he had to deal with this fucked-up dude, Dr. Death. This guy was hurting him. More importantly, Dr. Death was hurting the community. And another thing: there's this myth that a drug dealer is some kind of a cross between a gangsta rapper and basketball player. The truth is he's like me—a kid just old enough to hold a rock.

Jessica sat in Jerome's mean apartment, soaking in the environment. The kid, to hear him tell it, was virtually a one-man benevolent association.

"From the first to the fifth each month, tha's when mos' of the money rolls in, when the welfare checks arrive," Jerome informed her. "A dealer can make pretty good money after his customers get their benefits, and that's a fact. By month's end though, cash is long gone, baby. When they gets paid, I gets paid. What I'm sellin' now, I'll probably have to give out on credit. But I trust my customers. My people."

As he said this, Jerome tapped his chest, evidently to indicate the repository of his feelings. Jerome then took time out from his tale of hardship to dump the dregs of his cocaine into a jar of steaming water. With a kitchen mitt, he set the glass container inside a blackened saucepan, heating the solution until it lumped together into a pale gray wad. He grinned at his guest and proudly displayed his handiwork: a handful of crumbs from the bottom of his stash had been recycled into a $40 rock.

CHAPTER EIGHTEEN
HUMAN EVENTS

D'waine Jackson, aka Booger, was getting restless. He had languished in County Jail for two days and not one damned relation or homeboy had come by to bail his ass out. For a man with his responsibilities, this was an unpardonable indignity. The fuck was going on?

Perhaps his people hadn't heard, he reasoned to himself. Loretta, his sister's eldest daughter, certainly seemed to understand his dilemma when Booger used his one phone call to reach Gwen: Uncle D'waine was in lock-up and needed mom to come down and bail him out. It wasn't as if this were the first time Loretta had taken such as a message. And Gwen always responded promptly.

The following day he was reluctantly given a second phone call. But his homeboy Ahmed, who like Booger was an Arden Street Gangsta, wasn't responding to his beeper. Only later did he remember that Ahmed was in County Jail himself.

Enough of this shit, thought Booger. He decided he'd trade a story for freedom. He'd tell the police he knew who Dr. Death was. That ought to get him out. Only he wanted more than simply to get out. He wanted a cash reward for himself, protection and relocation money for his mom, three sisters, several cousins—he'd have to think about who deserved to be on that list—along with the five children he had fathered with three women.

So he told the police about this weird mother-fucker he knew. Now D'waine was no hype, you understand., but occasionally he liked to score. Kind of a way to relax, him being a man with a lot of responsibilities. So one night, after he scored at the shooting gallery behind the Rose Tattoo Bar, which was in an alleyway off Washington, he'd drifted off a while. When he came to, he told the cops, he saw two dudes arguing. One was Denzil, a dope dealer. The other guy was this weird mother-fucker. Suddenly this weird guy stabbed Denzil with a needle. Not a fuckin' word was said after he did it neither. He just stabbed him. Boom. Done. Fortunately, the weird guy didn't see him.

Why was he weird? The cops wanted to know. Because he was a white guy on the street, man. And not just a white guy but a guy who didn't belong. He didn't live on the streets. Junkies who live on the street smell. And they don't' care if they're dying. This guy, he didn't smell and looked like he cared about a bunch of stuff.

Because it was his civic duty, Booger wanted the police to know about this incident. Booger'd have reported this earlier only he forgot.

Of course, Booger knew the dude's name. He'd seen him around. Never questioned why he was hanging. It's a free country 'n' all but he was a *weird* mother-fucker. Yeah, yeah, his name Dean Thurber.

Booger knew mention of Dean Thurber would have an impact. It was common knowledge on the street that Dean had been arrested for attacking Pedro Javier. A drug deal had gone south and Dean took offense to Pedro's comments about the sexual acts his mother would have to perform with Pedro if her son wanted any more of his blow. Just one of those things, but Dean was arrested after he and Pedro beat the crap out of each other. He was charged with one count of assault with a deadly weapon. The deadly weapon, in this case, happened to be the only one Dean had on hand—a needle.

Booger was also counting on Dean Thurber's personality in his quest for freedom: Dean, something of a mental misfit, had an ego the size of Dodger Stadium. He claimed to be the meanest fucker around. The baddest bad ass. The most vicious bitch abuser. The most vengeful ass-kicker.

But he was white! What could be more fucked up than a honky thinking he's a nigger gangbanger? Must be the drugs made this fuck so delusional. The drugs and that temper. For Thurber, who had a really bad habit, hated pushers. They took all his money and always gave him shit, drugs so cut and fucked up they scarcely had any kick at all. He hated every dealer.

The police detective listened quietly to his tale, made a few notes, then said he would be in touch. This pissed Booger off. The cop should demonstrate more gratitude for his help in solving a major criminal case. Even greater was his annoyance when no one got back to him for a day and a half. Then, surprisingly, an assistant D.A. came to see him—she was much nicer—and wanted to open negotiations about a sentence reduction.

D'waine had been thrown into jail on a weapon possession charge. The 28-year-old had had enough dealings with the legal system to know how to negotiate and what to negotiate for. What he was most interested in was the district attorney's witness protection program. Unlike federal protection programs—in which those who testify get a new identity or plastic surgery or jobs in faraway cities—the county program usually offered first and last months' rent for a new apartment in a safer location. But D'waine bargained for more.

Eventually, the attorney agreed that should his information lead to the arrest and conviction of the junkie murderer, the city would augment the county program with extra funds. And once he testified at the preliminary hearing, prosecutors would drop the weapons possession charge.

***

Gary Parker made his second cup of herbal tea and focused on his terminal screen. He was on the trail of a real serial killer.

There were too many microbes loose in the world for even Parker to keep track of these days. Where most men keep tally sheets in their heads of their natural enemies — the boss, the in-laws, the guy whose wife they're banging — Parker's enemies list consisted of infectious diseases on the comeback trail.

It was an invisible world of viruses, bacteria and one-celled creatures with attitudes. Old ailments — diseases everyone thought had vanished long ago such as TB and whooping cough — were coming back in new and virulent forms. To say nothing of new plagues such as AIDS.

It was Parker's lonely task to chronicle the race for survival between humans and microbes. There were billions of single-celled creatures out there festering away each day, getting fully oxidized and living the life of Riley, waiting for their time to come.

"The question is," he typed on this bright, sunny morning, "will we get the bugs before they get us? We're beginning to lose ground."

In today's story, Parker went after the Jet Age. A ship bearing the cholera virus in its bilge water had infected shellfish in Peru. Then two days later, an airplane ferried a dozen sick people from Lima to LAX. You want instant travel, you deal with instant epidemics, he thought to himself as his fingers pounded the keyboard. He prided himself on being one of the few journalists at the Morning Snooze who knew how to touch type.

As he sipped his herb tea, he glanced at the piles of faxes, news releases and mail from around the country which sat on his desk. He must remember to spray his desk with disinfectant later. Catastrophes were lurking everywhere.

Parker saved his copy to his hard drive — he never trusted the Snooze's server — and pushed his rolling chair back from the monitor. He felt good. Even better, he felt righteously indignant. He got up from his chair, ready to eat a righteous lunch. He felt so good he decided he would treat himself to his once-a-month hamburger.

***

Jessica's telephones at work and home rang at about 2:15 p.m. to no response. Alex's urgent call to her beeper resulted in her quickly leaving the pet store, where she had picked up kitty litter for Trixie, to get to a payphone. This was how Jessica learned the police were ready to announce the arrest of the man she knew as Dr. Death.

Based on a tip, Alex told her, police had arrested a guy named Dean Thurber, already in jail for a vicious attack on a pusher.

"The best part is," Alex said, "the guy's made a full confession."

The late afternoon press conference was a zoo. Every reporter faced enormous deadline pressure caused by its late start. In the crush getting inside Parker Center, a KCOP television reporter was accosted by a woman screaming, "You killed Joan of Arc! All you people do is talk, you don't listen!"

When the reporter tried to walk around her, she grabbed his jacket from behind, pulling it down his arms and pinioning his hands. The police, as if they didn't have enough to do, were forced to arrest the crazy woman.

Inside, about twenty minutes later, Commander Fairchild read from a brief press release: His name is Dean Thurber. He's thirty-five. He lives in the Koreatown area. He was taken into custody four days ago and was booked on one count of attempted murder and one count of assault with a deadly weapon. Thurber is currently hospitalized in the medical ward of County Jail. He will be arraigned tomorrow morning in Superior Court.

Jessica made certain she got in the first question. Several hands shot up, but Fairchild was nothing if not a fair man. He called on the reporter who broke the story first.

"Commander Fairchild," asked Jessica, "is Dean Thurber the man known as Dr. Death?"

Fairchild sighed: "He says he is."

***

Big Bob already had his headline picked out:
   "Gotcha!"

This would scream at Los Angeles the next morning in a four-column, forth-eight-point banner. Thus, Jessica was sweating. She had to write a lead to fit that banner.

First, she wrote: "Dr. Death may have written his final prescription for murder," She then sat back and stared at her computer terminal for two solid minutes. The lead was shit. Jessica felt a presence behind her. She turned to see Bill standing there, reading over her shoulder.

"Congratulations," he said, his grin wide and genuine. "Looks like you scored a big one today."

"Thanks. I appreciate that."

"Your lead's not right though."

"I know," she muttered, hitting the back erase button until the offending sentence vanished. "Let's not be cute," she muttered to herself and typed:

"Los Angeles police announced Tuesday they have arrested the man they believe to be the serial killer known as Dr. Death."

"Accurate but dull," said Bill.

 "Got any ideas?" she asked.

"Let me think about it, okay?" said Bill. Before she could give that okay he turned to go back to his desk.

Jessica left her lead alone for a half-hour and banged out the story. Two other reporters called in "string"—a brief statement from the Mayor, background stuff about Thurber's part-time job at a Burger King, a few anonymous quotes from police sources—which she wove into the main body of the story.

Jessica characterized Thurber as a man motivated by a warped crusade to rid L.A. of its deadliest criminals—the drug dealers who drain the life from the city's youth, yadda yadda yadda…

A bell rang at her terminal. Bill had sent her a message on the Morning News' messaging system. It read:

"Dr. Death has lost his license to kill.

"Bringing one of the city's most riveting crime dramas to a stunning climax, Los Angeles police said Tuesday they have arrested a 35-year-old drifter on a charge of attempted murder of a known drug dealer. Police said the man later identified himself as the serial killer known as Dr. Death."

Jessica grinned. That worked.

***

Deadline was pushed back an hour to allow the Snooze's staff time to assemble a "Dr. Death" package. Big Bob grumbled to himself about not having foreseen this dramatic moment and ordering a full-scale work-up on the good doctor to be ready at short notice. But, frankly, he had only 90% believed in Dr. Death himself. Which meant he really only 80% believed in the original story.

So the staff went to work: A chart with a timeline of Dr. Death's probable murders was prepared, the main story and three sidebars were scheduled and Pages Four and Six were dedicated mostly to photos along with the Page One photo—Dean Thurber's booking photo, staring straight into a police camera with haggard eyes. Photo editor Guy Rutledge retouched the eyes to make them haggard yet defiant.

Along with the banner, reporter Arnie Benstein in his Page One sidebar interviewed Thurber's shocked neighbors and a guy in Texas who claimed to be Thurber's brother. The brother discounted the whole thing as a huge mistake by the police. His brother was no killer.

Jessica's copy got to city desk about an hour late as Don and Big Bob did "reads" before shipping it to copy editors. Everyone congratulated Jessica and after deadline, she was forced to put in an appearance at the American Legion bar. Applause greeted her at the door. The bartender scrambled around in the back room and came out with a bottle of bubbly.

Rounds of beers were consumed by Morning Snooze staffers. Jessica's head swam a bit and since her car was in the shop, Bill offered to drive her home. They stopped off in Larchmont Village where they grabbed a bite at Le Petit Greek. They started with Rolling Rock beers then moved to a bottle of Sonoma Valley Cab. Jessica's eyes sparkled with excitement and she couldn't stop talking. Bill had never known her to be so chatty. She ate her lamb and grape leaves with hearty abandon. She dipped into the hummus with her pita bread as she regaled Bill with tales of her mom's days as an actress and her multiple eccentricities.

Then, in Jessica's apartment, she opened another bottle of red before Bill could even ask for a drink. She laughed and told him what a great reporter he was and threw a video into the VCR. But they grew bored about a quarter of the way into the movie. She turned off the video, put on a jazz LP and they sat on the couch, sipping wine and talking shop. After a while, she excused herself to go to the bathroom. Bill decided to switch to beer.

He went into the kitchen to grab a bottle out of the fridge. He twisted off the bottle cap and moved back into the living room where he stood at the large picture window. Jessica's apartment off Wilshire was on the sixth floor and faced south. This provided an excellent view of the Santa Monica Bay and the twinkling light of the beach towns stretching toward Palos Verdes. Bill stood mesmerized as he watched jets on final approach for the runways at LAX.

So much was taking place out there at any given moment. News that might never even make its way into any local newspaper was happening. Human events marched on, irrespective of journalistic scrutiny. Guns fired, accidents happened, lives changed, people fell in or out of love and nobody was on the scene to report it.

If news happens and no one reports it, does it really happen? And if news gets reported in big bold headlines, does that really make that story any more important? Does the fact that one demented soul may have murdered a bunch of drug dealers matter in any real way? If no one had reported it, would anyone have noticed? And if that's true, does not the Story become more important than the story? Does not the reportage supersede its subject?

What is this human need to report the daily minutiae of our existence? What is this record that people fight to be on — or off? Is there an actual record somewhere, in some dusty archive, that sums up who and what we are? Is news reporting truly the first draft of history? Or is it a distortion on which history will later embellish, the way Homer's epic tales came down to us through centuries of telling and retelling?

Bill was aware that Jessica had come back into the room. But his train of thought was carrying him in such a strange direction that he did not immediately turn around. She joined him at the window and she too looked out on the winking city lights.

As he turned toward her, she did a strange thing. She reached her hand up to his neck and gently pulled him toward her. She kissed him on the lips, her tongue pushing against his. He could smell her red-wine breath and feel the tiny hairs on her upper lip. He pulled slightly away as if to determine that this person was indeed Jessica Tannenbaum.

"I adore you," she murmured as she gazed unsteadily into his eyes.

"And I'm wild about you," he said. "I didn't think you liked me."

"I do, Bill," she said. Then, abruptly, she sobered up. She broke away from him.

"This is totally inappropriate," she stated. "We work together, for Christ's sake. We're going to pretend this didn't happen."

She moved to a neutral area in the living room where she might contemplate her sins.

"We will not pretend this didn't happen," said Bill firmly. He went to her, grabbed her and claimed another kiss. She did not resist. Instead, she threw her arms around him and kissed him back. His right hand found her breasts, which he caressed. She murmured and her hand tightened around the back of his neck.

Moments later, she again broke away, declaring, "No, this is crazy," and hurried into the kitchen. Bill followed her. She turned to confront him: "You're not relationship material with a wife still in the picture and girls at the Women of Color bar and God only knows who else comes and goes in your life. And I may have a developing relationship of my own."

"My wife is not in the picture and I love you," he said half drunk.

"You're full of shit," she said sweetly.

"I am not," he said, walking over to her.

This time, she blocked his embrace. "I'm going to make coffee," she told him.

Bill eventually retreated to the leather couch in the living room and sucked down his beer. He followed this up with a cup of hot coffee, which had a soothing effect but also increased his desire for Jessica.

She poured a second cup and sat beside him. He threw an arm around her and kissed her hard. She gently pushed him away. Trixie jumped on the couch to join them.

"I need you to be my friend, not my lover," she said in a soft, calm voice. "Can you please do that? I'm sorry this happened. It won't again."

"Well, I'm not sorry it happened," he said as he took a sip of coffee. "Boy, can you kiss when you're excited." He took another sip of coffee. "What developing relationship?"

"None of your business," she said. "But can you be my friend?"

"I was the minute you walked into the newsroom," he said. "That'll never change."

He petted Trixie, who purred.

CHAPTER NINETEEN
COVERING THE CIRCUS

On its 11 o'clock news, KABC anchorman Forrest Bibby quoted "reliable sources" as stating that police had recovered a sharp knitting needle from a downtown trash bin that they believed was the murder weapon in one of Dr. Death's killings. The Daily News reported the following day that a Halloween mask had been recovered at the scene of another crime. Both reports later proved incorrect but were widely broadcast and discussed over the next two days.

Everybody wanted a piece of Dr. Death.

Phone calls from television producers flooded the switchboard at County Jail. Dr. Death T-shirts were suddenly everywhere. Thursday afternoon a skywriting airplane penned the words "I Love Dr. Death" on L.A.'s dirty blue sky. Members of the media team from the national Drugs Out of America organization—or DOA—pondered ways to use Dr. Death to bring more attention to its issues. Yes, everybody wanted a piece of Dr. Death. Everybody that is except for Bill Boyer. He wanted more of Jessica Tannenbaum.

But he was getting nowhere. She all but avoided him for the next two days at the office. On Thursday, when her car was ready, he offered to drive her to the Westside repair shop before it closed at six. With everyone else still on deadline, she had little choice but to agree.

Moments after pulling out of the employees' parking lot, Bill slipped a cassette into his car's tape deck. The sound of Wayne Shorter's saxophone drifted through the car. He noticed her extensive jazz collection that night at her apartment and made certain to stock his car accordingly.

"We're not going to be a couple, you know," she blurted out two blocks from the paper.

"No," he said, "I don't know that."

"Look, you've got a wife and that situation needs to be resolved. And I don't know if I can love anybody. I prefer guys like the wine at the American Legion bar—with expiration dates. I want you as a friend. I don't want to lose your friendship."

"But why not friends *and* lovers?" he asked and with that, the two plunged into one of those arguments that no one ever wins. After she picked up her car, they ate at a tiny sushi joint on Montana Avenue in Santa Monica.

"Look," he began, "we started something the other night when we—"

"No, we didn't," Jessica said weakly.

He looked at her, astonished: "What was it then?"

"It wasn't like we planned to."

"Just one of those things?"

"If you want."

"What I want is you."

"And what I want is my career."

"Since when are love and a career mutually exclusive?"

"They aren't—but in a way they are," she said, again in a defensive, uncertain tone. "I'm not concerned about being alone. I accept that."

"But why? You don't think I, a fellow journalist, would understand late nights and out-of-towners and weeks on assignment without seeing each other?"

"Oh, Bill, it's not like we'll ever get married."

"How do you know?"

He felt desperate. She was slipping away from him. Why was this happening? Why couldn't she simply love him and let time work things out? Suddenly, he had a thought.

"Is this about that damn cop?" he asked.

"You mean Alex?"

"Yes, I mean Alex what's-his-name. Is he the one you have a developing relationship with?"

"What if it is?"

"He's a news source, for Christ's sake! You don't have a developing relationship with a source. Any journalist knows that. If you cover the circus, you don't fuck the elephants."

Now she was angry. But she also knew Bill was right. It was one of the oldest adages in the news business. Christ, how had she gotten herself into these predicaments?

She finished her California roll, split the check with Bill and fled to her apartment as quickly as possible.

***

On the eighteenth floor of the Criminal Courts Building, District Attorney Ray Bowman was preparing to announce to the press that his office would prosecute Dean Thurber. The following year was an election year so for Bowman this was an opportunity to build up film clips for his commercials. As a consequence, he intended to seek the death penalty.

"I'm looking at a noon deadline and I'm sweating already," a TV reporter told the DA's press secretary, her voice reflecting a crisis mode. When Bowman arrived a good fifteen minutes late, all sense of order was wiped away by the shouted questions of reporters. The DA stood still until the shouts died down, then in a tone he and his voice coach had perfected in recent months, he began what he hoped was a solemn pronouncement.

In a courtroom five floors below, Odell Washington pleaded guilty to the felony beating of his small child and his girlfriend. Under a plea bargain, he was placed on five years probation and ordered to serve a year in the County Jail — minus time already served plus credit for good behavior. Which meant he would be out in 232 days. The child's mother, LaKeesha Williams, was terrified. Odell was, of course, forbidden from going within one hundred yards of her or their child when he got out. But what cop or County Probation officer was going to come down to Watts to enforce that? LAPD slang for incidents of domestic violence in African-American homes was "NHI." That stood for "no humans involved."

She shuddered. However, no reporter was in the courtroom to record her drama.

In the weeks that followed, the media turned Dean Thurber into something of a movie-of-the-week character—a tough, wisecracking man-child disgusted with the criminal justice system who had resorted to vigilante justice.

He made the covers of Time and Newsweek. Time went with his booking photo while Newsweek used an enhanced photo from his arraignment. Experts in ethics and criminal justice debated the moral of the "Dr. Death" story on the Op-Ed pages of newspapers around the country. A near fistfight broke out on one afternoon TV talk show between a crime victim and a liberal commentator.

In Los Angeles, Channel 13 ran a film series in the early evening hours featuring mass murderers from Jack the Ripper to the Boston Strangler. DOA staged a variety of actions including speeches, demonstrations and news conferences to bring attention to the issue of drug abuse. There was talk of creating a video game.

As the media constructed its myth about Dr. Death, it continued to work overtime to publish leaks and ferret out more details of Thurber's crime spree. Questions arose about several narcotics-related deaths in the San Francisco Bay Area two years prior. But no real connection could be established despite the best efforts of the Oakland and San Francisco papers.

The Los Angeles Times joined in the circus halfheartedly. Still smarting over getting beaten on the year's major local story—unless, of course, the Big One hit, which might salvage the year for the Old Lady—the Times managed to find many other stories vastly more compelling. But its initial skepticism on Dr. Death gradually and reluctantly gave way to a daily report—not always on Page One though—that summed up developments on the Dr. Death beat without the sensationalistic tone most of the other media took.

It was just another damned murder case to the Old Lady. She had seen thousands in her time. Meanwhile, things were looking very bad in Eastern Africa and the Times went into lascivious detail describing those horrors.

Sly took a different approach. He tried to bring a perspective to Dr. Death. Most journalists suffer from a kind of tunnel vision in which things unfold in the White-Hot Now. They fail to see the patterns and rhythms in human events, which have played out over and over again through out time. Crime, avarice, racism, corruption and power hunger are steadfast in the history of mankind. Only the modes of expression change. The climate of opinion may shift continuously but the weather systems remain in place.

Sly viewed Dr. Death as a pathetic reincarnation of Jack the Ripper. The crucial difference between the two was Dr. Death stood no chance of becoming truly legendary. Dr. Death's tragic mistake was getting caught, Sly noted in his first column on the subject. Jack's claim to historical fame was the elusiveness of his identity. Endless monographs, books and films had appeared in the past century about this sadistic albeit minor murderer because he had slipped through the cracks of time without a clear identity or personality.

To slink around Whitechapel in the late nineteenth century and murder a bunch of prostitutes did not require criminal genius. Anymore than does knocking off a bunch of drug pushers in Los Angeles in the twentieth century. What intrigues us about Old Jack was his mystery, not his deeds, Sly insisted. Dr. Death was now unmasked. He was just another mass murderer in a historical continuum running amok with such bores. He had ceased to matter.

"Plato said that no one would knowingly do evil," Sly wrote in a second column dedicated to the subject. "But Plato was a dreamer. I think people do evil all the time for all sorts of reasons. Evil has always given more pleasure than virtue. And do we like virtuous people? Would this so-called Dr. Death receive this much ink had he managed somehow to reduce the misery of drug addiction?"

CHAPTER TWENTY
NEW EVIDENCE

After work, Bill headed over to the Women of Color bar. As Bill drove through the nighttime streets, his foul mood deepened. He longed for the Bay Area, for Saturdays in Golden Gate Park and Forty-Niner football and Oakland baseball and barhopping on Union Street and quiet dinners at Chez Panisse and weekend jaunts to Napa Valley.

But this harsh and sun-bleached desert community paved over with asphalt and concrete was now his home. The town had long ago been put up for sale—to Detroit in the 1950s so its excellent transportation system could be dismantled to boost car sales; to developers in the 1960s and 1970s to rip out the old and construct the new; to Arabs and Japanese in the 1980s who bought up so much real estate they forced the market higher and higher.

Los Angeles was always for sale. It was a town designed for and by scoundrels. Old was forever being torn down and replaced by newer and cheaper. Crackerbox apartment complexes of eight- and ten-units were jammed onto single lots, a blight to neighborhoods and breeding ground for crime.

Los Angeles had few landmarks, old haunts or historic monuments. Everything was built quickly as though Angelenos might awaken from their slumber and demand their city back. The town was being given over to strip malls and high-rises. As the tax base eroded and city services shut down, an underground economy in everything from drugs to labor to street vending sprang up.

On his way to the bar, Bill drove past signs that read *lavanderia, pupuseria, farmacia*. He drove through a world where refugee children of U.S.-sponsored Central American wars joined the 18th Street gang or formed the Mara Salvatrucha gang and brought a new kind of warfare to the streets of *Norteamericano*.

Passing a recycling center in Koreatown, Bill had to smile. The addicts were bypassing the middleman by exchanging shopping carts full of cans and bottles directly for their next piece of rock.

Yes, he missed the Bay ferry that, after a hard day's work, would take him past Alcatraz toward Sausalito nestled in the hills of the shore and a fog bank that often mounted the seaward Marin hills and came creeping over their summits like a mysterious force slowly reaching down for the town.

L.A. never had this mystical effect on Bill. On the other hand, L.A. made him want to write something of significance; it strengthened his cynicism and focused his scrutiny. More and more, he saw his role as a despoiler of myths and a seeker of truth. He wanted to force readers to confront the perversion of L.A., not its mythos of romantic corruption and Technicolor sensuality.

He parked his car a few doors down from the Windsor Arms and went inside. He knew Sophie was off tonight so any melodrama could be avoided. He waved at Rosario as she danced on the runaway and walked along the bar where he found a stool near the beer tap. Maria, the bartender, had a Rolling Rock opened on the counter before him moments after he sat down. He smiled and threw down a ten.

He took a gulp. He glanced over at a lantern-jawed man in his mid-forties, who sat two stools down from Bill. His skin was lean and leathery as if he spent time outdoors. He wore a flannel shirt, beltless blue jeans and a cardinal-and-gold USC cap. He looked at the dancers occasionally but did not seem to take much interest in their presence. He stared at the TV broadcasting silently from its perch at the back of the bar over brightly colored liquor bottles.

He raised a beer bottle to his lips and took in several gulps. He drank with a steady intensity of purpose. Bill was about to turn away from this dull character when he was surprised to see an animated expression take hold of the man's face. It was a look somewhere between happiness and anger. His eyes narrowed. He put his beer down hard on the worn counter.

Bill followed the man's intense gaze to the TV. None other than the visage of Dean Thurber graced the screen. Something like a smile creased the man's face; his head slowly, almost imperceptibly, shook back and forth. A short, ugly laugh escaped from his throat.

"Idiots," he murmured. "Stupid idiots…"

Before Bill had time to think, he found himself asking, "Who are?"

The man jerked his head sideways and stared at Bill as one does a bug on the wall. The stare lasted for what seemed like a full ten second before the man barked, "What?"

Bill had no choice but to persevere: "Who are the stupid idiots?"

The man startled Bill with a hearty laugh. "The cops! The cops…the D.A.….the media — they're all idiots."

"Why?"

"Why?" The man inspected Bill as if searching for signs that he was being challenged. Finding none, he issued an abrupt, harsh snort. He pulled a cigarette pack from his shirt pocket and shook loose a smoke.

"Why?" he repeated. "Because they're stupid. That guy didn't kill anyone. Look at him. He doesn't have the balls!"

Bill looked but a commercial for sanitary napkins had interrupted the newscast. The woman on the screen looked cool and dry and self-confident. She certainly didn't look like she had the balls to kill anyone.

The man lit a cigarette while Bill considered his last statement before replying: "But the evidence—" Bill started to say before the man cut him off.

"The cops faked it to get the politicians off their backs. And the TV and newspaper guys go along with it. Nobody gives a damn."

Bill was always interested in how the public perceives newsgathering to take place. He asked: "Why would the TV and newspaper guys go along with the cops?"

"Don't be so naïve. Because they're pals. Cops give news guys tips to write their stupid stories and news guys believe everything cops tell 'em. It's real cozy."

Bill was amazed: "The cops and the media are pals?"

"Damn straight. They need each other. But who gets screwed while those two form their mutual admiration society? The citizen who can't drive the streets without fear of getting shot or carjacked. The cops stand around donut shops and news guys eat up everything the cops feed 'em."

"Really?"

The man fixed him with steely eyes. "You think I'm crazy, don't you?"

"Not at all."

"Well, I'm not. My wife was on those streets. I know what they're like. And I know what cops are like. They only hassle the weak; they only jam guys who won't give 'em any real trouble. They keep the streets safe for drug dealers."

"Then who did kill those junkies?"

"You mean pushers, don't you?" asked the man, who sucked deep on his cigarette. "Hey, *señora*," he called to Maria. "*Otro cerveza, por favor.*"

Maria, who was Filipino, smiled and opened a Bud for the man.

Rosario finished her dance set and moved along the bar, trolling for tips. Bill's interlocutor brought the new bottle to his lips for a long gulp. Rosario plopped down next to Bill and hugged him.

"I love you," she said to Bill, who turned to kiss her on the forehead.

"Buy me a drink?" she asked. Bill nodded to Maria, who stood nearby waiting for that nod. She served Maria a highball made up of weak fruit juice and tiny alcohol for which she charged Bill a dollar more than she would a customer.

The man two stools away left shortly thereafter, no doubt uncomfortable in the company of anyone who didn't understand that cops and news guys were best buddies.

***

Sharon Morgan's body was found sprawled obscenely in her Mercedes. The garage door was shut and the engine still running. She had been dead about two hours, the coroner figured. Andy found out about the tragedy a day later when he read about Sharon's death in Metro. It made Page One since she was a porn star.

Andy immediately thought back over his recent conversations with her but could detect no plea for help or signal that anything was wrong other than that IRS investigation into her nightclub earnings. There were hints in the obit of a troubled childhood and low self-esteem—the usual bullshit when a reporter doesn't have time to investigate thoroughly. But nothing to indicate suicidal desires.

Of course, she did tell Andy once or twice she might kill herself. But she was laughing when she said it. Damn, he was going to miss talking to her and laughing at her wry jokes. He was going to miss her items too. Andy threw down the Morning Snooze and rubbed his eyes with his right hand. He was getting sick of his job. And he was getting very sick of Darlene Temple.

The affair had been exciting at first—an older woman, a savvy news pro who could teach him things in and out of the sack. But this was a Temple in which he no longer wished to worship. She really was an older woman—she hadn't been to a rock concert in years—and had taught him just about everything he wanted to learn from her news-wise. And, hell, she should do herself a favor and get implants for those granny tits.

Hazel said something to him the other day about transferring him to a new role in Metro. He hadn't said anything about a raise, though, and Andy's review wasn't due for another seven months. If a transfer and raise could be arranged, Andy would have no problem with that.

What about Darlene? She would be crushed. She loved his cock. She even jokingly promised to dedicate her book, "Great Hollywood Pricks I Have Known," to Andy.

As it happened, he and Darlene were scheduled that night to go to the Beverly Hilton for some bullshit dinner honoring a guilty film producer who gave a lot of money to charity. Andy let most of the no-host cocktail hour slip by before telling Darlene he didn't intend to stay for the rubber-chicken dinner. Her eyes widened.

"You're not staying?" she asked, unable to keep the surprise out of her normally controlled voice.

"Don't worry," he quickly replied. "I got enough for the column."

"I'm not worried. It's just that it should be a lovely dinner."

"Hey, knock yourself out. I ate a big lunch."

"What about later?" Darlene was never one to pull punches.

"I'm going to meet some friends, have a couple, then crash," he said with what he hoped was pointed indifference.

"Friends." She was back in control of her voice. The tone was not friendly.

"Yeah, I got some, you know," he said. "Not easy though with the hours I put into this job."

"Is that a complaint?"

"No, a statement of fact. I work for you about eighteen hours a day."

Darlene's face visibly reddened. One didn't have to be a whiz at math to calculate what those hours of "work" included. Hurt, she turned from Andy and strode into the ballroom to search for her table. Andy smiled thinly and walked to the lobby. There would be hell to pay tomorrow.

***

Harvey Brillstein, Dean Thurber's lawyer, knew how to work the media. He was himself a celebrity, having represented several headline-making defendants. He made certain to charm all reporters, not merely those working for the Times, wire services and O&O stations.

Brillstein in appearance looked like a radical though rich Yuppie. He wore a full beard, one earring and stylish Italian cut double-breasted suits with carefully matched shirts in fashionable hues. His long hair ended in a ponytail.

Early in his career, Brillstein had perfected the art of the sound-bite interview. The trick was the setting. After visiting an infamous client in jail, an attorney would find TV crews formed in a semi-circle, effectively blocking any exit from the building. An attorney is therefore backed against a wall or doorway with light glaring in his eyes and microphones thrust in his face. Not very attractive.

So Brillstein developed the habit of telling reporters in advance that he would make a statement at the end of his visit and would then direct them to an area *outside*. His preference was for a lawn with trees.

Brillstein would talk to the print media first, which allowed time for him to compose his thoughts. He, therefore, was prepared for TV interviews, of which only ten to fifteen seconds would ever make it onto the evening news. By then, he had boiled his thoughts down to perfect sound bites.

He never bothered with whether his answer precisely addressed the reporter's question since only the answer would be aired. He also never lowered his head or looked at mikes since this causes the eyes to close and gives a dazed appearance. Consequently, he would try to look over the cameras.

The moment he sprung to Dean Thurber's defense — and competition among Los Angeles criminal defense attorneys to represent Dr. Death was fierce — he tried to turn Jessica into his best buddy. She created Dr. Death so in a sense she created this job and its attendant publicity for him.

Frequently, he would slip a tidbit to her he withheld from the other reporters. More importantly, Brillstein was determined to "turn" Jessica. For he was truly convinced his client was innocent. So many factors didn't add up including Dean's insistence he was the junkie killer. In Brillstein's experience, only innocent men insist they're guilty.

Brillstein had made several phone calls to Jessica over the past week. He told her Dean had no recollection of several of Dr. Death's alleged house calls. Another time he hinted Dean had "failed" a lie detector Brillstein insisted he take: he wasn't telling the truth when he confessed.

Jessica refused to play up these exclusive tips. Rather she would bury them in the third or fourth graph of her daily Dr. Death stories. She understood the game Brillstein was playing. Getting Dr. Death off would be the ultimate feather-in-the-cap for a lawyer.

This is why Jessica was curious about Brillstein's latest phone message: he wanted to meet her at Eddy's.

Eddy's Saloon on East Sixth was no longer the downtown hangout it once was, which probably explained why Brillstein wanted to meet Jessica there at the unfashionable hour of 4 o'clock. They would be virtually alone.

The booths at Eddy's were worn and scarred, some of the chairs could use retirement and the waiters were cranky. At least the jukebox was full of Frank Sinatra, John Coltrane, Smokey Robinson and Louis Armstrong.

Two fake Tiffany lamps hanging over the bar were the only lights in the cocktail lounge. Save for Fourth-Round Charlie, an aging heavyweight who lasted four rounds against Scrap Iron Johnson in his one big fight, and Liquor Louise, who could put 'em away with the greatest drinkers, Jessica and Harvey were the only customers in the lounge.

He ordered a Cabernet while Jessica settled for Pellegrino. Small talk engaged them while Harvey lit a Between the Acts little cigar and the bartender filled their order.

After drinks arrived, he put the cigar in the slot of a glass ashtray, his elbows on the table, folded his hands underneath his bearded chin and smiled benevolently at the reporter.

"Jessica," he said, his voice purring like a kitten lapping warm milk, "I wanted to speak to you off-the-record and as a friend. You did a brilliant job of tying together the deaths of these narcotics dealers as the work of a serial killer. You have excellent sources in the LAPD. I was very surprised to learn you've been on the beat for only three months. Maybe that's one reason why you're been so successful. Reporters who have been on a beat a while tend to get lazy. The news more or less comes to them."

He picked up the little cigar, took a long puff, exhaled away from Jessica and continued.

"Because I respect your enterprise, I want to give you a heads-up about a development that will undoubtedly play a key factor in the case over the next few days. It may even end it quite prematurely."

Jessica's eyebrows rose involuntarily. She had concentrated on keeping as placid and unreadable a face as possible for this conversation, but that last remark got her eyebrows to twitch. End the case? What was this bullshit?

"I know, I know," said Harvey, his head nodding and his hand putting the tiny cigar back in the ashtray. "I don't expect you to accept any of this on faith. I can only urge you — for your own good and the good of the Morning News, a paper I have enormous respect for — to listen and do with the information I am about to give you what you deem appropriate."

He took a sip of his red wine.

"From the start, I've been convinced of two things," he continued. "One, a perpetrator has killed several narcotic dealers by stabbing them with hypodermic needles loaded with highly concentrated heroin. But, two, the person arrested by the LAPD, which was under enormous political pressure to collar somebody — anybody — to play the role of 'Dr. Death,' is not the right man."

"So you've been telling me for some time," said Jessica.

He raised his left hand, palm out, and nodded his head. "I know, I know, you can't cry wolf often if you're to be credible. That is why I brought you this."

His left hand slipped inside his white double-breasted coat and pulled out several folded sheets of paper. Jessica was momentarily reminded of magic tricks where the magician pulls handkerchiefs and animals or birds from sleeves and pockets. The hand slid the papers across the sticky tabletop toward her. She hesitated a moment, then picked them up.

She opened the folded pages, which appeared to be photocopies of a fax. She saw they were from the Tarrant County Sheriff's office in Texas, prisoner release forms that stated Dean Thurber had been a resident of the County Jail from August 13 to August 30 of this year. He was held on a charge of disturbing the peace. That charge had been dropped by the D.A.

Another photocopy was from the Morning News: It was one of Jessica's first stories following Thurber's arrest, which detailed the charges against the suspect. A yellow marker highlighted a paragraph that indicated that two of the murders took place in Los Angeles on August 18 and August 29th.

Jessica looked up at Brillstein. Now it was his turn to raise eyebrows, although in his case with a certain bemusement. A gentle smile creased his face.

"So," she began, "a couple of the murder counts may be wrong..."

"No-no, my dear," the attorney replied, the smile never leaving his face. "It's a house of cards. Take one charge away and they all collapse. It's the same MO, as you so correctly reported, and the same perp. Those release papers also reflect my belief that Dean Thurber was in North Texas during the early days of Dr. Death's crime spree. I am reasonably convinced that I will shortly turn up other documentary evidence of Thurber's whereabouts during much of this time and it will not be in Southern California. I expect to discover he was in the Dallas-Fort Worth area until early September."

Jessica knew she was taking oxygen in short bursts, and she could feel her heart pound. This wasn't happening. She suddenly recalled how the voices during Dr. Death's telephone calls to her sounded differently. If the early deaths were unrelated — all that connected them was Alex's suppositions and theories — then the later deaths, those after her first story ran, might be the work of someone copying news accounts of the early "murders."

"Your stories may not be wrong but the police simply have the wrong man," said Harvey helpfully.

"When do you plan to show these to the D.A.?" she asked.

"Tomorrow morning," he said. "Then I intend to hold a news conference at noon. I'm guessing that all Thurber will be charged with is one count of assault for his attack on Pedro Javier. Since the guy is a drug dealer, the D.A. will probably look for a plea deal."

"What about Denzil Dulin?"

Harvey looked momentarily puzzled, then his face lit up and he laughed.

"Oh, you mean the drug dealer Mr. D'waine Jackson identified as the victim of my client. Well, all that puts Thurber at that murder scene is the word of a gangbanger and pathological liar. I don't expect the D.A. to jeopardize his re-election chances by relying too heavily on Mr. Jackson."

***

At that particular moment, the gangbanging pathological liar was being treated like royalty. City officials had housed Mr. D'waine Jackson at a hotel the city had acquired after a developer defaulted on a city loan. The city also paid for three meals a day and D'waine's telephone.

Since he couldn't as yet collect on the $40,000 city reward offered for information leading to the killer's conviction, D'waine kept agitating for "relocation" money for his mother and his many children. To shut him up, the city slipped him a $3,000 check to be reimbursed from the county's witness protection funds. Only D'waine refused to recognize this sum as his relocation money. This was "walking-around" money, which he promptly blew in Las Vegas.

One evening when a security guard at the hotel discovered him assaulting a hotel cigarette machine, D'waine was nearly kicked out of the hotel. Then when D'waine's cousin Willie was injured in a gang brawl, D'waine claimed the injury was in retaliation for his fingering Dr. Death and was threatening not to testify at the preliminary hearing unless police paid him additional family relocation funds.

A half-hour later, as D'waine was remonstrating over the phone with a clerk in the D.A.'s office, an emergency meeting took place in Big Bob's office that included the ME, Jessica, Hazel, Wersching and Bill. The Tarrant County Sheriff's office in Texas had confirmed the information in the fax she held in her hand.

"At least we can break the story first," Big Bob was saying, "playing up the poor, deluded drifter angle. This Dr. Death was really Dr. No—that sort of thing."

"My concern is how to handle this on the editorial page," said Wersching.

"Aggressively," replied Big Bob. "The police bungled it—they arrested the wrong guy. They've got to find the right guy."

"Are we afraid to admit we—I—may be wrong?" asked Jessica.

Big Bob stared at her, his jaw quivering.

"I told you the voice of the second caller sounded different than the first one," said Jessica. "The first caller had a—"

"It's a little late, isn't it, for us to argue that the calls to you may have had nothing to do with these crimes?" said Hazel. There was no kindness in his voice.

"I'm arguing that Dean Thurber is simply the wrong man," boomed Big Bob.

"But what if there is no right man?" said Jessica. "What if these aren't murders but simply drug overdoses?"

"We have a maverick homicide detective who says different," said big Bob.

"Not anymore he doesn't," said Jessica.

Her first call had been to Alex, who was shocked by the news. He too realized the implication of this "bombshell." The linkage among the various deaths was tissue-thin. There was more conjecture than evidence that connected these random deaths. Jessica's initial story sat right on the edge of wishful thinking: one cop's theory, a few unnamed sources and a shrug rather than a flat denial from a police official had turned wishful thinking into printer's ink. There it would have died but for a couple of phone calls and a murder that could be traced…not to other murders but a possibly fanciful story in the Morning News and therefore someone who was copying a false MO.

Copycat murders were certainly not unknown to the police. What made the whole damn thing a true banner story was Dean Thurber's righteous confession. With the validity of that confession now in jeopardy, Dr. Death ceased to exist.

Which didn't prevent Big Bob from proclaiming: "Alex Valesquez has been silenced by the department!"

"He wants to continue being a police officer," said Jessica. "Just as I want to continue being a journalist."

"Meaning?" snapped Big Bob.

"Meaning I may have blown it," said Jessica. "I followed a tip up a blind alley."

Big Bob glared at her for a moment, then refocused on the assembled brain trust. He sucked in air through his nostrils causing his chest to swell. His face turned a florid red.

"I believe in Dr. Death," said the managing editor. "The Morning News is foursquare behind this story. If this city's Keystone Cops and dippy D.A. have again bungled an important case, then we go after the sons-of-bitches! We certainly don't back down. And Jessica—"

Here he turned to her with a look more of sorrow than anger.

"—since you have lost confidence in your reporting, I'm taking you off Dr. Death and will reassign the story to a more— to another reporter."

"Fine," was all she could manage.

"Bill," said Big Bob, now turning to the one staffer who had remained silent during the meeting, "I want you to write this story. It's tomorrow's banner."

***

The next day, the Morning News informed the startled citizenry of Los Angeles of the latest twist in the Dr. Death case. The story read:

DR. DEATH SHOCKER:
COPS HAVE THE WRONG MAN
By Bill Boyer

Panic gripped City Hall and Parker Center Wednesday when news hit that the LAPD may have locked up the wrong guy in the Dr. Death case. For it now appears that Dean Thurber's confession that he is Dr. Death is as phony as a three-dollar bill.

Startling evidence obtained by The Morning News demonstrates that Thurber was in a slammer in the Fort Worth, Texas area when at least two of these murders—on August 18 and August 29—took place. His release papers show that he was incarcerated in the Tarrant County jail from August 13 to August 30.

"The cops bungled it," said an angry Harvey Brillstein. The ace attorney represents Thurber, who so far has "confessed" to the murders of seven drug dealers. However, informed sources have told The Morning News that Thurber may be released from custody as early as tomorrow.

Top cop Ned Sinclair, whose face must be redder than a late September sunset, failed to return phone calls seeking comment. Randi Millar, a spokeswoman for the D.A.'s office, declined to comment since Dist. Atty. Ray Bowman has not yet reviewed the documents. Mayor William Warren was traveling in Europe on a trade mission. His office declined to comment.

The killer, known as Dr. Death and first reported by The Morning News,

evidently stabbed his victims with a
heroin-laced hypodermic needle in a
killing spree that ran from July to
October of this year.

     Brillstein stated that these documents
"prove that my client is innocent." He
said he would demand that Bowman drop all
charges against Dean Thurber and release
him immediately.

     Deputy Dist. Atty. Michael L. Terzian,
who is expected to run against his boss in
next June's elections, attacked Bowman for
his "rush to judgment" and his failure to
check out the phony confession.

***

The following day the Los Angeles Times filed its report. While
harrumphing about the role of other "press" and "media" in the
unfolding shocker, the paper clung to its dignity and fine
reporting without mentioning its rival newspaper. It read in
part:

MAN CLEARED OF 'DR. DEATH' CHARGES
By Leslie Holtz

     Admitting they were duped by a bogus
confession, Los Angeles prosecutors
dismissed all but a single assault charge
Thursday against a man accused of slaying
seven local men—charges that some police
officials said were filed in haste when
details about the suspect began to surface
in the press.

     Dean Thurber will be released shortly,
according to LAPD spokesman Commander
Anthony Fairchild. He must still fight one
charge of assault stemming from his
original arrest in September.

"I think the suddenness of the inquiry and questions from you guys [in the media] put pressure on the D.A. to file," said Police Chief Ned Sinclair, who was among those flanking Dist. Atty. Ray Bowman when the charges were announced last month. Sinclair admitted that the September news conference was "put together hastily."

Added Fairchild: "There was a lot of pressure to put the story out because of rumors that Thurber was involved in the deaths of several drug dealers."

In an interview, Bowman acknowledged the media played a role in determining the timing of the filing of charges but said the decision was not made in haste.

"It had been a matter that had been investigated for several weeks. The fact that members of the media became aware of it meant that it was no longer possible to do any confidential investigating."

Attorney Harvey Brillstein, who represents Thurber, said the wrong person occasionally gets accused of a crime when prosecutors and police don't do their homework.

"It happens frequently that innocent people are arrested," said Brillstein. "But it seldom rises to the level of a press conference being called to announce that someone is guilty beyond a reasonable doubt."

"At no time did the defendant ever say he had an alibi or that he was in a Texas jail," noted Bowman.

***

However, KNBC news commentator Forrest Bibby didn't bother mincing words in his commentary that evening:

"The so-called 'Dr. Death' case represents a scandal for the city's beleaguered Police Department, for the District Attorney's Office, but most of all for the media in Los Angeles. Yesterday's revelation that Dean Thurber falsely confessed to the killing of seven drug dealers has many investigators saying that Dr. Death never existed—that he was created by the writers and editors of the Los Angeles Morning News. Note I did not say 'reporters.' For that publication fabricates rather than reports the news. Seven horrible human events led to the creation of the so-called 'Dr. Death'—the deaths of seven drug addicts who may or may not have been dealers. But people dying of drug overdoses on the mean streets of Los Angeles is not enough for the fiction writers of the Morning News. No, these deaths must be the work of a serial killer. Why? Because it sells newspapers, that's why. In these occasional commentaries, I like to think of myself as a media ombudsman, safeguarding the public against sloppy work by police and prosecutors—and reporters. The very phrase, 'the Fourth Estate,' implies we are part of a self-governing process in our society. Inherent in this function are vast powers and concomitant responsibilities. It is an abuse of journalistic responsibility to hype quotes from a news source or to twist facts to generate controversy."

And so Dr. Death was shoved off Front Pages and network television. If Dean Thurber wasn't the good Doctor, no one cared any longer to learn whether or not there ever was a Dr. Death.

CHAPTER TWENTY-ONE
THE JUMPER

Police cars, an ambulance and four fire trucks, all with lights flashing, clogged the street in front of the aging downtown building not far from the garment district. The crowd milling about in an area cordoned off by yellow police tape was growing restless. Everyone was waiting for something to happen.

Police radios squawked and automobile horns sounded. News helicopters buzzed overhead. The intersection was a mess with traffic backed up in all directions. Traffic cops were doing their best to untangle the gridlock and more were placing temporary detour signs several blocks from the scene to reroute traffic until the emergency was over.

The building was a hotel for transients, although rooms would rent by the hour to accommodate hookers. The only permanent residents were vermin and various forms of rodent and insect life. The structure itself appeared to remain upright more through force of habit than any architectural attributes.

On the steps of the building across the street, a homeless man offered regular updates to passers-by. "He's well dressed, ain't no homeless guy," the man told people, rattling a foam cup for spare change. "'Course, either way, he's doomed. Lord say, a soul ain't yours to give and ain't yours to take away."

The Jumper, dressed in a coat, tieless white shirt and baseball cap, stood with a strange calmness on the sixth-floor ledge, the kind made prominent by Harold Lloyd movies in the 1920s. His unshaven face was lean and without much expression, a dull glaze covering eyes underneath brows that grew in undisciplined directions.

Were he to jump, he could pretty much guarantee his death since he could easily dash from one side of the building to the other, thereby avoiding the netting firefighters had in place. The police were keeping the sidewalk directly beneath him clear of people except for emergency personnel.

A gasp came from the crowd as the Jumper dangled one foot over the edge.

Blocks away, a Yellow Cab crept along the nearest cross street where traffic could move at all. No longer able to tolerate this exasperating pace, Sly paid his Armenian driver and got out. He walked briskly along the sidewalk, threading his way among office workers and shoppers. The beeper lodged on his right hip vibrated frequently to announce urgent phone calls. They all were going to have to wait.

Sly knew he had a big story. He often fantasized about a collection of his best columns being published in a book that would stand the test of time as good journalism *and* good literature. Tomorrow's column was going to be one of his best. He could feel it.

Sly reached the scene six minutes after quitting the taxi. Officer Nyman, who was looking out for Sly, waved him through the security line. A reporter from the Times complained loudly about this, unaware of the special nature of Sly's visit to the news scene.

As he escorted Sly to the building, Officer Nyman told him: "He won't talk to any of us. He refuses to see a clergyman or a psychologist. He insists upon seeing his favorite columnist."

"Now I know who my readers are," Sly joked. The two men shared a quick laugh.

"What's his name?" asked Sly.

"We can't get anything out of him," replied the officer.

"Where are your crisis negotiators?"

"They're all out training," said Nyman sheepishly.

Sly and the policeman took the elevator to the top floor where police personnel was stationed. Sly briefly greeted each, several of whom declared themselves longtime readers of his column.

Sly was composing his column even as he experienced the event, noting the flora and fauna on the walls and struggling to locate in his brain the right words to describe the smells inside this wretched dwelling. The Jumper was in room 666, which caused Sly to shake his head in disbelief. What a gift, he thought. Room 666? There is a God, he thought to himself as he went through the doorway.

Two female officers occupied the bedroom and Sly momentarily wondered if the LAPD believed that female cops were more sensitive to the anguish of the distraught. He swiftly took in the room—the unmade bed, stained sheets, peeling paint, functional 1940s plumbing, filthy throw rugs and worn flooring—so he could poignantly describe it in a few well-chosen words. He moved to the window.

He poked his head outside and immediately felt a blast of smoggy air. He glanced to his right, along the ledge, where the Jumper stood. The mere appearance of a second person sent a tremor through the crowd. Several indistinguishable cries drifted up from below. The Jumper caught the changed mood but did not initially see Sly.

"Hey, there! What's goin' on?" Sly called to the Jumper, nearly causing the startled man to fall off the ledge right then and there. Retaining his balance, the man turned toward Sly and cried out, "Don't come any closer!"

"Thought you wanted to talk to me," said Sly.

The man immediately grinned. "You're Sly's Life?" he asked eagerly.

"I am Sly of Sly's Life," replied the columnist.

'It's great to meet ya in person and all," said the Jumper.

Sly pulled his considerable bulk through the window and now he too perched precariously on the ledge. He would, of course, do this much more nimbly when he wrote of these events later.

Sly sensed the crowd below was in a tizzy but forced himself to concentrate on the despondent man who shared the ledge with him. He could only hope the guy wasn't drunk or on drugs. There would be very little he could do with that.

"What's your name?" Sly inquired.

The man continued grinning at Sly and only responded after several seconds, as though sound waves reached him at a vastly different speed than they do with most people.

"George," he said. "My name is George."

"Always glad to meet a reader, George. But, Jesus Christ, couldn't you have picked a lower floor?"

"Sorry, but I'm really glad ya came," said George the Jumper.

"Hey, man, you saved my ass. I didn't have a column for tomorrow," replied Sly not insincerely. With this, he pulled a reporter's notebook from his jacket pocket and flipped it open to the first blank page. "So why are you threatening to jump?"

"Oh, I'm not threatening. I'm goin' t' do it, Sly. Was just waitin' for you to come."

"Thank you," said Sly. "I'd be happy to put you in my column. But I don't have any story yet. A guy jumping off a building is a backpage item. My readers need to know who you are and why you're doing it and what led you to this drastic action. And look, George, be as candid as possible. I can't be sitting back at my desk several hours from now with you flat as a pancake and my not knowing certain relevant facts about why you committed the ultimate sin. So, George, why are you jumping?"

The man furrowed his brow. "I'm tired," he said slowly. He looked at the gray buildings across the street as he spoke. "I lost everything. I'm alone an' people are after me."

"What people?"

"People," he said as if repeating the word would make things clearer. He narrowed his eyes. "I got no reason to live. Lost my job a while ago…lost my family…what else is there?"

Sly's heart sank. To George the Jumper he said: "We need something punchier than that."

"What?" asked the man, who turned to look at Sly, a puzzled expression replacing the one of abject sorrow.

"Guy loses his job and family, then jumps off a building is no big deal. I can't make a column out of that," said Sly.

"Oh," said George. "Well, what do you suggest?"

"Oh, hell, let's think about it," sighed Sly. "You could be protesting developments in the Middle East or maybe some long-ago crime has caught up with you…or, say, you could've gotten radiation poisoning at a Nevada nuclear test site."

The Jumper appeared genuinely confused by all this. "Gee, Mr. Sly, I dunno. I've never been to Nevada. Won't the truth do?"

"Look, George," said Sly, "here's the rub. People don't want to read about some Joe who jumps off a ledge because he lost a job. That's depressing, of course, but…well, no one is going to have any sympathy for you. You got a raw deal. So what? Everyone gets raw deals all the time. What makes you so high and mighty that you can take up valuable ink in the Morning News with your death?"

The man laughed. "Well, I am high up, ain't I?" he giggled. Seeing that his joke had not gone over well, he ceased giggling, letting a puzzled expression dominate his face one more.

"No, George, we need a better hook," Sly continued. "Let's focus on your unemployment. What kind of work did you do?"

"Oh, my last job was, it was over at the recycling center. I picked out bottles an' cans, see — "

"I mean a nine-to-five kind of job," Sly interrupted impatiently. "Did you ever have one of those?"

"Fuck, I had a million of 'em. I'm sorta a handyman, you might say. I worked in a shoe repair store once an' then I was a plumber's assistant an' got this job at the Hollywood United Methodist Church fixin' stuff for room an' board an' when I was a kid I was a grease monkey, y' see."

He stopped at this point and looked at Sly expectantly, hoping that the writer had heard the thing he was looking for.

"Hmmm," said Sly, shaking is head. "No real job, chronically unemployed—this is a challenge. Tell me about your family."

"Well, my mom was from Nebraska—"

"No, I mean the family you said you lost," interjected Sly.

"Oh. Well, I was married once if that's what you mean."

"That's what I mean."

"She left me 'bout two years ago…not quite two years ago." George slipped off his cap and dangled it over the side. "She was younger 'n me and kinda restless. Name was Martha."

Again, Sly sucked in his breath. Martha? George and Martha? A second gift. Shit, this column was going to write itself.

"She wasn't beautiful but I loved her, y' know? We had a kid once but it died after a week. No insurance for a hospital an' the doctor was a complete fuck-up. She was different after that, y' know? Didn't wanna screw or nothin'. But she stuck with me an' if I coulda kept that job as a plumber's assistant, I think she woulda stayed wi' me."

George the Jumper glanced over at Sly to see the impact his story was having on the columnist. But Sly merely nodded and appeared lost in thought. George at this moment turned and narrowed his eyes.

"This is it," he announced. "I'm goin' to do it."

Sly held up his hand. "I appreciate your resolve," he said, "but grant me a few more minutes of your time. Please. I don't know what happened to you recently to cause you to want to jump today."

"Told you," the man replied wearily. "People are after me."

"What people?"

"Jus' people…" The man fidgeted with his cap and glanced down at the street. Sly sensed he was running out of time.

"Do you believe in God?" asked Sly.

The man shook his head. Sly tried a different approach: "Well, you know, the story might improve if you didn't jump."

George's head snapped and he stared at Sly suspiciously.

"No," he said flatly. "Then it'd look like I wasn' serious, that I never intended to jump."

"You're missing the point," said Sly. "Your not jumping gives the story a note of redemption so people who have lost jobs and families will feel a little better about themselves."

Sly could see this was not working. The man kept shaking his head and looking at the distant ground.

"Also I could do a follow-up column later about how you regained your dignity."

George's head swung back to Sly, a startled look on his face. "You mean you'd do two stories 'bout me?"

"That's exactly what I mean," said Sly, letting a note of triumph creep into his voice. "Why I bet my first column will bring you job offers. After my second column, I wouldn't be surprised if the mayor ordered a parade through downtown for you."

The man met his eyes. Sly suddenly noticed how tired the man looked. George said, "Can I get that in writing? Can I get you to promise me you'd write two stories 'bout me? I don' want to live for nothin'."

Sly flipped to the next page in his notebook and scribbled:

"I, Francis Sylvester, promise to write two columns about you, George."

Sly tore out the page and held it out to the man. George then edged close enough to grab the paper. He stared at this for several seconds before turning back to Sly.

"Francis?"

"Yeah, that's my name," Sly said.

The man stared into space for several more moments. Sly sensed he was once again losing him.

"Look, my friend, let's have a resolution to this dilemma. I've got a deadline. If I don't leave soon, how am I going to get your story into tomorrow's paper?"

"If I do it now, you could be back at your paper real soon," said George.

"No, if you jump, I don't think I'll write about you."

The man's face reddened. The sound barely came out of him: "What?" he whispered.

"The only way I'm doing your story is a two-parter, one tomorrow and one after your redemption," said Sly.

"But you'll write two stories if I come down?" asked the man, a note of desperation in his voice.

"Yes, you hold my word in your hand."

The man began to cry. Sly got up and held out a hand.

"This is the time. This is the time to come down. I'm going to step closer to you and give you my hand. Will you take my hand?"

On the ground, the crowd fell eerily silent. The Jumper took a step forward and grabbed Sly's hand. The two men smiled at one another. George inched closer to Sly and the two men maneuvered their bodies closer to the window until each was able to slip back inside. They hugged each other.

"Thank God," murmured a woman on the ground.

CHAPTER TWENTY-TWO
THE RESTLESS

Darlene nodded to Sly as the red-faced columnist hurried through a newsroom celebrating his exploits. She even managed a go-get-'em smile. Sly had semi-jogged back to the Morning News as he could find no unoccupied taxi in the downtown traffic jam. Normally, Darlene would be bursting to find out what happened on that ledge. She along with the entire newsroom had watched the events on television. Newscasters had broken into the daytime soaps to bring "live updates" from the scene and everyone working cityside saw the Morning Snooze's very own Francis Sylvester talking the would-be suicide jumper down from that ledge.

Yes, normally she would have been among the first to hear every juicy detail. But Darlene was too damned depressed.

Andy Reynolds had been a tough one to get over. Why was that? She dumped guys, guys dumped her and so it goes. No big fucking deal. Why did she ache so for Andy, a punk who had hustled his brief gig with her into a plum assignment in Metro? If he used her, she certainly used him too and used him, well, sometimes long into the night. So why all the schoolgirl grief? Snap out of it, you horny bitch, she told herself.

Alas, it did no good. Worse, her column lacked its usual sparkle. This, she had to admit, could only partially be attributed to the loss of Andy's contacts. Darlene felt burnt out. The fling with Andy — and his contributions to the column — had perhaps only disguised a deeper malaise.

The column had become a grind. Every damn day she had to reinvent the wheel. Every damn day she had to telephone contacts, smother them with false good cheer and use every means in her extensive bag of tricks to extract dish from this sorry lot.

And for what? For the you-heard-it-here-first news that some TV actress was pregnant?

She glanced longingly at a pack of menthols lying on her desk. To get a nicotine hit, though, Darlene would have to take the elevator to the sixth floor and climb the stairs to the roof. Or go down to the alley. Too much fucking exercise for this time of day.

What she needed was a vacation. But who was there to run off with? Since Andy's abrupt departure from her life, she had remained celibate. She even turned down an offer from a young actor who was moving up in Hollywood. He was just looking for some ink, she figured.

Then there was Don Hazel. He had asked her to lunch twice the past week. What was that all about? At first, she worried she had made a major screw-up in her column and that the paper was once more being sued because of her. That still gave her nightmares. But were that the case, the ME or Whitcomb himself would have called her on the carpet. No, Hazel was an errand boy — for only small errands.

Fortunately, she had lunch dates with industry sources on both occasions. But the puzzle remained: why was he asking her out? He certainly couldn't have the hots for her and besides another fling with a colleague was simply out of the question. Unless, of course, Bill Boyer could be distracted from his crash-and-burn lifestyle. Darlene had a thing for rogues and since his wife left him, Bill had gone rogue.

***

"I'll take one card," said Jessica. Rose Tannenbaum, who was dealing, slid a card across the table. Jessica discarded one of her five cards, then said, "I'll raise you a dollar."

"A whole dollar? My goodness, I do have a wild and reckless daughter," sniffed Rose. "I'll raise you five dollars."

"Seven."

"Eight."

Jessica grew alarmed. "I'll see you," she told her mother.

Rose dropped her cards: three kings. Sheepishly, Jessica revealed hers: two queens and two sevens. Rose shook her head and used both hands to rake in the pot.

"Dear, never bet heavily on two pairs. I swear, if I played you more often, I could pay off my account at Saks."

"Mother, I've never been any good at poker," said Jessica.

"Well, it would stand you in good stead in the business world," said her mother. "It's not only a game of money management but a study in psychological behavior. Do you want another drink?"

"No, thanks."

"Well, I do. You shuffle."

With that Rose got up and went to the wet bar while Jessica gathered in the cards. Mother and daughter got together about this time every month so the evening had been planned without reference to the Dr. Death fiasco. And there was an unspoken agreement between the two women to make no mention of the unfortunate incident.

Jessica had driven to her mother's apartment in Pasadena through Highland Park where the Latino community was preparing for the celebration of *Dia de los Muertos*—Day of the Dead. There would be a procession later that night. Minstrels would play under Day of the Dead lace patterns and children would take turns trying to smash the *piñata*. People would give friends or relations a sugar *calavera* or skull bearing the recipient's name. In homes, families would light candles at altars covered with bright marigolds, a likeness of the Virgin Mary and favorite dishes and drinks of the deceased to entice the spirits. The souls of children would descend the first night and the adults would come the second.

Jessica was unaware of all this activity along the main streets beneath the Pasadena Freeway as she made her way to the San Gabriel Valley. Her life since Dr. Death had been filled with restlessness and melancholy. She went to work, filed her stories and scurried home as swiftly as possible. She no longer joined in newsroom banter and refused to rise to the bait of Danny Evans' mock insults.

The sad blur of her daily routine reminded Jessica of the days following her father's death when she went through the motions of living without really experiencing life. If her mother had asked, she probably couldn't recall the stories she had worked on that week.

Big Bob had left her on the police beat since to remove her would so demoralize the young reporter she might never recover. Besides nothing about the Dr. Death embarrassment caused him to doubt her basic reportorial instincts. Big Bob continued to believe in Dr. Death. Someone killed those hypes; the city bulls just got the wrong guy, he insisted.

"By the way, what's happening with you and your cop?" Rose asked Jessica while pouring a double shot of Glenlivet.

"Would it do any good to say it's none of your business?" asked Jessica.

"Of course not," replied Rose. "A child's happiness is always a mother's business."

"I thought as much. Well, there never really was anything between us."

"I thought—"

"I know what you thought and, believe me, I regret even mentioning Alex to you."

"Now, Jessica, if Alex isn't the one for you then you should look elsewhere for a mate."

Jessica sighed. "Mother, I'm not looking for a mate as you so quaintly put it. I don't like going to bars and the only people I meet on the job are criminals, the mentally unstable and fellow journalists, none of whom I find suitable."

"What's wrong with bars?" asked Rose. "I met your late father in a restaurant bar here in Pasadena."

"A bar was just about the only place you could've found Dad," replied Jessica. "Besides, I thought it was at the Pasadena Playhouse."

"Technically, yes, but we would meet at the bar after rehearsals and that's where I got to know your father."

Rose returned to the card table where she eyed her daughter's method of shuffling—holding half the pack in each hand against the table and clumsily trying to mix them.

"What are you doing?" asked Rose.

"Shuffling," replied Jessica.

"Lordy! Give 'em to me. I'll shuffle," said Rose, taking the deck away from Jessica. "Even as a child, you were no good with your hands. Your tinker-toy arrangements always looked like Rube Goldberg contraptions."

Once she sat, Rose shuffled the cards expertly. "You know, Jessica, I'm a staunch advocate of women's lib. Nevertheless, a woman needs a family."

She handed her daughter the now shuffled cards, which Jessica cut.

"Mom, I enjoy living alone. I don't have to fix a meal every night. I don't have to clean up or sew buttons. And being single has had everything to do with success in the news business."

"Rubbish," snapped Rose.

"No, really. Being single has helped me advance quickly. If I had a husband, I wouldn't have nearly the energy on the job. I come home exhausted too many nights to be sweet and loving to a man. My job is at the core of my life."

"Acting was the core of my life," said her mother, "yet your father enjoyed a hearty dinner every night in a clean house and in clean clothes with no buttons missing."

"Oh, Mother," said Jessica, growing more exasperated with the conversation, "that was all very different. You didn't have to support yourself with your acting. My only point is that living with someone takes up a lot of creative energy. Living alone is a kind of freedom."

"Yes," said Rose. "Freedom to be lonely."

"Mother, shut up and deal."

Dona Rosa, Alex's maternal aunt, had died a little over eight months earlier. But her spirit still restlessly roamed the little house in Boyle Heights she had inhabited for over thirty-six years of her mortal life. Neighbors heard her pots and pans banging and could smell beans cooking on the sturdy O'Keefe & Merritt range. Neither of her broken-hearted sons wanted to touch a thing in her house. It had stood for these eight months as a memorial to Dona Rosa. Her glasses, her knitting, her aging hi-fi and mariachi records that reminded her of her childhood in Sonora, Mexico, all these things were as she left them on the warm February evening she passed from this world.

Alex remonstrated with her sons, Jorge and Diego, that it was not right that their mother's spirit still inhabited the family house. How could they rent the old place with their mother not at rest? Jorge and Diego understood the need to get income out of the house so they agreed to Alex's plan to construct a large altar for her on this *Dia de los Meurtos*.

So now a fiery trail of marigold petals led from the street to the door of Dona Rose's home. Inside many candles lit the living room. Offerings of the finest tequila, tobacco and flowers were left at the altar. Photos of Dona Rosa, her family and especially Rafael, her long-departed husband, surrounded the altar. As a final touch, Alex convinced Jorge to cook his mother's favorite dish, chicken in a dark red mole sauce.

After everyone else cleared the house that night, Alex slept on the living room couch. The wind blew softly outside. At about seven-thirty, he awoke as the sun climbed the hill behind the house and sent its light into the kitchen and parts of the living and dining rooms. He arose from the couch and slowly approached the altar. Nothing appeared to be touched, not even the tequila, which surprised him given his aunt's penchant for late-night nips. He felt the sting of disappointment deep within his chest. What had gone wrong?

Then he noticed a speck of mole on the altar. Alex grinned broadly. Dona Rosa had feasted on the chicken. News traveled throughout the neighborhood by midday. Soon everyone leaned that Dona Rose would no longer haunt the house.

***

An hour earlier that same morning, Bill rose to work on his novel. With his third cup of coffee, the caffeine hit him full force. He felt jumpy and alive and creative. His fingers twitched as they hovered over the keyboard. His eyes stared intently at the PC's black-and-white monitor. He hadn't eaten any breakfast so the coffee took effect quickly.

Bill was determined to write a Newspaper Novel. Only the novel was mysteriously turning into the story of unrequited love between two cityside reporters.

Bill wasn't certain why he was writing this story. He knew what he wrote in the Morning Snooze was, as Ruth so succinctly put it, birdcage liner. So perhaps this was some kind of quest for immortality. It is not enough to pass through life, to feel and act and let those actions evaporate. There must be some kind of permanent record left behind or else that life fades into nothingness. Bill wrote, or so he imagined, so that a particle of himself might lodge in the collective conscience of mankind. Whether that particle entertained or irritated, it at least would find a home.

He was no longer content to be a reporter; he wanted to be a writer.

Then again, he might be writing the novel simply as a means of working out his feelings for Jessica and for Sophie and for his wife. It was all so complicated.

Jessica. How he yearned for her. How he wanted her milky skin and long, dark curly hair. She remained fixed for Bill as the perpetually close and yet perpetually receding object of desire and idealization. It was a kind of romanticism stretched into its lyrical and lush limit before breaking into something darker and more fragmented.

Sophie. The mental image of her passing through his brain ignited his passion. He loved being in bed with her dark skin and white teeth and bright brown eyes. He had never known such physical desire for a woman. But something, perhaps her being from such a different culture, stood between them.

His wife. He no longer dreamed of Renee. As far as he could tell, he ceased to dream at all. He slept well, wrote in the early morning hours, showed up early at the Snooze and hadn't missed a deadline in weeks. In a final act of liberation, he removed the ax from the trunk of his car.

***

A commitment ceremony?

Damn, thought Francis "Sly" Sylvester, newspaper columnist and professional curmudgeon. The very thought of such an exercise filled him with fear, repugnance, misery — and weird titillation. He couldn't determine if the way in which his whole body trembled was caused by horror or excitement. Maybe it was the same: horror-excitement. Maybe it was one's excitement over committing the ultimate folly. Didn't heterosexuals call marriage the triumph of hope over experience? Was it any different for us homos?

How had he gotten into this situation? Were he to write a column, he could trace the course of events in less than 450 words easy. That first encounter at the Water Grill, the first night, the tender days and nights which followed, the gradual need to make some sort of declaration to the world about their relationship and his eagerness to wage war against the Morning Snooze's discriminatory insurance policies regarding longtime companions. Ah-hah, he thought. That was it! It wasn't just a commitment ceremony but a political statement. He felt much better with that realization.

Still, the mystery remained: how had he been seduced into a commitment ceremony? "Seduced." That was the word. He'd been seduced. Seduced by Charlie Moller. Seduced by ecstasy. Seduced by love itself. What horror-excitement there was in that word.

As he watched from the second story window of Bill Boyer's modest Hollywood Hills home, he replayed in his mind the time and place when he and Charlie knew it had come to this. Late one Monday, Charlie's day off from the restaurant, Sly had returned to Charlie's Brentwood condo his usual disheveled self. Only more so on that particular early evening for the minute he walked in the door. Charlie took one look at Sly — jacket rumpled, shirttail out, hair flying and sweat drenching his flushed face — and exclaimed, "What the hell happened to you?"

Sly glanced in the entry mirror and saw what Charlie saw. "Oh," he said, "I was chasing a story and fell down."

Charlie laughed at this remark, but his laugh was filled with such bright, good cheer that both men looked at one another. Sly joined in the laughter and the lovers embraced.

"You're funny," Charlie said.

"I'd better be. I'm a columnist," he replied.

"I love you."

"Nonsense. I'm not lovable."

"Oh, but you are, kind sir."

"You been drinking?"

"Not at all. I've been thinking."

"Even worse. A dangerous thing to do."

"If you think that's dangerous, wait till you hear what I've been thinking about."

And so it happened. The idea of a commitment ceremony was broached and, for some inexplicable reason, Sly found his body tingling with excitement. And not one single objection escaped his lips. He had instantly agreed and now he found himself looking down into Bill's rose-lined garden moments before this ceremony.

Bill knocked and entered. "It's time, my friend," he said.

"Any possible escape route?" asked Sly.

"Nope. All are carefully guarded."

"No call from the governor?"

"He's on vacation?"

"No way out?"

"No way out."

"Dead man walking," mused Sly, who exited through the door.

As the two men walked toward the stairway, Sly said, "I look at it this way. I'm assured of getting the best table at the Water Grill for the rest of my life."

"This commitment thing must be good for you," remarked Bill. "I've never known you before to look on the bright side of any tragedy."

CHAPTER TWENTY-THREE

REVIVING DR. DEATH

It was going to be one of those days. Firestorms had struck Malibu two days earlier and new ones flared in Ventura and Riverside. Then unseasonable Santa Ana winds whipped up a 600-acre brush fire north of San Bernardino. Half of the city room was out on assignments covering the stories. The other half complained about the dry heat.

"Get used to it," chortled Gary Parker to the newsroom. "It's the early stages for worldwide warming. If you keep increasing carbon dioxide that our fossil-fuel-burning civilization insists on adding to the atmosphere, expect to see a lot more heat in years ahead."

First Dr. Death and now Dr. Doom, Bill mused to himself.

"How long is that story of yours?" Danny Evans called over to Bill. "Keep it down to ten inches, will ya?"

Bill was writing about a man who left his baby with a stranger he met in line at a North Hills mini-mart while he went looking for cocaine.

"That'll be tough," Bill called out. "There's a lot to say."

"Well, then there will be a lot to cut," snapped Danny.

Bill got up, walked over to Danny and put his hand on the copyeditor's shoulders. "Danny," he said, "you know your word is law but, unfortunately, around here, we break the law all the time."

For once, Danny was dumbfounded.

Meanwhile, several feature writers were grumbling to one another about Big Bob's edict that the entire staff must contribute stories for the damn gardening issue.

"What do I know about gardening?" muttered one writer. "My house plants all die."

Sly, who was exempt from such a contribution, was lost in thought. He was contemplating the plight of a 75-year-old woman, furious that a developer was poised to tear down her longtime home for sleek new condos. It was up to Sly's Life to rescue Thelma Albertson.

Winnie's desk sat empty. She suffered from what the doctor called cellulitis on her leg. She had acquired this staph infection while trampling about in a Riverside field during a rock concert the weekend before. Something infected a cut sustained the previous day when she ran into her living room glass table. She was said to be heavily medicated although, as Ruth pointed out, Winnie was always heavily medicated. The question was whether it was physician-prescribed.

Jessica's phone rang. She waited a couple of rings before picking up. "Jessica Tannenbaum," she spoke clearly into her headset.

"Hello," said a male voice. Then nothing.

"Yes? Who is this?" asked Jessica.

"Don't you recognize my voice?"

Indeed, she did recognize the voice and had begun the tape recorder attached to her phone the moment she heard it. But what she said was: "I'm sorry, I don't. Who is this?"

"You don't recognize your old pal, Dr. Death?

"Sorry," she said. "I'm not covering that story anymore."

"Looks like you and me have been sidelined," said the voice.

"What do you mean?"

"You're off the story and a good killing has gone unnoticed. Not a single line about that hippie pusher in Van Nuys. I thought it was one of my better clean-ups."

"What about Dean Thurber?"

"Oh, Jessica…Dean Thurber…I nearly died laughing. I never called you to correct the mistake. Forgive me for that. Fact is, I thought it might be good for someone else to take credit for my work. Things were getting tough on the streets for a while and my opportunities to finish the job were narrowing rather precipitously. If the pushers thought the good doctor was behind bars, I figured my job would become a little easier."

"What job is this?"

"Making L.A. Clean again. Remember? Hey, you really can't recognize my voice?"

"The job of making L.A. clean might take years. Think of all the pushers out there."

"True…true," the voice mused, with an inflection of regret shading into a sigh. "But I never for a minute intended to eliminate every single pusher. That would take a determined citizenry and police force, neither of which exists. My only goal was to—what shall I say?—eliminate a select few."

"Which select few?"

"Those who took advantage of people who were sick and dying, people addicted but not depraved. In other words, scum!"

The last word rang in Jessica's ear like a gunshot. Her mind was racing. What was he trying to say?

She asked: "Don't all dealers take advantage of people?"

"Yes, of course, they do. Maybe it's just fate. You sell shit to this junkie and she dies and you sell to another and he's okay and maybe one day he'll even kick the habit. But a customer does die and that scum should pay for it with his life."

"If you say so."

'You don't believe me?"

"To tell you the truth, I'm sick of Dr. Death."

"Don't blame you," the voice softly said. "That's why I called—to apologize. You were misled by a copycat and then by a false claimant and I never called to warn you. I'm really sorry. I just didn't think this Dean Thurber would get exposed as a fake so quickly. I was hoping he would remain in the media limelight for a while. Bad luck for both of us."

The line went dead. Jessica hit the off button on her headset and stared for a moment into space. She dialed the Van Nuys police station commander, got confirmation of a junkie overdose the previous night, then dialed a four-digit inner-office number. Once she got the library on the phone, she asked for printouts of all Morning News stories on Dr. Death.

A couple of hours later, after she had filed her final copy of the day, Jessica intently studied printouts from the archive of Dr. Death stories. Something the guy said on the telephone kept ringing in her head, the part about people who were sick and dying, people addicted but not depraved. What did that mean? She drew up lists of new hypotheses and phone calls to make. Then she went to see Big Bob.

***

Big Bob was extremely dubious about letting Jessica back on the case. The tape recording meant little to him and her new scenarios, scenarios which a week before may have seemed perfectly valid to him, now sounded like wild fantasies. Frankly, he too had lost his enthusiasm for Dr. Death. Brush fires made much better news. An editor didn't need to rely on reporters' sources to confirm their existence. The issues were clear-cut. No one sought a morality tale in a brush fire; it simply needed stamping out. If Dr. Death reappeared in the pages of the Morning News, the evidence had to be ironclad. Only when Jessica suggested using her growing unused comp time to investigate did the managing editor relent ever so reluctantly.

The next step for Jessica was to gain Bill's help, not an easy task in light of the disruption of communication between them. Bill had been solicitous on the day following the Dr. Death fiasco. But after that, silence. She knew he resented her unwillingness to follow up on that one unfortunate late-night episode. She needed somehow to use his silly schoolboy crush on her to entice him back to her side without fully arousing that tricky libido of his.

After a couple of beers at the American Legion bar, he was much more amenable to her entreaties. Bill had the next week off, which he planned to use for an all-out assault on his novel. Instead, as she hoped, he volunteered to assist Jessica part-time while putting in four hours daily on the writing.

The first couple of days yielded little. Using the Thomas Guide Zip Code Edition maps to L.A. County and extensive coverage from not only the Snooze but also other papers, Jessica mapped out the quadrants of Dr. Death's alleged exploits. She and Bill then canvassed the areas, hitting, bars, nail parlors, clubs, barbeque joints, motels, markets and the pushers themselves when they found them. For their efforts, they got mostly "Huh?" and "Who?" On the street, Dr. Death was already yesterday's news.

They then moved off the street to talk to relatives and pals of the overdose victims. Nice sob stories but little else. They were getting nowhere.

The third day, which was an unusually warm one, Bill and Jessica stopped at a Salvadoran *pupuseria* in a Koreatown mini-mall. Bill loved *pupusas*, those soft hand-patted, griddle-baked corn cakes stuffed with cheese, pork or the pungent vegetable *loroco*. He hungrily ordered all three while Jessica picked at her fried *yucca con chicharrónes* with its chewy deep-fried pigskin draped over a mound of cabbage slaw.

The hours of closeness, the legwork and surveillance had brought them together in a curious way. Easiness developed in their friendship. She found herself able to focus better when she was around Bill. With Alex, she had felt a need to inspect each thought before giving it utterance. With Bill, a calm clarity pervaded her being. This soothed her because she knew it meant she was not in love with Bill. Love meant anxiety, stratagems, distress, watchfulness, role-playing, loss of appetite and hysteria. Love, she knew, never induced calm.

Thank God she never fell in love with Bill. Not really despite that one mistake. Journalists probably should never fall in love. There were married people at the Morning Snooze but they were mostly editors and people in circulation or advertising. There were a few married reporters, but they weren't very good journalists as a rule. How could they be? You can't focus on what's important when someone else is forever demanding your attention. At least there was room for camaraderie like the one evolving between her and Bill, she thought as she bit into a crunchy tuber dressed with mild tomato sauce.

Their newly established rapport spurred her on. You didn't have to be a lone wolf in the news game, she realized. Teamwork could get you there twice as quickly. Yes, that's it. It was teamwork she most enjoyed as she worked with Bill. She was sure it was better than sex with him.

For his part, Bill was chasing a Big Story. He could feel the energy flowing through his body; his fingertips tingled. Why did everyone want to brush this story under the rug? Why did it inconvenience so many people and institutions, from Parker Center and City Hall to the drug trade and the addicts themselves? Why did everyone breathe a sigh of relief when Dr. Death vanished? Everyone was so eager for him not to exist. Maybe that was the story.

There were so many possible angles on this thing. He hated to go to sleep at night. Sleep could be such a waste of time. Even now, his mind was chewing over the facts once more.

"Trouble is," he said, moments after swallowing the last of his second *pupusa*, "is that nothing connects the victims and any potential perp. What have we got? They were all men from the lower class or lower middle class and, yes, all were connected to drugs but so what? We knew that before we started. Why were they targeted—if they were targeted? Were they junkies or pushers?"

"I'm convinced they were all dealers," said Jessica.

Bill shrugged. "I need proof. Besides some people deal drugs simply to get drugs themselves. They're not hard-core dealers."

"Let's say I'm right," said Jessica. "It'll speed things up. Better to head in a direction, even the wrong one, than in no direction at all."

"Okay."

"Remember in the Times piece when the police admitted Thurber was the wrong guy, there was something about other credible leads that had not been explored?"

"Vaguely."

"That makes me wonder."

"What do you wonder, my dear?" asked Bill as he sank his teeth into a third *pupusa*.

***

Jessica got back to the office around 3. She immediately put in a call to Alex, who was out but called back an hour later. The conversation was their first since she came off the Dr. Death case. The tension in each of their voices was palpable.

"Hey, I want no part of your Dr. Death," he interrupted before she could finish her carefully planned greeting and inquiry. "I'm in the biz bag with my supervisor."

"Biz bag?" she asked.

"The doghouse to you civilians," he explained.

"Don't you want to be proven right about these killings?" she asked.

"That would add insult to injury."

"Well, I would like to be right. I got a mother who thinks of me now as a National Enquirer reporter."

"What do you want?"

It came so quickly she took a second to recover and formulate her questions. "Is anyone at the LAPD continuing to investigate these overdoses?"

"Fuck, no," snapped Alex. "My superiors now believe a Mexican trafficking ring has flooded the area with cheap and highly pure heroin and this caused a spike in deaths."

"You believe that?"

"It's more than plausible. This stuff is sixty to eighty percent pure. You know what that means? Usually, the purity of Mexican black tar heroin has been thirty to forty percent."

"Tell me what this unnamed investigator quoted in the Times meant when he said other credible leads had not been explored."

'Haven't a clue."

"No?"

"No, I don't," he said, weariness slightly slowing his speech. "Look, we had compiled a profile for a possible 'Dr. Death,' a guy working alone and on a mission and, believe me, Dean Thurber was never a comfortable fit."

"Who is?"

The silence on the other end was deafening. Finally, Alex signed: "What do you want? Me to turn over every department memo and secret file on the case to you?"

Jessica fought her instinct to respond positively to this less-than-serious question. Instead, she said: "Look, that guy called me again, the one who made the first call. He said he's back in business and has killed a dealer in Van Nuys. Sound familiar?"

She figured Alex might know about the overdose in the Valley.

"What else did he say?" asked Alex, his voice softening ever so slightly.

"He claimed his targets were not just drug dealers but drug dealers who—and I'll quote him to you—'did real harm, who took advantage of people who were sick and dying, people addicted but not depraved. In other words, scum.'"

"I can't believe you're still taking these crank calls seriously."

"I'm sure this was the same voice I heard the first time," she insisted.

Another pause on the line was followed by a drop in Alex's voice to a matter-of-fact tone: "I know I'm going to regret this, but at one time there was a general belief among those of us working on the overdose cases that somehow DOA might be involved."

"DOA?" she said with astonishment. "You mean Drugs Out of America? That group?"

"That group."

"Involved how?"

"That's all I can tell you and I shouldn't have told you that much."

"Oh, come on," she pleaded, suddenly thinking she sounded like a high-school kid asking for the keys to her parents' car. "You gotta tell me what I'm looking for."

"I don't gotta do nothin'," he shot back. "After Thurber's arrest, we dropped the idea. All I'm telling you is that our abandoned profile fits that group. Or at least it would fit a member of that group. Now what I do gotta do is get back to work. Let me know if you come up with anything."

He hung up. Jessica stared momentarily at the notepad on the desk in front of her. She had said none of the things she wanted to say. She felt awful. She had been all efficiency and business, pressing a source for information. She wanted to tell him how sorry she was for all the grief she had caused him and what a swell guy he was and what she wanted to do was to make him a meatloaf.

***

Roy Rogers — not to be mistaken for the singing cowboy star of the same name and don't think the poor fellow hadn't spent a lifetime hearing bad jokes about his unfortunate name — was the Morning News' chief librarian and virtually the only soul in the building who understood the paper's database.

The Snooze had computerized its morgue but in a cost-saving move purchased a cheap and inadequate NEXIS-like system that never seemed to work properly. But Roy could, magically, retrieve most information requested by reporters from the reluctant server.

Bill approached Roy about his request on Saturday. Bill knew Roy always came in on the weekend to use the library computer to write homosexual pornography to boost his meager income. Bill, therefore, knew Roy would not only be in the office but would be compliant about Bill's time-consuming search request since Roy's use of the paper's computer for a second job was, strictly speaking, a violation of company policy.

Roy fussed about the request, naturally, but Bill was one of his favorites since he was a good guy and never made remarks about his name. So Roy took a break from his chronicles of the back-alley exploits of Randy Lance and began a keyword search for Drugs Out of America. As was anticipated by Bill, the painfully slow search came up with enough story hits that it would take the better part of the afternoon to willow them down. Roy and Bill divided the task with the understanding that in an hour Roy could return to the adventures of Randy and his drag queen bitch, Gloria Hole.

By the end of the afternoon, Bill had a still substantial fifteen stories that needed further research although one, in particular, intrigued him.

On a hunch, he had typed the search keys "depraved" and "drug overdose" on the template on his screen. A nearly two-year-old story popped up about the drug overdose of one Cathy Bruening. It was a backpage item—only four graphs—and probably wouldn't have made into the Snooze had she not chosen the AMC multiplex in the Century Square Shopping Center as the scene for her departure from this mortal life. Her husband, Martin, was quoted as saying his wife had a longtime drug-abuse problem. The story let him rail for another sentence about the depravity of drug dealers and their disregard for human life.

Using "Martin Bruening" and "Drugs Out of America," Bill came up with another hit, a story several months later, in which Bruening was again quoted, this time as a spokesman for DOA. He quickly checked city directories in the library. A Martin Bruening—fortunately, a fairly unusual name—lived in the West Adams area.

Thanking Roy Rogers profusely, Bill left the building, got his car out of the company parking lot next to the American Legion and drove west on Washington Boulevard. He wanted to see Bruening's house although he wasn't sure why.

The West Adams district contained many Craftsman homes from the early part of the twentieth century. The construction of the Santa Monica Freeway in the 1960s divided the area while gobbling up many of the finer homes of what was then Sugar Hill. But because the area was predominantly black by then, banks and other lending institutions had "red-lined" the entire district, meaning no major loans in that area. Ironically, this also meant no major development, which had the effect of preserving the remaining homes in their original glory.

For the past few years, middle-class whites, unable to afford real estate prices in the suburbs, had moved back into the area to restore the now valuable older homes and turn West Adams into a historic district. The area became the most racially mixed district in the entire city, comprising black, white, Asian, Latino, straight and gay families in about equal measure.

Turning from Washington, Bill drove two blocks south before coming to the address. He coasted past the two-story Craftsman and parked half a block away. The place looked as if its owners had restored it in the last few years. It was painted dark forest green with the trim in moody brown. A generous front porch ran the length of the front.

A 1963 Chevy sat up in the driveway—apparently, the owners liked old things—but no one appeared to be home. Bill sat in the heat—ridiculous for the end of November—watching the house for an hour. Then a late model blue Buick came down the street and turned into the driveway, parking behind the Chevy. A man, medium height and angular, got out and pulled laundry fresh from the dry cleaners from the backseat.

Bill grabbed his Canon from the camera bag and focused on the man, who was climbing concrete steps to the front porch. He unlocked the large wooden front door and moved inside the house without Bill being able to get a shot. The door remained open though and moments later the man re-emerged.

Bill fired off several shots as his target moved back toward the car. The man opened the truck to remove two bags of groceries. Closing the lid, he turned toward Bill who furiously refocused the telephoto lens. This time he got several shots of the man's face before he turned to go back into the house. The door closed.

Bill lowered the Canon and stared at the house, a puzzled look coming over his face. Bill felt he somehow knew — or at least had seen — the man. But where? Where had he seen this guy?

Unfortunately, Bill had a journalist's memory bank. Names and faces were associated with physical locations and stories. Bill usually drew blanks when confronted with a person he knew but out of context. A neighbor once turned up at a press screening at the Academy of Motion Pictures Arts and Sciences' Samuel Goldwyn Theater and Bill simply didn't recognize the man when he came up to Bill. More embarrassingly, at a Santa Monica cocktail party, he failed to recognize a Valley woman he pursued across two fruitless dates.

Bill's mind raced through the many beats he held on the Snooze since he joined the paper — City Hall, police, urban affairs — but came up with empty. He slipped his camera into its bag and turned the car's ignition key.

Bill drove north on Western to Third Street to grab a beer at the Women of Color bar. Twenty minutes later, as he watched Alice, as one Thai woman called herself, dance with nonchalance on the stage, his eye drifted to the TV screen over the bar. As a news program flashed on the screen, something clicked inside Bill's head

He sat frozen, staring dumbly at the TV screen. What was it? Somewhere in the back of his mind, a connection struggled to get made. The TV screen, a beer, the Windsor Arms bar — shit, what was it? He shook his head, swallowing a good mouthful of cold beer, then glanced at Alice. Misunderstanding his look of concentration, she playfully fondled her breasts. Bill forced himself to smile, then looked back at the TV.

The TV screen, a beer, the Windsor Arms bar and…then it hit him. He was sitting here about a month ago when some guy wearing a USC cap watched a newscast about Dr. Death. Stupid idiots, the man had said. Then Bill asked him who are the stupid idiots and the man had laughed and said the cops and the D.A. and media were stupid idiots because Dean Thurber hadn't killed anyone. Or something like that

Bill pressed the thumb and middle finger of his right hand against his temples as if trying to squeeze more information out of a tired brain. What was it that guy had said? Something about Thurber not having the balls for the job?

Bill dug into his coat pocket and withdrew Roy Rogers' printout of the Morning News' story about the drug overdose death of Bruening's wife. Cathy Bruening was found in the corner of the last row of a Century City movie theater, her lips blue and eyes staring at the ceiling. She was pronounced dead at the scene by a doctor who happened to be in the complex. Her husband told police she had a drug-abuse problem. Bill recalled that the guy in the USC cap had said something about his wife having been on the streets.

Bill Boyer didn't realize it but his jaw dropped a good inch as he stared unseeing at the television. "Shit," he said out loud.

Could it be? Was his drinking companion a month ago Martin Bruening? The same Martin Bruening who called drug dealers depraved just as Jessica's caller had? A tenuous connection at best. Maybe no connection at all.

Bill's mind raced. Should he phone Jessica? Or maybe Big Bob? Should this wait until Monday? Did he have anything at all here? Did a brief conversation in a bar a month before add up to anything? Could he be certain that guy in the Windsor Arms was Martin Bruening?

***

In the end, Bill waited until Monday. He drove by Bruening's house twice, Sunday and heading for work Monday, but never caught sight of him. When he did arrive at work, more electrifying news was in store for him.

The front-page story in the Morning News was written by Richard Azari, a second-year reporter who handled all Thornhill press releases:

THORNHILL ANNOUNCES MAJOR RESTRUCTURING
By Richard Azari

Thornhill Publishing unveiled a corporate overhaul that will return the New York-based media company to its fundamental operations while eliminating more than 650 jobs at its newspapers.

Besides the restructuring, which the company said will result in charges of several hundred million dollars in the second half, Thornhill Publishing said it will close its multimedia division and buy back up to 10% of its common stock. The firm, which publishes the Los Angeles Morning News, also announced an anticipated sharp drop in fourth-quarter operating earnings.

"We have made a very clear decision to focus our efforts, activities and investments in our core businesses," Gordon Janeway, Thornhill Publishing president and CEO, said.

The move is part of a broad cost-cutting campaign that includes 45 newspaper jobs at the Morning News. That newspaper, which has already cut 10 of those jobs, has struggled through rising

```
newsprint  costs,  an  uncertain  Southern
California economy and flat revenues.
    About half the job cuts at the Morning
News will come through layoffs resulting
from 'product discontinuance,' the paper's
publisher, Duke Whitcomb, said. This will
mean  that  several  services  and  sections
will be discontinued.
    Thornhill  will  retain  its  NewsLink
electronic  service  but  will  review  all
non-core business assets including efforts
to  develop  a  cable  TV  programming
business.
```

***

Funeral parlors exude more cheer than the Morning Snooze newsroom. Stunned journalists and other employees read and reread the story. Even Big Bob lumbered rather than strode through the newsroom to his office, where he immediately shut the door and wouldn't be seen again until lunch.

Who's job was at stake? Journalists mentally calculated the month and year of their hire, how many had come aboard since and the number of jobs to be pruned. Older hands smiled only for smiles to evaporate with the thought that these smilers might work for a section headed for product discontinuance or have a large enough salary to get "offered" a buyout.

Bill didn't talk to Jessica until lunchtime when they braved the culinary disaster that awaited them at the American Legion. As it turned out, Jessica never touched her meal. She couldn't stop asking him excited questions as he explained the vague link between Martin Bruening and the guy at the bar. Bill had thought she might be skeptical. Instead, her eyes sparkled and skin color glowed as her enthusiasm mounted.

"We need a plan," she said as words tumbled from her mouth at the speed of thought. "At the moment, we don't have anything—not enough for Alex to look into the situation, assuming he'd even bother, or for Big Bob to spring us to investigate further or for Duke Whitcomb to back us up. We need some way to get to this Martin character without him wising up. We need to talk to this guy somehow."

"Risky business," Bill interjected. "If Martin Bruening *were* Dr. Death, he'd be wary of talking to any reporters. And I don't take him for anybody's fool."

"Couldn't we approach him as a DOA spokesman and say we're doing a series on the drug epidemic in L.A. County? We know he lost his wife to drugs from a story we wrote a couple of years ago, and we need him for anecdotal evidence of the toll drug abuse takes on citizens."

"Which one of us? He might remember me from that day at the bar. And he would certainly link your byline with the Dr. Death saga."

"You," she shot back swiftly. "I agree my name is tarred by Dr. Death. In your case, maybe he'll remember you and maybe he won't. Either way, there's nothing to suggest you're not doing exactly what you say you are—a newspaper series on drug abuse in the county."

Bill sighed. "I don't know. I wish there were some way of doing surveillance on him rather than approach him directly."

"Like what—a 24-hour stakeout like in a cop movie? Sure, Big Bob would spring for that. Spare no expenses—only, wait, we're cutting back on everything. Did you happen to read today's paper?

"I read it."

She looked at him, not unkindly but with an intensity that made him uncomfortable.

"How have things been left between you and Alex?" he asked.

Her eyes blinked. "What?" she asked.

"Are you kaput or what?"

"Why ask now?"

"To gauge how much we can count on him?"

"Not much, okay?"

CHAPTER TWENTY-FOUR
TRUE CONFESSIONS

Bruening proved to be highly cooperative on the telephone. While he did ask if the Morning News series was at all tied in with Dr. Death, he nonetheless welcomed the opportunity to unburden himself about the loss of his wife.

Meanwhile, Bill and Jessica did convince Big Bob to let them do a three-part series on drugs in L.A. so his phone call to Bruening was legitimate. Bruening agreed to be interviewed the following afternoon when he returned home from his work as a stockbroker downtown.

If Martin Bruening recognized Bill when he opened his door, he made no sign of it.

"Mr. Boyer?" he inquired pleasantly, picking Bill out from the two men confronting him, the other being Morning News photographer Tim Pollack.

"Yes," said Bill, pulling a card from his billfold and handing it to Bruening. The man glanced at the card and slipped it inside a vest pocket. Still dressed from work, he wore a tasteful silk tie, a beige and white vest over a powder blue shirt and brown slacks. Quite a difference from his attire at the bar. He moved aside so Bill and Tim could enter. They all went into the adjoining living room.

The house had been lovingly restored with dark wood molding setting off pale green walls in the living room. A dining room with pocket doors beyond the living room featured wainscot paneling of slightly lighter oak. Original plate rails held decorative plates and a few framed photographs. Indeed the home was filled with either genuine antique furniture and appliances or those designed to look turn-of-the-century or slightly later.

Bruening motioned Bill to a light pink love seat. As Tim grabbed his shots so he could leave for another assignment, Bruening politely asked if he would get either gentleman anything to drink.

Tim declined but Bill volunteered, "Well, if you're having tea or coffee —"

"Why don't we have some Earl Grey," said Bruening, who then called out, "Carmen!"

A middle-aged Latina appeared at the dining room entry. "Yes, Mr. Bruening?" she inquired with a slight Mexican accent.

"A pot of tea, please, Carmen," he said. "Earl Grey."

"Yes, Mr. Bruening," she said and disappeared back into the kitchen via the dining room.

The two men contented themselves with small talk while Tim and Carmen went about their respective tasks. Bruening was very interested in Bill's newspaper job. He asked many questions about it and the downsizing at the Morning News. When the tea arrived, Tim declared himself finished and departed. Bill pulled out his notebook and placed a cassette tape recorder on a glass table between them.

"First of all, thank you for seeing me," Bill began. "I know this isn't easy. Not everyone can talk about their grief."

"When you called, I knew instantly I must talk to you," said Bruening in measured tones. "No one seems to be doing anything about the drug pandemic in this city. I see cops dive right by drug buys on the streets. I see judges letting users off with stern warnings. I see homeless activists refusing to talk about drugs because it risks destroying political support for their constituency."

"But, as you say, it's a pandemic. Where does one begin when a boat is flooded and you have only a teacup?" said Bill, gesturing with his cup of Earl Grey.

Bruening pursed his lips and frowned, his hands coming together in a triangle beneath his chin. "It seems to me that statement is a recipe for disaster. If everyone did *something*—save a friend, turn in a dealer or simply refuse to have anything to do with even the mildest of gait-way drugs such as marijuana—then clearly the pandemic would be reduced to an epidemic and the epidemic could be curtailed and eventually eliminated. But people prefer to do nothing. Or to make jokes about it."

Bruening spoke in a coolly analytical manner, choosing his words with care and articulating them calmly.

"Out of curiosity, what do you do?" asked Bill.

"Many things besides working with DOA," Bruening replied. "In my search for my wife, I did become acquainted with all sorts of people on the street and especially those struggling to prevent further damage from drugs. I donate time, for instance, to the Pico-Union Drug Addiction Treatment Center, which does a lot of good. I recommend you speak to one of their best councilors, José Díaz, in your reporting of this story."

"I will, thanks," said Bill. "Tell me about your wife."

"Cathy was the most beautiful woman I ever met," said Bruening. "She came from Ashland, Oregon—you know, where they have the Shakespeare festival—and I don't think she ever got used to this big, ugly city. I wish now I'd moved to Ashland after we married. There was a moment—well, the point is we met at USC in our senior year, got married and bought this house a couple of years later before gentrification hit West Adams. It was very affordable then. We spent our weekends restoring the house to its former luster."

"You did a fabulous job," said Bill.

"Thanks," said Bruening. "Can you believe it, it took over three years? Just stripping the paint from the woodwork took forever. Anyway, that's not what you want to hear. You want to hear how a perfect and beautiful woman from Ashland can wind up on the street, filling herself with poison."

The man shifted in his seat and stared for a moment into space. "It all began when she fell down the stairs right here," he said matter-of-factly, pointing to the stairway leading to the second floor from the entry.

"She tore up her left knee pretty badly. After surgery, she got her first taste of Demerol. She loved it. In the hospital, she had one of those machines where you can dose yourself by pushing a button, and when they came to take it away, she started hanging on to it. She said, 'You can't do this. This is my friend.' I thought she was joking. So did the nurses.

"After she was discharged, she had access to enough pain pills to continue feeding her habit. I finally caught on and put her into rehab. She got better for a while, then she relapsed. This time it was cocaine.

"My wife, Mr. Boyer, was a professional person with what I would call a strong will. She wasn't a weak sister or a welfare chiseler or a depraved person. You must understand how virulent these drugs are — how strong a hold they have over an individual."

"What did she do?" asked Bill.

"She was a casting director when we got married. Afterward she went back to SC to get her law degree. She wanted to be an entertainment attorney. But she never finished school."

"What happened after she got into cocaine?"

"Well, that led to more rehab in a methadone clinic and at Cedars-Sinai's chemical dependence wing and eventually Narcotics Anonymous. When that failed, we tried psychoanalysis and family counseling. Nothing lasted very long, I'm afraid. Sometimes she would look at me and say, 'Why me, Martin?'

"She spent $3,000 a week, I reckon. She believed she wouldn't get along without it. She got so she couldn't remember whether she went to the supermarket or not. She used booze — which she formerly hated — to bring her down from the coke.

She took codeine, sleeping pills, Dilaudid, marijuana and even heroin. She plundered our bank account and stole prescription painkillers out of friends' medicine cabinets."

"Whom do you blame for this?"

Bruening jerked his head toward Bill as if shaken from a reverie. A frown bit into his forehead.

"Blame? I blame every mother-fucker—excuse my French—who sold her drugs. I blame every physician who prescribed her pain pills and every law enforcement official who failed to do his duty. She was murdered, Mr. Boyer, and the pushers, doctors, cops, lawyers and judges were accessories to that homicide.

"Do you know what she would do? She would cook a chunk of this shit they call 'Mexican tar' in a few droplets of water and inject the mess into her veins. A doctor told her if she continued using her arms as a pincushion he might have to amputate both arms. Finally, she disappeared on me."

"Where did she go?"

"The street. I can only imagine what her life was like. I filed a missing person report with the police and searched every day for her. The cops, I'm sure, never even bothered to look. I eventually found her living in a seedy motel in North Hollywood. She sold everything she had of value—stereo, clothes, rings, a nineteen-inch color TV—everything just to get drugs."

His voice halted here for the first time in his recitation. He looked away from Bill.

"I'm pretty sure," he then continued, "she was selling her body by the time I located her. She denied that, of course, but…well, I think she was. You see, the goddam 'voice' of those drugs was leading her along, soothing her, telling her everything was okay. It gets to the point where, if you can afford it, a junkie doesn't even want to sleep.

"What I'll never forget though was the smell about her when I found her—the stench of the street, the smell of death. But she didn't care if she was dying. She just wanted that poison.

"By the time I got her to the hospital, she was in the terminal phase of her addiction. She weighed less than ninety pounds. Her heart was about to fail and so were the rest of her organs."

His words suddenly ceased. He was again staring into space. He sat that way for several moments, oblivious to Bill's presence. His sightless stare reminded Bill of the first time he saw Bruening downing beers at the Windsor Arms. When he spoke again, his voice was so soft Bill couldn't even hear his first words.

"…escaped and, as you know, she was found dead in one of the movie houses in Century City." His voice again faltered, then ceased altogether.

"I'm sorry," said Bill. He let several moments pass before asking his next question: "After she died, how did you cope with the tragedy?"

Bruening turned to him, his eyes blazing wet with impossible anger. "What makes you think I did?" he asked.

"I'm sorry if these questions disturb you," Bill quickly said. "Please understand your story may help someone else to avoid drugs altogether."

"That's why I'm talking to you, Mr. Boyer. I want people to understand what drugs do to the human spirit. I want people to realize how drugs rape your body. No, not rape, they gangbang your body. They fuck you and fuck you and fuck you until your body is a mass of blood and sores and pus and excrement. I want people to understand that my wife was *murdered*."

"What can be done about her murderers?" asked Bill. He had to tiptoe into this dangerous territory. Bruening shifted in his seat so he could reach his cup. He brought the cup of now lukewarm tea to his lips and took a quick sip before replying.

"First of all, I would like to see a mandatory death penalty for hardcore pushers," he answered. "But that's only the tip of the iceberg. There are so many people along the drug distribution network. They're all murdering bastards."

He put down his cup and fixed the journalist with a look Bill associated with judges handing down sentences.

Bill cleared his throat. "I'm not sure whom you're going after with your death penalty," he said. "The pipeline you mention runs from deep in South America into our streets. Do you go after the Andean farmers whose economic misfortunes cause them to raise and harvest coca leaves? Or the ghetto kid whose own economic misfortune makes him willing to risk standing on a street corner with plastic bags of coke? Or the guys in the middle, the ones who control the pipeline?"

"Yeah, I hear you," said Bruening. "It's a lot easier to nab a kid on a corner than a drug lord. But that gangbanger who gave that kid drugs to sell — you nab him and maybe he'll lead you to a drug lord."

"A snitch in the ghetto? I doubt that'll happen."

"So you do nothing?" Bruening said with an accusatory tone of voice.

"No, not nothing. I'm going to talk to drug enforcement cops to see what they are doing, but I suspect they're overwhelmed by the sheer quantity of the shit coming into Southern California."

Almost as if he hadn't heard Bill, Bruening interjected: "And then there are ACLU types who defend these fuckers. I know bleeding hearts feel sorry for gangbangers and turn victims into criminals. Maybe some people blame my wife for her addiction. After all, nobody forced her to take drugs, did they? So it's all her fault and she got what was coming to her."

Abruptly Bruening stopped his voice at the peak of its crescendo. His face had turned red and a tiny bit of saliva oozed from the corner of his mouth. The tick of a wall clock in the entry echoed like a drumbeat through the living room.

Was Dr. Death emerging from the mask of Bruening? But who wouldn't react this way over the death of a loved one? This was a guy who was angry and justifiably so. It didn't mean he was a murderer.

"Many people seemed to feel that Dr. Death's solution was not a bad one," Bill ventured tentatively.

"Not enough," snapped Bruening, the color fading from his face. "You in the media equated him with the Night Stalker and the Hillside Strangler, and the cops spent more energy trying to catch him then ridding the streets of pushers."

The tape recorder continued to purr on the table between the two men. Bruening's eyes bored into Bill, causing him to stir in discomfort. For once, Bill couldn't decide what his next question should be. Perhaps sensing this, Bruening relaxed his gaze and allowed a smile to penetrate his face.

"I'm sorry if I came on a little strong there," he said, his voice resuming its analytical model. "I simply get so frustrated with the casual attitude our society has toward drug usage. A holdover from the Sixties, I guess."

"And yet the Morning News did a poll during the Dr. Death episode—you may have seen it—in which fifty-seven percent of the people in L.A. County looked favorably on Dr. Death and nearly seventy-five percent of the people polled felt the County wasn't doing enough to counteract the drug problem."

"Polls don't mean anything," said Bruening. "Depending on how you phrase your questions, you can get people to agree or disagree with anything. Let's face it, your paper had a good ride with Dr. Death. It was in your publisher's interest to get an instant poll lauding the death of those pushers. I bet circulation went up dramatically during Dr. Death's reign. And I bet it's gone back down now that Dr. Death is dead."

"Is he?" Bill asked.

"The LAPD seem to think so," said Bruening.

"Are you happy or sad about that?"

Bruening shrugged and raised his hands with a who-knows gesture. He picked up his cup and drained the remainder of his tea. Bill did likewise, stalling for time. The trouble was he wasn't thinking like a journalist. The questions for a series on drug abuse were obvious. But these weren't the questions Bill longed to pose.

"I notice you called the overdose victims in these deaths 'pushers'," Bill finally said. "Maybe they were simply victims of drug abuse like your wife."

"Oh, come on," snapped Bruening. "In almost every instance, the bodies were found with enough drugs and paraphernalia to supply a small army. A hype doesn't walk around with all that. Those fuckers were pushers, believe me. Besides, what does any of this have to do with the story you're doing? Are you trying to resurrect Dr. Death or are you interested in getting at the root of the problem?"

Bill understood Bruening's mounting suspicions precluded any more questions in this area and swiftly changed the topic. The rest of the interview stuck closely to the facts of Cathy Bruening's life and death. Twenty minutes later, Bill shook Bruening's hand and said goodbye at the front door. He walked to his car with a sinking feeling.

***

That night, Bill played the tape several times for Jessica at her condo. She then played her tapes from the conversation with the man who phoned anonymously. They couldn't help notice the vocal similarity between "Dr. Death" and Martin Bruening. But this wasn't enough evidence to get the Morning Snooze back in the Dr. Death business.

Jessica stood up from her kitchen table, absentmindedly petted Trixie and poured another scotch for both of them.

Bill took a grateful swallow, then said: "You know what you have to do, don't you?"

She turned to look at him quizzically. "No, Bill, tell me what I have to do."

"Go to Valesquez."

"What on earth are you talking about?"

Bill twirled the glass of scotch in his hand. "Look, he said to let him know if you came up with anything. Well, you have."

Her face reddened. "That's not an option," she said quietly.

"Of course, it is," said Bill. "The police still have eight unsolved deaths on their hands. You can ask him about Bruening and DOA. He said the police profile—"

"Damn it, I don't want to keep calling that man."

"Okay, *I'll* do it. I'd love to know if Bruening was the kinda guy who did fit their 'profile'."

She slumped into her chair opposite him and took a large gulp of scotch. "Oh, Bill, please don't ask me to."

"Jessie, we've got no choice. If you have a better plan, I'd love to hear it."

"I have no better plan," she said with a sigh. "I don't even think he'll meet me."

"Use your animal magnetism," suggested Bill.

"It's all used up where he's concerned."

Bill stood up and took her cordless phone from its cradle near the microwave. He handed her the phone.

"Fuck you, Bill," she said as she took the phone.

She dialed Alex's home phone. After leaving a message on his voice mail, she hung up.

"By the way," she said, "since when do you call me Jessie?"

***

Nick's Café on North Spring sat near the former rail yards, a basic breakfast joint intact from the 1940s with wood paneling and old railroad signs. Nobody who ate there remembered who Nick was. The place was owned by a couple of LAPD homicide detectives and served as a morning stop for cops starting on patrol or coming off an all-nighter as well as guys who made factory runs and the occasional downtown businessman looking for a hearty breakfast.

The smell of fried ham and drip coffee hung in the air. Alex and Jessica sat at a window table. She could look past Chinatown to Dodger Stadium as the morning fog lifted. The specials were noted on a chalkboard: Denver omelet, tri-tip sandwich with gravy and mash potatoes, steak and eggs.

Alex, who was getting off night detail, ordered steak and eggs along with black coffee. Jessica stuck with herbal tea and an egg-white omelet. The guy taking the order looked at her funny but said nothing. When he left, Jessica outlined the situation. Alex listened attentively, an occasional smile playing on his face. When she finished, he drank some coffee, then put the mug down.

"What happened to us?" he asked.

Jessica was stunned. Of all things Alex might say, this was the least expected. "What?" was all she could manage and that came out weakly.

"What happened to us?" Alex repeated. "I seldom get this kind of thing wrong. I just knew we were somehow going to get together. Even this Dr. Death nonsense shouldn't have prevented that."

"Alex, I—" She was stumped for an answer. She finally said: "I think our jobs rule our lives."

"You know I used to think I was obsessed with my career. Then I met you."

"That bad, huh?"

"I think two workaholics could make it together, all right," he continued. "Maybe it's just that our jobs—cop and reporter—don't mix."

"I guess I could've transferred to the food section."

He laughed. "No, you're good at what you do."

"Thank you. Do you know what someone called me the other day? A post-modern Brenda Starr."

"Oh, yeah? Well, then I must be a post-modern Dick Tracy."

This made them both laugh. Hard. After a few moments, Alex stopped and looked at Jessica, not unkindly. "We'd have been at each other's throats all the time," he said.

"I like you, Alex. Why is it that when I like someone...it never works?"

"You want an answer?"

She hesitated. Did she?

"Yes," she heard herself say.

"You don't trust your emotions. You don't open up. You're very careful…too careful."

He took a sip of coffee, then stared out at the street. Two truckers in tired blue jeans ambled toward Nick's, looking eager for hot food. He continued:

"When it comes to being a reporter, you're fearless. You don't take crap from anybody whether it's me or the mayor. But when it comes to letting yourself be admired—loved—you're scared to death. You're afraid of something. I have no idea what but you are afraid. Oh hell, I'm just an overly suspicious, self-centered cop. What do I know?"

"No, you're right," she was all too quick to say. "I don't open up to people. I stand aloof, analyzing, questioning, but never participating. I must be a real pain in the butt."

"Yes, you are, but you'd be more than worth it to the guy you would let love you."

He gulped the rest of his coffee and signaled the waiter for a refill. The guy nodded. Somehow whenever Alex signaled waiters, they saw him. Why was that? Jessica wondered.

"Now, as for your suspicions about the dead dopers, yes, they were dealers. Every last mother-fucker. And there's a connection between Dean Thurber and Martin Bruening."

"What?" exclaimed Jessica.

"Bruening is known by certain elements on the street. Searching for his wife, he relied on hypes, gangbangers and the homeless. Somewhere we think he may have met Thurber. My sources tell me he used to see 'em together. Not often but once or twice."

"So who's investigating this connection?"

"No one is. Didn't you hear, the coroner has ruled all the deaths were due to overdoses?"

"But we can revive the case. "A story in the Morning—"

"Forget it. The brass doesn't want Dr. Death to exist. He became too much of a poster boy for vigilante-style adventurism. The streets are bad enough.

'Sides, we never established any real link other than unreliable gossip and now it's a dead issue, you should excuse the expression."

The waiter arrived and Alex momentarily stopped talking as he poured steaming hot coffee into his mug. Jessica shook her head no when he asked if she would like another herbal tea.

When the waiter left, Alex resumed: "When your compatriot visited Martin Bruening the other evening, I assume he tape-recorded the interview?"

"Yes," she said.

"And did you happen to record any of your phone conversations with Dr. Death at the newspaper?"

"You know legally there must be prior verbal notification of all parties to record a telephone conversation in California," said Jessica.

"I know," he replied.

"Yes, of course, I taped Dr. Death's calls without his knowledge," she said.

"And how do the two voices sound?" he asked.

"Similar," she replied.

He nodded. Taking a tentative sip of the hot coffee, he gazed thoughtfully out the window. "You need to call Lt. Robin Wakefield at Parker Center. He headed the task force until it was disbanded. He might be willing to give you help off the record. You might be able to share information. That's up to you two. As you know, I have no involvement in any of this nor did we ever meet today."

She wondered why he would insist on the latter condition when he chose a place frequented by cops. But instead, she said, "I'll give Lt. Wakefield a call."

"Good," said Alex. As if on cue, their breakfast arrived.

A half-hour later, Alex paid the bill at the register and the two parted company. Jessica drove the downtown streets to the paper with a dizzy feeling in her head. Was she back in the Dr. Death business? Had she snatched victory from the jaws of ignoble defeat? Would Big Bob buy any of this?

When she arrived, Bill suggested he would write up everything that connected Martin Bruening with Dr. Death while she telephoned the officer. They needed to put together a package that Big Bob would find irresistible.

CHAPTER TWENTY-FIVE

SOURCES

When Lt. Wakefield returned Jessica's call early that afternoon, he was unusually helpful. He confirmed the men who died were narcotics dealers, but that would have to remain off the record. He agreed all of the deceased were probably the victims of foul play, but that too would have to remain off the record. He told Jessica that Bruening was a person they were planning to interview, but he couldn't say that on the record. All he would say on the record was the task force was no longer investigating these deaths.

She asked about the profile the task force had of their potential perp, which momentarily angered the officer until Jessica could convince him she had read this in an LA Times article. He then agreed that Bruening was a better "fit" than Dean Thurber.

Noise on the street, which Lt. Wakefield characterized as "rumors and shit," indicated low-level drug dealers had a profound distaste for DOA. The general belief was that, somehow, the radical organization or someone close to it was behind the slayings.

What about the recent death of a dealer in Van Nuys? Jessica wondered.

An isolated case, said Lt. Wakefield. Off the record, of course.

Jessica stared at the notes of their phone conversation on her VDT monitor for several minutes. She was oblivious to the renewed warfare between Ruth Treadway and Winnie Yankovich over Winnie's review of a rock concert that included words Ruth couldn't find in any English dictionary or the sniping by Danny Evans from his foxhole that picked off every reporter past deadline. All she could think about was whether she had enough to convince Big Bob.

She did not.

***

"Why you like me?" Sophie asked Bill.

He put down his bottle of beer and looked at her for a moment. "You're a beautiful, smart, resourceful woman and a very brave one for coming to a foreign country to make a living," he said.

"Some smart," she said. "I speak English very bad." She was not certain what "resourceful" meant and she was tired of men telling her she was beautiful.

"You'll learn. It takes time," said Bill.

"I have no time," she said. "I work 12 hour a day five days a week."

"You're up to five days now?" he asked.

"I need money, honey."

He gave her a ten.

"Thank you," she said. "You didn't answer my question."

"What?"

"You say you like me. Why? How much you like me?"

He looked at her. She wore a frown but that did little to undercut the sheer prettiness of the smooth brown face. Unflattering reds and blues from a neon beer sign caught wrinkles creeping in around her eyes and did little to enhance her eyeshadow, mascara and eyeliner. Yet she was pretty, no doubt. He loved that face.

But did he love her? What honwas there ever to talk about? World politics? The Lakers? Actually, she did like basketball and would watch games on the TV over the bar.

"I like you very much," he said as he kissed her rouged cheek. "You know that."

"I don't know that," she came back at him. "I know you like to fuck me. That not the same thing."

"What do you want me to do? Go to Bangkok with you and meet your parents?"

She was startled. "My parents not in Bangkok. They in Ayutthaya. You don't want to meet them. But I like you to go with me to Thailand someday. I show you my country."

"Okay, maybe we will," he said, then took another swig of Rolling Rock. He paused for a moment. Hey, maybe that wasn't such a bad idea. Then he remembered why he had come to the bar this night.

"Sophie, I need your help."

Again she was startled. "You need *my* help?"

He reached inside his coat pocket and extracted photos he had brought with him from the Snooze's photo lab. After he wiped away any stickiness from beer spills, he laid them on the small round table where they sat on bar stools. These were his photos of Martin Bruening, taken surreptitiously with the telephoto, and from the previous day's photoshoot. Two sides of the man as it were. He spread them out.

"Have you ever seen this guy in here?" he asked her.

She looked at the photos. Her frown deepened. She nodded.

"Yes, I know him," she said. "He come here sometimes. The girls no like him. He disrespects them. And he no tip."

"What does he do?"

"He drinks beer, watches TV and sometimes guys meet him."

"Really? What kind of guys?"

"Freaky guys. They sometimes smell and have tattoos. Usually Latinos. They no like skinny Thai girls like me. They like fat girls."

"How often does he come here and meet these guys?"

"A lot long ago. Not so much now.

"Did you ever sit with him?"

" I no want to. He's weird, for an American.

"And you're sure? This is the guy you've seen here?"

"Yeah, I'm sure."

"Hey, does your boss Miss Lily still have that closed-circuit TV working in here?"

"Yes, she no trust girls to not hanky-panky with customers."

"Good. I think I want to talk to Miss Lily."

***

Big Bob was in meetings all morning so Bill and Jessica didn't get into his office until lunchtime. He acted distracted, almost not hearing their carefully rehearsed presentation. He nodded and occasionally stared at his punching bag as though he would rather be hammering it than listening to two of his reporters. When they finished, he scratched his head with a pencil that seemingly had no other use and looked at the two as if they were discussing comp time rather than potentially the biggest story of the year. Then he sighed.

"Look," said the ME, swiveling the chair containing his bulky body so it faced slightly away from his reporters. "I'm under strict instructions that any story involving Dr. Death must be run by Duke Whitcomb personally. I have also been told that your series on narcotics in L.A. is a no-go per Duke's instructions. As far as the Morning News is concerned, we now live in a drug-free zone. If the mayor himself ODs, we have to phone the Duker before we can write about it."

"What's this all about?" asked Bill.

"I would say our publisher is personally embarrassed by our Dr. Death stories and especially by the way I handled the situation," said Big Bob. "We had our version of a Cultural Revolution last weekend at which Chairman Whitcomb invited his senior editors to indulge in the healthy exercise of self-criticism. While not wishing to stifle our natural aggressiveness in the news-gathering process, Chairman Whitcomb feels—no, I would say 'insists' is the precise term—Chairman Whitcomb insists we refrain from inventing serial killers for the near future."

"'Inventing'?" Jessica all but shouted. "Somebody is killing drug dealers in L.A. I didn't invent that!"

Big Bob patiently held up his left hand. He swiveled the chair to face the two reporters, one of whom had a very red face. "I was referring to myself and my poor management decision to name your perpetrator Dr. Death. As I said, Chairman Whitcomb is a firm believer in self-criticism."

"Let Jessica call her contact, Harvey Brillstein, Thurber's lawyer," said an anguished Bill. "He might be able to strengthen the link between his client and Bruening. And let's forget about calling him Dr. Death."

Big Bob shrugged. Or maybe it was closer to a shudder. He swung his body out of the swivel chair and stood, looming over his orderly desk. "Make your case to Duke Whitcomb, not to me. If you want to take it up with him, you have my blessing. Now I've got calls to return."

Thus dismissed, the two reporters slumped out of Big Bob's office. They walked back to Bill's desk where they huddled close together.

"I say we go to Whitcomb," said Bill.

"Sure, fine, but who makes the call?" asked Jessica.

"I've been here the longest and I once talked to Whitcomb at a company Christmas party," reasoned Bill. "He's a nice guy."

"Okay," said Jessica.

Bill picked up his phone and dialed the publisher's office.

***

The six-mile stretch along Mulholland Drive between Coldwater Canyon and the San Diego Freeway is a row of guarded-gate communities. Thanks to a city policy aimed at minimizing grading, L.A. ordinances governing hillside density encourage developers to pack homes into clusters surrounded by buffers of open space. That space is often sold or donated to the Mountains Conservancy, thus creating a crazy-quilt stretch of cross-mountain parklands.

Duke Whitcomb's home was in the community of Paradise Estates about half-way between Coldwater and the 405. Bill and Jessica rode in his car past the various wrought-iron curtains. They had spoken very little during the drive from downtown, each lost in his or her thoughts about the impending appointment. Neither, of course, had ever been to the Whitcomb's home. Indeed, Big Bob himself had been there only once for a party Duke threw to welcome himself to the position of publisher and introduce himself to L.A. society.

Their summons caught the two by surprise. They had imagined they would see Whitcomb in his chambers, hidden away in the upper recesses of the historic Morning News building. These had been the domains of Oakleigh Benet. Legend had it that Benet maintained a secret bedroom next to his office where he could screw his mistresses. Or where he maintained his Prohibition-era wine cellar. The legend varied according to who told the tale. Danny Evans long maintained that Mickey Cohen used the chambers to hide out from the sheriff whenever the heat came down, Mickey being a regular pal of Oakleigh's and all, to say nothing of being one of the best news tipsters in town.

Bill had genuinely hoped to visit this inner sanctum and maybe learn the truth. But Whitcomb, who rarely if ever turned up in the newsroom, was working at home and asked the two reporters to "drop by" after 4:30.

Bill and Jessica took some measure of encouragement in the summons. If the Duke truly wanted no part of Dr. Death, why would he go to the trouble of a summons? The two went into overdrive to get their deadline stories done by 3:30 so they would get on the Hollywood Freeway before rush hour clobbered traffic.

After clearing the Paradise Estates guard gate, Bill drove a wide, steeply sloping street lined with mature camphor trees planted to create the illusion of a neighborhood that has been growing for twenty years instead of six. Although technically in Sherman Oaks, the homes nevertheless had the prestigious

90210 zip code. Without a Beverly Hills Post Office address, home prices would fall drastically.

Once inside the Paradise Estate compound itself, the streets flattened out and gave unusually generous views of the Valley from the mountainside. The developer had cleverly sliced the property's central ridge by seventy feet and used that one million cubic yards of dirt to fill in and flatten an adjacent canyon. The grading thus led to the creation of flat streets in otherwise rugged terrain.

Man did not belong here. Not within the fire ecology of the Hollywood Hills and Santa Monica Mountains. Bill knew this from a two-part series he wrote a couple of years back that contrasted the virtual army of firefighters and disaster relief subsidies employed to keep the wealthy secure in their gated hilltop suburbs to the scant attention paid by the city to remediable fires in the inner-city. Bill mused that such a series would be impossible now that Duke Whitcomb was the Morning Snooze publisher.

The Duke's house proved to be one of those fake adobe affairs with white walls and a red-tile roof. Once Bill identified himself at the intercom located at the foot of the driveway, a wrought-iron gate swung open and admitted the car to a circular drive lined with shade trees. This brought them to the Spanish-style front of the two-story house. A man in a dark windbreaker and Angels baseball cap hurried from a side door and directed Bill to park his car in one of several visitor spots.

The two reporters were then pointed toward a massive oak door that magically opened as they approached. Another servant, this one female in a blue housekeeping dress, gestured a reluctant welcome and ushered them into a two-story circular entry hall, edged in hand-hewn timbers and stained glass. Imported tiles were artfully embedded in the white plaster walls and a massive chandelier shaped like an old wagon wheel hung from the cathedral ceiling. Stairways on either side led up to the second floor and connected in a clerestory balcony at the rear. Two antique chairs sat on the red tile floor at the base of each of the two stairways. Modern paintings lined the walls as in a museum. One, Jessica was surprised to note, looked like a Picasso. Could it be?

The woman led them through a generous archway into the living room. Again, the feeling was one of expanse with the room towering two stories before the ceiling peaked with exposed, hand-hewn beams. A log burned quietly in an enormous adobe fireplace. The furniture was Spanish oak with matching Mediterranean floral prints. A woolen Mexican rug lay on the polished oak floor. Beveled glass doors led to a back patio that gave way to a spectacular view of the Valley. A wet bar occupied the far wall just to the right of this view.

The woman asked Bill and Jessica if either would like a drink. Both asked for water even though Bill was dying for a scotch. He wasn't certain if he wanted the Duke to realize his reporters would even allow themselves to drink during work hours. He eyed the wet bar longingly.

The woman crossed to this bar, took a pitcher of ice water from a small refrigerator and poured water into two tall glasses. She brought these to Jessica and Bill, smiled, then told them Mr. Whitcomb would be with them shortly. They took their seats on a beige sofa with dark oak arms and waited.

The wait lasted longer than fifteen minutes, which created mild distress in the pits of their stomachs. The euphoria of reviving Dr. Death gave way to the sinking sensation that they were being allowed to cool their heels as well as their ardor. When Duke Whitcomb finally did appear, he made no attempt to apologize but merely grinned and waved them back to their seats. To Bill's disgust, he clutched a highball glass that contained what certainly appeared to be a generous shot of scotch.

Whitcomb was a tall man with graying reddish hair that was beginning to thin on top yet made up for this by sending out tendrils in several directions, up, down and sideways. The hair had a look of studied carelessness that was coming into fashion among businessmen who felt a need to declare a difference between themselves and the old school of short hair and clean-shaven conformity.

His face with its ruddy complexion, bright blue eyes and relaxed smile expressed ease and friendliness that warmed the room. His gray slacks were casual as were his black Salvatore Ferragamo loafers but he wore a dress shirt with gold cuff links. He appeared as if caught unawares, changing his clothes for the evening but willing to stop all activity to entertain his guests in as hospitable a manner as possible.

"So," the Duke said as he lowered himself onto an antique straight-back dark wood chair with a velvet seat. "You wish to talk to me about this serial killer story, I believe."

"Yes, Mr. Whitcomb," said Jessica. "We have new information that Big Bob—I mean, Mr. Patterson—thinks you should be made aware of."

"Please, Jessica, call me Duke, will you?" implored the publisher. "I don't stand on ceremony with my colleagues at the Morning News."

"Of course, Duke," she said. "How much time do we have?"

"As much as you wish my dear," he replied. "I don't have to leave until six. I'm afraid I do have to be at a gala at the Beverly Hilton given by some conference of Christian and Jews honoring some Buddhist for his opposition to the Communists in China. Or maybe it has something to do with Tibet. I forget. Anyway, Richard Gere will be there."

Jessica got so lost in the Duke's answer that she wasn't certain how much time that gave her. She decided to go with the shorter version of their investigation.

The Duke listened without speaking as Jessica summed up their investigation to date including the highly encouraging off-the-record comments by Lt. Robin Wakefield of the LAPD. The Duke smiled once or twice—or so Jessica imagined—and nodded his head vigorously when she stoutly defended her newsgathering practices that led to the Morning News' initial reporting about the serial killer. She made no mention of "Dr. Death."

When she sensed his attention waning, she quickly wrapped up her account with a flourish that included Bill's recorded interview with Martin Bruening, his possible link to Dean Thurber and the two reporters' near certainty that Bruening's voice was identical to the voice that tipped her to the existence of—she nearly said Dr. Death but caught herself—a killer of drug dealers.

The Duke took a long swallow of his scotch or whatever that intriguing liquid was in his highball glass, put the glass down on a side table and gazed up into the vast expanse of his living room ceiling.

"Jessica, do you have any idea how the cost of newsprint has soared in just the last year?" he asked.

The question caught her off-guard. She stammered a no, which caused the Duke's head to bob up and down in a firm nod.

"No, I'm sure you don't," he said, his voice assuming the authoritative air of a professor gently guiding young students toward a discernible truth. "Well, our newsprint bill has soared twenty-five percent this year. I've had to radically cut costs in other areas to offset this increase. The rise in newsprint has hiked expenses by as much as twenty million this year. You see, worldwide demand for newsprint has given paper producers the leverage to dramatically raise their prices. The price climbed from four hundred and forty dollars per metric ton in February to five hundred and fifty in November. But that's the cost of doing business, isn't it?

"My job—my only job as I see it—is to purchase newsprint and to sell it for a profit," he continued. "It is not my job—nor yours—to solve crimes or capture criminals. I don't allow the police department to edit copy for the Morning News. So I do not expect my reporters to make arrests for the LAPD. It's that simple."

He turned toward Jessica and Bill, his blue eyes glistening with the vigor of a preacher who has just finished his Sunday sermon.

Bill took the bait. "But, sir—" he began but got no further.

"Enough said," said the Duke abruptly. He stood and gazed down on the two reporters with a look that was not unkind.

"You two did terrific reporting and I intend to commend that work to Bob Patterson. It's people like you that make the Morning News a great read. But in this instance, we must let the police do their job as we do ours. Now I'm afraid I do have to get dressed for this damn monkey-suit affair. Mustn't keep Richard Gere waiting now, must we?"

He turned to exit the living room. Halfway across the room, the Duke pivoted back toward them and said in a warm voice, "Bill, do fix yourself and Jessica a drink before you leave. I think you could both use one."

CHAPTER TWENTY-SIX
GUM-SHOE

As Bill and Jessica limped back to the city, an air of gloom pervaded the car. Bill stopped off at a little Mexican diner to order a kilo of *carnitas* to go. Along with the pork, sweet and crunchy the way he liked it, he picked up lard-infused refried beans, flour *tortillas* and chunky fried pigskin. Each man has his own way of committing suicide.

The two dragged themselves into the American Legion to consume Bill's meal of distress with a gallon of beer. Sly, who helped them munch on the chips and guacamole, was unwilling to share in their self-pity. Sly was of the opinion that getting fucked on a story by management was part of being a journalist. And perhaps it's just as well.

"If we could print what we knew to be the truth, there would be daily rioting in the streets," said Sly as he grabbed a pork-rind. "In a way, it would also kill the art of journalism. One has to shade meanings to get at the truth."

"Oh, shut up, Sly," said Bill.

"Your trouble, Mr. Boyer, is that you want to be a celebrity," said Sly, untroubled by his friend's rebuke. "You want to uncover a new scandal every week and have your own talk show. But, remember, more journalists have been ruined by self-importance than by liquor."

"What self-importance?" snarled Bill. "We got a damn good story that got tainted by a fake confession. I have a half a mind to tip off the Times."

"They wouldn't be interested," sighed Jessica. "And you know what?

"No, what, my darling?" said Bill with a vocal flourish to undercut the endearment.

"I'm losing interest as well," she said, raising a beer mug—Jessica refused to drink from a bottle—to her mouth. "What say we let this guy go his merry way? I've got any number of murders and assaults to write about. Fuck Dr. Death!"

She drained her mug in a mighty gulp.

"Mind if make a few inquiries on my own then?" Bill asked.

"Not a bit," she said. "Who you gonna ask and what about?"

"Well, I'd start with Brillstein. He's your contact. Do you mind?"

"He's not my contact," she said. "He'll talk to anyone if he's got a good reason. You gotta give him a reason, is all."

***

Bill Boyer gave Harvey Brillstein's paralegal as many reasons as he could imagine over the next few days but no phone calls got returned. So he dropped by Brillstein's office on the sixth floor of a South Hill Street building that looked at least seventy years old.

The office resembled Harvey Brillstein in almost no way. Where Brillstein was always nattily dressed and smooth as silk, this cramped office was jammed with boxes containing legal briefs and his paralegal worked out of a tiny cubicle that was the outer office. She explained her boss was on a call and Bill would have to wait. She did go in to deliver a scrap of paper on which she had scribbled Bill's name. So Bill waited. Quite a while.

Approximately a half-hour after the note was delivered, Brillstein barged out of his inner office and, briefcase tucked under his left arm, was heading out the door.

"Mr. Brillstein," said Bill as he jumped up, "I'm Bill Boyer of the Morning News—"

"I can't talk to you now, Mr. Boyer. I'm due in court in under an hour."

"Are you on your way there?" asked Bill as he followed him out the door.

"Where else would I be headed, Mr. Boyer?" asked Brillstein.

"Mind if I walk with you? I could use the exercise," asked Bill.

The lawyer glanced at Bill, who caught up with him and was matching him, stride for stride, toward the elevator.

"I suppose not, Mr. Boyer. It's not a long walk to the Criminal Courts Building, but I have to go so damn early because the elevators there are so excruciatingly *slow*."

Brillstein punched the down button on his own building's elevator and turned to face Bill.

"That's what happens when you take the lowest bid on a works project," said Brillstein. "The elevator company did a crap job, then went bust the minute the job's done and whenever you need repair work or spare parts, good luck getting any of those elevators fixed."

Minutes later, the two men walked north at a steady pace through relatively heavy pedestrian traffic as they headed toward West Temple Street. Seemingly half the traffic consisted of lawyers, either pulling briefcases on wheels or clutching leather satchels jammed with documents.

"I never heard back from you," said Bill. "I left you several messages."

"I'm very busy, Mr. Boyer — "

"Please call me Bill."

"I'm very busy, Bill, so I don't always have time to chat with reporters. What is it that you want?"

"Your client Dean Thurber, why did he confess to a crime he didn't commit? Do you know?"

"Is this off the record?"

"Yes, it is."

"You're talking about a man with a low I.Q. and even lower self-esteem. Suddenly he's a big shot. At least for a week until a good lawyer checks out his story."

"Does he know a man named Martin Bruening?"

Brillstein stopped in mid-stride, then turned to face Bill.

"Martin Bruening? I *know* Martin Bruening as a matter of fact."

"Really? What do you know about him?"

"You understand, Bill, that my clients often come from the street as it were," said the lawyer, choosing his words carefully. "Bruening is known in certain circles on the streets. He works with the organization known as DOA, as you probably know. He speaks fluent Spanish and has become somewhat intimate with the underground drug culture due to his work with DOA."

"Does Dean Thurber know him?"

"I imagine he might. A nodding acquaintance perhaps. I don't know for sure."

"May I speak to your client?"

"Why?"

"I want to know about his connection, if any, to Bruening. I'm following up on a story about Bruening. I interviewed him last week."

"No, Mr. Boyer, I do not want you to speak to my client. He's still got an assault charge I'm trying to bargain down to disorderly conduct. I don't need your linking him in the press to anybody such as Bruening. Good day, Mr. Boyer."

Bill wanted to ask why linking Thurber with Bruening would be harmful to Billstein's client, but the lawyer abruptly turned and walked up the street in a manner that left Bill with no avenue for further conversation.

Bill was not without further options, however.

***

"My man, 007!" called out a Salvadorian immigrant known as Lil Strangler when he saw Bill Boyer walk into Mariscos Ensenada, Señora Rosa's seafood café. Lil Strangler sat as he regularly did, in a dark red and tattered booth toward the back of the cheerfully lighted place, drinking strong coffee and flicking cigarette ashes into the remains of shrimp in spicy tomato sauce.

Lil Strangler liked to call Bill 007 since he was one of the few white men and certainly the only journalist who dared to enter such an establishment in Pico-Union, a section of Los Angeles rife with drugs and gangs both black and brown. Señora Rosa's café was by common consent neutral territory and a haven in which to devour some of the best seafood in L.A. Yet when he first met him, Lil Strangler thought Bill was such a brave dude he dubbed him 007, a regular James Bond. Those were the only white movies the gangbanger liked to watch.

Lil Strangler was an upbeat and mostly friendly banger with tattoos snaking around his body like so much foliage. A single teardrop hung beneath his left eye but more elaborate tattoos covered arms, chest and other places not immediately visible in the Mariscos Ensenada café.

Lil Strangler liked to help the reporter on his stories. 'Bout time white folks got some reality into their damn newspapers, he figured. Plus he liked the man.

Bill settled into the booth and ordered a coffee too.

"Hey, wha's up, 007 dog?" asked Lil Strangler.

"Need to run a few things by you, Lil Strangler," said Bill. "You know a guy by the name of José Díaz."

Lil Strangler frowned. "Know a Sneaky Díaz, think his real name José. He was runnin wit the Loco Drifters, a feeder gang for Varrio Eastside 23rd Street. Motha fuckas. Those motha fuckas ain't 'bout *nada*! Foos wanna bang fuckin' kids, let anyone walk through their stank-ass *varrio*. Bitches! Flappers are only good for suckin' cock, being rats and target practice!"

"This Díaz might work at the Pico-Union Drug Addiction Treatment Center as a counselor or something like that," said Bill.

The frown deepened. "Yeah? The Drug Center? That place got somethin' messed up with DOA, right?"

"I don't know. Maybe. What's the word about that organization, DOA?"

"Those foos as fake as fuck."

"Why?"

"People runnin' it, they all Eme. They hate MS."

Bill considered this for a moment. Maybe Dean Thurber was a dead end. Maybe he was the nobody his lawyer said he was.

"You remember that string of deaths of drug dealers a while ago?" Bill asked Lil Strangler.

"You mean that Dr. Death shit?"

"Yeah. Did you know any of those pushers?"

"All MS gang," said Lil Strangler, referring again to Mara Salvatrucha that started in Pico-Union about eight or nine years before. "Differen' clicks but MS fo' sure."

"So they were all from the same gang?"

"Never thought 'bout it. Shows some *putos* are scared to bang wit La Eme," he said, referring to the Mexican Mafia. "Bunch of weak-ass taggin' crews. Fuck fakes."

"Do you think these deaths were because of gangbangers and not some righteous dude trying to clean up L.A.?"

"Fuck," Lil Strangler laughed. Then the smile vanished from his face. He thought for a moment. "Yeah, come t' think of it, I know this fuckin' *vato* Díaz. He and other shit-stains from La Eme infiltrated that fucked-up center. They skim from alcohol and drug programs to juice their pussy-punk gang."

He stopped and looked straight at Bill.

"You sayin' that gay hoe behind this shit?"

"I'm not saying anything. I'm just trying to figure it all out."

"Everything's so fucked up. So many dead *vatos* on the streets. I'm OG but people wanna be crazy like hard-ass Eme. Fuck, I'm cool with black an' white an' Latino but jus' let us all live!"

"So maybe someone at this drug center, someone who's skimming money and knows who's pushing what in the hood, maybe this *vato* trips off this Dr. Death or whomever about this hype or that pusher and that *vato* gets whacked? Possible?"

"Like to know who doin' that. You say this shit-stain Díaz?"

"No. I'm *not*. I'm asking questions and I plan to go to that center and ask this guy more questions. It's an investigation. No immediately solutions."

He could see blood boiling in Lil Strangler's brain. Not a good sign.

"Trust me for a few more days, okay?" he asked.

"Yeah, sure. Fuck, a few more days," murmured Lil Strangler as he flicked another cigarette ash into his plate.

***

The Pico-Union Drug Addiction Treatment Center occupied a drab windowless graffiti-smeared building not far from Señora Rosa's seafood café. Since he had an appointment with José Díaz, Bill was ushered past a crowd of treatment seekers, nearly all Hispanic, who sat, stood, paced or smoked in a narrow reception area. He was brought to a compact office down a gray-green hallway past the swinging door.

José Díaz entered the office within a couple of minutes. Tall with pock-marked skin and a quick smile, the man, who Bill guessed to be in his late twenties, wore dark creased pants, short-sleeve white shirt and black tie. He could easily be mistaken for a Mormon on an overseas mission. If he had tattoos, they weren't visible.

"Mr. Boyer, glad to meet you," said José with enthusiasm.

Bill, who has risen from his chair to greet José, shook the proffered hand, which clutched his with extra firmness. The two sat down, Bill in a chair opposite a functional desk, José in a chair behind the desk.

"Martin was especially eager I meet with you and explain all that we're trying to do here to help the community," said José.

"Thanks for seeing me on such short notice," said Bill.

"Not at all," said José.

"Does Martin come by here often?" asked Bill. "How does he contribute to your facility?"

"No, not that often," replied José. "He's a righteous dude though. He donates money more than time. He does attend a monthly counseling session where he speaks of his wife's experiences and his own experiences trying to find her on the streets. We're blessed.

"Y'know, he *hates* drugs. By the time he finishes talking at these sessions, you hate drugs too. If you sat on a chair and a rattlesnake were coiled on a chair next to you and a needle and shit on the chair on the other side, my man, you'd lean toward that snake."

"That powerful."

"Oh man, I tell you, that fucker gets going and you see how drugs rape you. That's a word he uses a lot — rape. Folks get it. Hey, I'm not sayin' they walk outta here clean or anything but they walk out determined to get sober, I tell ya.

"He also comes with me out on the streets to talk to folks. Him being a white man, people take notice. They think he's a cop, of course, only he doesn't look like a cop as you know."

"No, but he's DOA," interjected Bill, "which has often been criticized for its militancy about dealers."

"Yeah, I know but I respect that," said José. "We're all in the same fight. Different weapons is all."

"Okay, but are you on the same side as a vigilante willing to attack dealers?"

"No, here at this center we're about love, not hate. We're trying to help victims."

"A lot of dealers have died around here recently."

José cocked his head and looked at Bill strangely. "Yeah, I know. That's nothing to do with us."

"All MS."

José stared at Bill for a moment before shrugging. "'Round here it would have to be."

"But around 22nd and Central and the Eastside and Westside and now Van Nuys? C'mon."

"What's your point?"

"You were once on the street, no?" Bill asked, making the question seem more like a statement.

"I've been pretty open about my past but—"

"La Eme, no?"

"What's this got to do—"

"When did you leave La Eme? I have the impression one doesn't resign from a gang the way you resign from a job."

"I got out, okay? Yeah, I got a death threat and, fortunately for me, I'm an orphan so they couldn't threaten *mi familia*."

"Maybe you never left. Maybe you still belong. Maybe you got into this Center to skim money from drug prevention programs for La Eme."

José stood up, color coming into his face that even brown skin could not mask.

"Hey, man, I thought you wanted to know about the Center and—"

"You know a *vato* named Lil Strangler?"

Now the blood drained from that very same face.

"Yeah, I know him. Why?"

"I'd say he's a ticking time bomb. See, I went to see him at Mariscos Ensenada yesterday and we carefully went over the strange circumstances behind this rash of murders of MS boys. The two of us played a little Sherlock Holmes, I'd guess you'd say. We put one and one and one together and came up with three.

"One, the first murder, as far as we know, was of a guy believed to have sold heroin to Cathy Bruening. Okay, things happen. No connection to anything. Two, this guy like every other subsequent victim that can be attributed to a vigilante were MS members. All right, a coincidence. No big deal. Three, Cathy Bruening's husband is very connected to this Center and to José Díaz, who says he left La Eme, a rival to MS, but still maintains a close connection to the street, to dealers and gangbangers. He intimately knows who's dealing what and where; he knows who makes an easy target. One, two three."

José snorted.

"You ever read Ian Fleming, the guy who wrote the James Bond novels?" asked Bill.

José Díaz looked bewildered. "What? Shit, no," he said.

"I did as a kid. I admit it. In one book, can't remember which one, he said, "Once is happenstance. Twice is coincidence. Three times is enemy action.""

José stared at Bill, his mouth open with incredulity.

"What do you want? This is no newspaper interview, I take it."

"What I want is to keep Lil Strangler in the dark about your involvement in these deaths of MS *vatos*. I'm guessing you and Martin don't go out on the street yourself and do anybody. No, I'm guessing you get someone else to do it for you."

"You think I got a gang of assassins?"

"No, you don't need a gang. You just need someone willing to do a job for one of Martin Bruening's donations of the Center or maybe a little blow."

"You're *loco*, you know? You got no proof of any of this shit," José said, the color coming back into his face.

"Yeah, you're right. I only got one, two, three. And Lil Strangler, of course. He's pissed by the way.

"That shit-stain's a fuckin' fool! *Mierdosos me pelan la verga*! I'm not scared a Lil Strangler."

"No, I'm sure you're not. I'm also sure you don't want any gang war to break out in Pico-Union right now. So can I make a suggestion?"

José regarded Bill contemptuously. He brought his two hands away from his sides, palms up, in a let's-hear-it gesture.

"How do you recruit your hitmen?"

José shook his head.

"Okay, let's try this another way. I want you to recommend a new guy."

***

Bill's request brought out the artist in Konstantine Theosophus. He rummaged through rack upon rack at Alphonse's Costumes to find the right outfit and accouterments to fit Bill's description of a punk/white trash/junkie/rebel/nihilist.

The henna artist understood that the temporary tattoos should be masculine and bold so she went with basic Russian prison culture tattoos. She sprayed a mix of lemon and sugar juice on the designs to get a better stain.

For his performance, Bill drew up a combination of Marlon Brando in "The Wild One" and Martin Downey Jr. in "Less Than Zero."

Miss Lily was hesitant to let even a favorite customer of hers at the Windsor use her CCTV for his purposes. But Bill's remonstrations and a generous tip finally got her to position the cameras at a slightly different angle for a night to focus on a far table, better lit than usual, she kept "reserved" for Bill, and to discreetly place a directional mike where it wouldn't be noticed.

Things went off without a hitch. When the two met in the bar, Martin Bruening failed to recognize Bill nor did he take any notice of Bill's nervousness. Perhaps all Bruening's hired help were nervous when asked to kill people, especially gangbangers.

Once Bill had the VCR cassette in his hot hands, he telephoned Martin Bruening for a follow-up interview.

Bruening was surprisingly calm and quiet when Bill played the tape in the VCR player in Bruening's den. The man even smiled and shook his head as if a victim of a silly prank. When it finished, he looked at Bill for several moments before saying anything.

"I don't understand, Mr. Boyer," he said finally. "Why did you show me this tape? Why don't you take it to the police?"

"The police don't need to see this," said Bill.

"No? Why not?" asked Bruening.

"For one thing I consider my performance far too hammy and would be embarrassed if this were played at any trial," said Bill. "But what you don't want is for this to be played to a fellow named Lil Strangler. Or for any members of Mara Salvatrucha to gain knowledge of this tape's existence."

"I understand," he said quietly.

"Many lives would be lost," said Bill. "And you must now realize José Díaz played you for a fool. You were getting rid of gang rivals for him."

"How ironic that I trusted that punk," mused Bruening. "I thought I was so street smart."

He laughed a soft self-deprecating laugh, more to himself than to his guest.

"What do you want me to do, Mr. Boyer?"

"I want you to retire," said Bill.

"Retire?"

"Your vigilante days are over. Have any deaths brought back Cathy? No, of course not. Have any deaths decreased drug trafficking in L.A. by even one gram? No, of course not. Have any deaths done you a damn bit of good?"

"I get your point."

"Do you? Do you see why you have to retire now or else start a gang war and go to prison for God knows how long?"

"Don't you want a scoop, Mr. Boyer?"

"No, I do not. Not this time. The Morning News wouldn't even appreciate it. Besides, I believe you to be a good man who went through a hell I cannot imagine and reacted badly. Your rotting away in a prison cell would do no one any good as far as I can tell. Just fuckin' retire!"

Martin Bruening sat up straight and sucked in air through his nostrils. His face relaxed.

"What happens to the tape?" he asked.

"I keep it. No offense but I'll be scanning the police blotter regularly for some time to make certain your retirement isn't like Frank Sinatra's."

Bruening laughed for the first time since Bill had met him.

"Okay, Mr. Boyer. You're a sane man and you make good points. Plus you have the VCR tape. Oh, I'd better eject it from the player."

He reached for his remote control and did as he said he would.

"Take the tape, Mr. Boyer, and I'm sorry you won't get your scoop."

"Mr. Bruening, if there's one thing I've learned is that scoops aren't all they're cracked up to be."

***

Bill Boyer threw back his bourbon and followed it swiftly with a beer chaser. Jessica raised an eyebrow but said nothing. Sly was too busy with his nachos to notice.

The only thing that constrained Bill's buoyancy was his inability to describe his unalloyed joy over the demise of Dr. Death. Meanwhile, Jessica was, yet again, bitching about Big Bob and his top-down dictates.

Sly giggled softly and shook his head. "What on earth do you expect? He's an *editor*. He can't help being an asshole. Jessica, did I ever tell you the story about the cannibals' cafeteria?"

Jessica groaned at the thought of one of Sly's stories but the columnist would not be put off.

"Well, you're going to hear it anyway, and I think you might even enjoy it," said Sly.

Sly drained his beer mug and glanced toward the bartender who was looking in the wrong direction. As it would interfere with the rhythm of his storytelling, Sly shrugged and looked back at Jessica and Bill.

"Well, there was this cafeteria for cannibals," Sly began, "and one day they had a special on journalist's brains. So this cannibal goes in and the waiter tells him that copyboys' brains go for five dollars an ounce, reporters' brains for ten dollars an ounce and editors' brains for fifty dollars an ounce. The cannibal understandably protests. Vigorously. 'Why the hell should editors' brains be worth that much?' he demands. The waiter looks at him and says, 'Do you know how many editors we have to kill to get an ounce of brains?"

Jessica laughed in spite of herself.

Danny Evans showed up a few minutes later and to everyone's surprise, lingered. He had two pieces of grand news. First, the Linquest et LePierre Gallery on La Cienega was going to exhibit his paintings and he wanted everyone at the paper to come to Tuesday's opening night. It must be understood this was the first anyone who worked with him had ever heard about his secret life. Questions filled the air.

"Oh, I've been toyin' with finger painting since I was a young-un when my mother was away on maneuvers with the Marines," was all Danny would say. Questions flourished for so long that no one thought to ask him about his second piece of news until he got up to leave. Then Sly remembered to ask.

"Oh, something very mysterious happened," said Danny. "My grenade turned up today. I wonder where it's been?"

With that, he quit the American Legion to head home to his trailer park in the Valley.

CHAPTER TWENTY-SEVEN

30

In January, there was a civil war in Africa. This was followed by a terrorist bombing in Belfast and a plane crash in Arizona, killing ninety-two people. The crime rate in Los Angeles was heading down, but pundits questioned whether this was caused by less crime or new methods of crime reporting by police.

In February, a Marshall High School senior died when a classmate laced his lunch with more LSD than was necessary for a practical joke. A West L.A. man was arrested on suspicion of torturing his girlfriend with a cigarette lighter and cigarettes and keeping her handcuffed in the closet for ten days.

The news continued to roll into the Morning Snooze in vast, unstoppable waves. The news was always there, reborn with each morning's paper. It continued to roam restlessly through the day that followed until it could be pinned down by writers, slugged for delivery to editors, revised by the copy desk and assigned news holes for the following day's paper.

In March, in the shadow of an abandoned building splattered with graffiti, two assassins lay in wait, AK-47 assault rifles at the ready. They had been alerted that José Díaz was in the area driving his new Chevy Suburban.

When José rolled by, the gunmen unleashed a thunderous blast of more than thirty rounds. The Suburban, its steel doors strafed by thumb-sized bullets, slammed into a pole spray-painted with more graffiti.

It was a hellish scene even by the crime-hardened standards of the Rampart Division. Díaz's body was slumped in the front seat with shell casings and skull fragments strewn over half a block.

In April, Sly did the unthinkable. He moved Sly's Life down the street to the Times. The combination of a buyout by the Morning Snooze's downsizing and a generous offer from Times management was a one-two punch the columnist could not resist.

The column needn't change, Times editors assured him: He would go after anything or anybody he wanted. Just to test them, one of his first columns accused Cardinal McIntyre of wasting too much of the archdiocese's money on a lavish lifestyle. Catholics were enraged — with Sly. A later attack on the Jewish Defense League brought death threats. Sly couldn't be happier.

The riot in May began in the terraced hillsides that form Boyle Heights. A teenager with gang ties was fatally shot by a police officer who said the youth pointed a semiautomatic pistol at him. The anti-gang officer, who was white, shot Julio Hernandez four times in the upper torso. Residents who claimed to be witnesses sharply disputed the LAPD version of this tragedy, saying the officer fired on the unarmed Hernandez without warning. Others said Hernandez did have a gun but tossed it over a fence when police arrived at the scene of a gang dispute. This was not a good area for a cop to shoot a kid, even if he was a gangbanger.

In the initial hour, mostly teenagers and people in their twenties hurled bottles and rocks, set trash dumpsters afire and screamed insults at police. Some bought bottled drinks at stores, threw them at advancing officers, then scooped up the shards from the street to throw them again. Police citywide were put on tactical alert after more than a hundred officers, some in riot gear, found themselves in a mile-long street battle. About twenty-five people were arrested, mostly for assault and disturbing the peace, before things took a more serious turn.

Latinos had never had a Los Angeles riot to call their own. In the Zoot Suit Riots, the most famous L.A. civil disturbance in which they were involved, they were the victims, not the perpetrators. So the shooting in Boyle Heights brought the community together as never before with political activists, gangbangers and working-class alcoholics united in their fury over this brutal shooting of a Latino kid by a white racist cop.

Jessica along with reporters from every TV station and newspaper in Los Angeles was on the scene by 3 p.m. when things grew ugly with gangbangers and others joining in the fun. Chanting "We Want Justice" and other slogans in Spanish, the crowd moved in when police pulled about ten bottle-throwers from an apartment, whom they handcuffed and sat on a curb.

SWAT members and officers from other divisions arrived. They chased down and tackled some protestors. Officers marched in a riot line to break up the crowd, but protestors kept running into stores and buying bottles to throw. The merchants never had it so good.

Around 4:30, things were getting sufficiently out of hand to inform the Mayor. Hizzoner was raising money at a Brentwood barbeque though and wasn't able to come to the telephone immediately. By 4:50, when television reports were better informing the Mayor, he reluctantly climbed into his chauffeur-driven car and headed for City Hall. Nutty Ned too was caught out of position by this line drive: He was attending a California peace officers conference in San Francisco on community relations.

By 5 o'clock, a full-scale riot was underway.

Angelenos sat glued to their TV sets for most of the night. Thanks to the quick imposition of a curfew by the Mayor, the riot was mostly contained within twelve hours.

The best reporting on the riot and its aftermath was done by the Morning News team led by Jessica Tannenbaum. Many thought it should've won a Pulitzer. Her series of news articles and features about the riot's origins and aftermath did, however, get Jessica a job a couple of months later as a political analyst for ABC's Channel 7 News.

One evening in June, Bill was sipping scotch and listening to a jazz band at the lounge of the Grand Hyatt Erawan Hotel in Bangkok. He flirted briefly with two beautiful Thai women who sat nearby but soon realized they were friends with the guys in the band. Besides Sophie was arriving the next day to show him the sights.

At 11, Bill left behind the cool sounds of the music and stepped outside into the humid Asian night. He climbed an overpass that took him to the other side of the thoroughfare where he could more easily walk back to his room at the Amari Watergate. As the strolled past the World Trade Center, a chaotically organized mall of shops, commercial offices and department stores, he hummed a tune that had been rattling around inside his head for the past couple of days.

As night settled over Bangkok, the traffic eased only slightly. Cars and buses jammed with commuters crawled by at a snail's pace with people hanging out the windows to gasp for polluted air. Noisy *tuk-tuks* and motorbikes darted in and out between larger vehicles. The footpath, potholed and strewn with rubbish, was congested with pedestrians who navigated past the irregularly placed lines of food stalls. A dog meandering aimlessly on the broken sidewalk sniffed oily puddles.

Odors assailed Bill's nostrils—incense and spices, motor exhaust, dog shit, smoke from braziers cooking meat as evening strollers grabbed snacks. Pedestrians approaching a main intersection grabbed the sleeves of their blouses or reached for handkerchiefs and pulled these over their mouths for relief from the filthy air. At one intersection, a building was being torn down and dust from the site added to the devil's brew. Bill crossed Petchburi Road, where the sidewalk stalls of the Pratanam market were closed for the night.

Bill had two more beers at the Amari Watergate's downstairs bar, glancing about at the curious mix of foreign and local customers and watching the bartenders perform their beer-bottle juggling routines. Then he went upstairs to his room for a good night's sleep.

In the months that followed Bill's retirement of Dr. Death, he had grown too restless to continue working at the Morning News. He cast his net out and drew in a surprising number of offers, the best of which came from the Asian edition of Time magazine in Tokyo. Here was a new beat with a chance to roam the cities of Southeast Asia.

He had husbanded his comp hours and days off so he could make this run to Thailand and meet Sophie. She wanted to take him up north to show him its pagodas and forests. He couldn't wait.

***

In the months following the Boyle Heights Riots, no one noticed if any more drug dealers died. Drug selling continued freely but dealers had mostly moved indoors.

With cops posing as buyers, collecting hours of surveillance videos and reinforcing their patrols, the dealers got smart. They got beepers and later those new cellular phones. They insisted that customers call in. Which meant the streets became a little safer for citizens and dealers didn't have to worry so much about cops.

Undercover cops used to a high rate of collars from no-hassle, walk-up street sales now had to wade through layers of telephone security checks set up by wary dealers.

Competition forced the price of the cheapest drugs such as rock cocaine down as new cut-rate stimulants came on the market. This, in turn, caused a mild recession in the "narco-villages" in the high plateaus of the Sierra Madre, two-hundred-and-fifty miles south of the American border, and in the Huallaga Valley deep in the Andes in South America. Life got a little bit harder for everyone along the distribution networks.

Meanwhile, as the cost of drugs declined, the cost of newsprint reached seven hundred dollars per metric ton, causing Duke Whitcomb to spend several nights in Cedars when his blood pressure rose to alarming heights.

Two of Danny Evens' paintings sold in the high six figures, causing him to retire from the newspaper to devote himself entirely to painting and his pet rabbit. The American Legion bar experienced a sharp downturn in business since neither Bill nor Jessica nor Sly patronized the establishment any longer. And rumor had it the cost of editors' brains had climbed to one hundred dollars an ounce.

ALSO BY
KIRK HONEYCUTT

John Hughes
A Life in Film: The Genius Behind *Ferris Bueller, The Breakfast Club, Home Alone,* and more